LIES OF MEN

DANA KILLION

Obscura
Press

1

"**I**s it my fault that my client was stupid?"

Two women at the end of the jury box shifted uncomfortably in their seats. If Gavin Wright thought ignorance would be his saving grace in these embezzlement charges, comments like that would only pulverize his defense. I could feel the prosecution's glee from my vantage point six rows back. It was week two of the trial; the prosecution had rested, and the defense was waging equal battles between the substantial evidence presented by their opponents and the defendant's narcissistic tendencies. Neither was helping their case.

Wright stood charged with embezzling over $500,000 from the estate he managed for his client, Isaac Sikora, and day by day he was adding a new definition to the word *chutzpah*. There was nothing more endearing to a jury than stealing money from grandpa.

I turned my head toward the administrative assistant who had discovered the alleged theft. Her hands were clenched in her lap, her head down, and she stared at some stain on the carpet, probably wishing she could sneak out the side door. Since Wright was her boss, she'd brought the financial irregularities to the attention of the victim's son, Nathan Sikora, but only after the elder Sikora had passed away. Nathan was now whispering furiously in the prosecution's ear. I imagined the expletives were flying.

Tension crackled in the room with each insensitive remark by Wright, but his psych profile prevented him from controlling himself. Oh well, two more points for the prosecution.

It was entertaining, but I was more interested in the jury's reaction. I furiously jotted notes for the article I would post later that day as I watched the circus unfolding. Despite her best efforts, juror number eight was showing her hand. She despised Wright, but as I knew, that didn't mean she was a shoo-in for the vote to convict. It wasn't unusual for a juror to dislike the accused or even the victim for that matter—after all, criminal cases didn't always involve the best and the brightest. Nonetheless, it was the jury's role to set aside personal feelings and bias and draw a conclusion based on the facts of the case, even when you thought the accused was a heartless SOB.

Wright sat back in the witness box, flicked a piece of lint off the sleeve of his custom-tailored Italian suit, then shot a look at his attorney that said, "I'd rather be on the golf course." His arrogance enveloped him like a storm cloud. As a onetime prosecutor myself, I'd met many an attorney who seemed to think "I" was the only pronoun in the English language, but it was a quality usually reserved for trial attorneys, not estate wonks like Wright.

I leaned forward in my seat, stared at Wright, and tried to come up with words to describe the undercurrent in his testimony. The flavor of the setting and the emotion in the courtroom were key components in adding texture to the story I was writing on this case for my employer, Link-Media. Facts were the primary elements, but getting my readers to feel the tension in the room was important for taking this story to the next level. Anyone could throw up five hundred words and call it done, but I was developing a reputation for going deeper. In my fourteen months with the digital news outlet, I'd broken a story about a casino scheme involving the highest levels of Chicago government and exposed a tainted energy drink product that had taken the lives of three people and nearly killed my sister. This wasn't the time to get sloppy.

The defense attorney made a move to get the questioning back on track, asking Wright about financial reporting cycles and the frequency of communication between him and Mr. Sikora. The legal strategy seemed to be a claim that this half-million sum was largely expenses related to administration of the estate over the seven years Wright and Sikora had been associated. Hell of a fee structure.

A reporter from the local NBC affiliate slid into the bench next to me. I couldn't help but shoot my eyes at the hideous lime-green-and-orange plaid tie knotted around his neck. Had he dressed in the dark, or was he color blind?

"Hey, Andrea," he whispered. "Do you hate this guy as much as everybody else here does?"

I glanced at my colleague and lifted an eyebrow.

"Nice tie," I said, then turned back to the defense attorney without saying more. Did he really think I would respond? The TV news guys seemed to think they stood on top of the pecking order and we peons in the digital world were just wannabes hoping for our shot. Sorry, I wasn't going to add any color commentary.

"Mr. Wright," the defense continued, "you testified earlier about the monthly administrative expenses charged to Mr. Sikora. How did these fees compare to those of other clients?"

"Every client is different," Wright replied. "We start with a base rate then make adjustments based on the number of man-hours put into the client's assets, the types of investments, the complexity of their personal tax situation."

"And was Mr. Sikora's tax situation complicated?"

"He was an aggressive investor and impulsive about buying assets." Wright shrugged, bored with the whole thing. "It was difficult to get a handle on his ownership stakes, let alone the tax implications on the estate when your client doesn't involve his partners. We were in constant contact with his broker, trying to get information on acquisitions. This went on for the entire time I worked for Mr. Sikora. Of course, that meant more work for my firm, and our fees reflect the work our client directed us to do, nothing more."

Wright tugged on his French cuffs and gave his attorney a practiced smile. *Slick* was the word that came to mind when I looked at him. There was an undercurrent beneath the polished exterior that was hard to identify, as if his poise were practiced rather than innate. Throwing punches in a bar fight or dining in one of the fine restaurants his lifestyle afforded him were two scenarios in which I could easily imagine him.

"I might also add," Wright continued, "that Mr. Sikora changed his mind frequently about how to distribute his assets upon his death. Some months his son was on the short list, others Mr. Sikora felt inclined to donate his wealth to charity. I can't take responsibility for the lack of communication between my client and his son or the quality of their relationship. I was simply following my client's lead."

Nathan Sikora jumped to his feet, his chair clattering to the floor behind him. "Liar!" he screamed. His face was as red as the burgundy sweater he wore, and his hands trembled with rage.

The judge slammed his gavel as the prosecution took Sikora's arm, attempting to calm him down, but he was having none of it. Rage and accusations spilled out uncontrollably as the courtroom visitors watched, erupting into a low rumble of their own. My seatmate chuckled and scribbled in a notebook, delighted with the show.

Two attorneys now whispered in Sikora's ears while he ignored them and continued his tirade. As his volume and agitation increased, Sikora pushed off his counsel and made moves toward Wright. Toward what end wasn't clear, but no one was taking the chance. The bailiff stepped forward as the legal team blocked his movement. With control of the courtroom at risk, the judge continued to call for order, eventually having no choice but to have Nathan Sikora removed from the courtroom.

As Sikora was led out of the courtroom, the room buzzed with shock and amusement. The judge called for lunch recess, and the jury filed out.

"Just another day at the carnival," my journalist friend added before rushing out of the room himself. I had a feeling Sikora was about to have his day in the press.

I exited the building into Daley Plaza, hoping the line at the deli salad bar around the corner hadn't yet gotten unbearable. Buttoning my wool coat against the sharp February wind, I pulled gloves out of my pocket and headed west. Twenty feet out I noticed a crowd building around a woman standing near The Picasso, a monumental fifty-foot-tall COR-TEN steel sculpture that anchored the square. Cameras and voice recorders pointed in her direction. Elyse Wright, the accused's ex-wife.

There was no mistaking the sharp line of her blonde bob and the impeccable wardrobe of the ad executive and former Mrs. Gavin Wright. Together the former couple had made a striking pair, she with her fair beauty and he with his dark skin and easy smile. They were photographed frequently in social pages, particularly for their support of the Lincoln Park Zoo.

As I reached the group, I heard Elyse reiterate—for the benefit of the evening news cycle—the same line of defense she'd used in court.

"Gavin, and Gavin alone, is responsible for the heartless betrayal of an elderly man's trust. I was duped just as completely as Mr. Sikora."

Today Ms. Wright was showing her survival skills. She had kicked her lying husband to the curb and wasn't about to go down with him. I knew the sentiment.

Her testimony had been as harsh and as deadly as a lethal injection, an impressive blend of victimization and "nail the bastard." Unwisely, she was now holding court on her own. But after hearing her testimony for the prosecution, I didn't imagine the defense wanted anything to do with her. If she could add a couple dozen more nails to her ex-husband's coffin, she'd do it in a heartbeat. This stunt seemed more about self-preservation, and I got the feeling she was a pro.

"Ms. Wright? Andrea Kellner from Link-Media." I pushed around to the side of the small group. "Can you speculate on a motive? Was your husband desperate for money? Were there financial problems in his business?"

Elyse Wright turned to me with a hard stare. "It was greed and arrogance. Nothing more. But you know all about arrogant men, don't you, Ms. Kellner?"

2

I walked into the Link-Media office, the deli takeout salad getting warm and limp in my hand. The diversion of Elyse Wright's impromptu press conference had cut into the break, and I had had to return to court, food not eaten. At least my soggy zucchini had amused the guys manning the metal detector. Elyse had responded to the additional questions I shot at her, but her comment about arrogant men was still sitting uncomfortably close to home. We'd never met, but I took her to mean she knew something about my history. Or maybe I was overreacting. Having been both an attorney and a journalist, distrust was my go-to reaction, until I developed lie detector superpowers.

The trial post-lunch break had been a bust. The judge and counsel had spent about an hour huddled at the bench over some unknown technicality before dismissing the jury for the day. I wasn't in love with the piecemeal nature of the trial, but it wasn't my show. Defense and prosecution both seemed to be holding their own, but unless there was some bombshell, my money was on this guy going to jail. The evidence was strong and had been solidly presented.

I also had a hard time imagining a jury feeling warm and fuzzy over a man who bilked grandpa out of a small fortune. It was the financial equivalent of beating the family dog, and both were in the category of reprehensible offenses.

I waved at Brynn, my former research intern who now covered the Metro beat and kept walking toward my office. Televisions hung from the ceiling throughout the loft space, playing the competing voices of CNN, Al Jazeera, and MSNBC in the background. Heads were down and fingers flying over keyboards as the staff pushed through final edits or drafts for tomorrow's news cycle. Being a digital outlet, our deadlines weren't as rigid as those of the traditional media, but we made up for it in volume. Couldn't have two hours go by without a story breaking, even if it felt like regurgitated dinner.

I had just set the salad on my desk and tossed my coat on the back of the door when my boss, Art Borkowski, stormed in. As usual, his shirtsleeves were rolled back and a tie left over from 1979 hung loosely around the open collar of his shirt. He'd come of age professionally in the 70s, and in his world little had changed other than his hairline, least of all his wardrobe.

"So, do we have a verdict yet?" he asked.

"Verdict? Are you kidding me? Wright and his defense attorney want to grandstand until everyone's so annoyed, he'll be acquitted on the grounds of flagrant narcissism. And the victim's family would prefer him to be publicly flayed. So, no, we aren't even close to a verdict." I sighed and took a swig of my Pellegrino, eyeing the salad longingly and wondering if I could spear a few morsels without Borkowski giving me shit. "Today became a free-for-all with Sikora's son ready to take Wright into the back alley and issue a little homegrown Chicago justice."

Borkowski crossed his arms over his chest, looked at me over the top of his tortoise-shell glasses, and made one of the clicking sounds he made when annoyed.

"The defense has only just begun their shot at the case," I said. "If we're lucky, they'll wrap up by the end of the week, then move into summation, but with this group, who knows. There's too much ego in that room."

"I hope you got good notes on the exchange with the son. Everyone and their dog has got coverage on how this old man got ripped off. 'Me too' won't be enough. You need another angle on this. Is there more dirt on Wright? Or the old man? Maybe Wright's been ripping off other clients? Find something. Anybody can get a transcript of the trial. A synopsis ain't good enough. We still don't know what he did with all the money. You know there's more out there. Guys like this aren't one-offs. Get creative."

I grumbled inwardly but only because I didn't like being told what to do; I assured him he had nothing to worry about. He lifted his reading glasses back to the top of his head and left me in peace with my salad. I pulled the Styrofoam salad container out of its plastic bag. Vinaigrette coated my fingers. I mopped up the spill, stabbed at the soggy arugula, and then picked up the phone.

I got Cai on the third ring.

"I hope you know you are the only human being I would answer the phone for on a day like today."

"That bad?" I asked.

"Taking over mid-case for someone else. You know I hate that anyway, but the client didn't tell me the case files would need to be delivered with a semitruck. I've never seen such a mess. The discovery files alone will take me two weeks to sort out, and even then I'll be lucky if I can use five percent of the material. The client thought his prior counsel was padding his bill; I'd say he was trying to make a year's worth of fees off one client. I'm tempted to pull out a shredder and start from scratch."

I laughed. Cai was my closest friend and longtime confidant. We'd met back in law school and had been near constant companions since. She'd coached me through giving up my law career for journalism, the divorce from my husband, the death of my husband, and every twist of the complicated professional life I now led.

"Then you probably need a break. How about a drink? Nico? Say seven o'clock?"

"You're on. Although I'll be tempted to order a martini. Make sure I stop at one. Well, maybe two."

An evening to look forward to arranged, I brought my thoughts back to Gavin Wright. The prosecution had made no attempt to introduce additional victims or to suggest that embezzlement was a more widespread problem. It would have been one of the first things they looked into, and if they found anything, I couldn't imagine they would've walked away from the opportunity. That meant I needed something else. I flipped open my file and paged through my notes.

"Andrea, can I interrupt you for a minute?"

I looked up. Wade Ramelli stood in my doorway. Shit. What did he want? Showing up unannounced wasn't his thing. Wade was the chairman of the board at Link-Media and technically my boss, although complicated was the only way to describe our business relationship. I had inherited the company my husband founded after his death and had been fighting against Wade ever since to maintain control.

I'd promoted Borkowski to managing director, giving him responsibility for day-to-day operations, knowing it was best for the business, while I concentrated on being a journalist. It was an unusual arrangement and, more often than not, complicated, but we were making it work.

Ramelli seemed to have other ideas and had proposed buying me out twice now, offers I'd politely declined. As the majority shareholder, in theory, I called the shots; however, Ramelli had developed alliances with a few of the other board members, and I sensed pressure was building for a change in leadership. If they wanted to vote in a block and make my life difficult, they probably could.

"Of course, Wade. Come on in." I flicked a hand at the chair across from me, and he stepped forward, closing the door behind him. Not a good sign.

As he settled his lanky frame into the chair, I felt my stomach knot. What had started as an empathetic offer to buy me out had moved into subtle undermining when I hadn't immediately jumped on board with his plan. I had a feeling today's visit would be more of the same.

"Andrea, I'll get right to the point," he said, smoothing his tie. "The board has decided to bring in a management consultant to help us formulate our near-term strategy. It's work that needs an outside point of view. Someone who can step back and offer an opinion in ways that insiders are unable to do. I'm sure you and Borkowski will give him whatever he needs."

There it was, the first step in minimizing my role. Heat rose up the back of my neck.

"Just a minute," I said. "Are you telling me that you and the balance of the board have made this decision and retained this consultant behind my back? It's fascinating how often you seem to forget that not only am I a board member, but I'm also the primary shareholder."

I glared at Ramelli, keeping my volume low but not holding back an ounce of the outrage I was feeling.

"Don't overreact, Andrea. You and I have discussed this in principle." He pushed his shoulders back into the leather, smiling at me with the confidence of a dentist about to drill, but his tone betrayed him.

"And you've totally ignored my point of view. Working

around me, even. We both know this is just the latest in your attempt to sideline me."

"It's nothing of the sort. For this company to survive, to thrive, we need a well-developed strategy. This is simply intended as an outside voice, a third party who can provide objective industry perspective. He'll work with you and Borkowski to develop a plan. I don't understand why you're being so defensive."

"Really?"

For a fraction of a second, a sheepish look crossed his eyes but was quickly replaced by the practiced nonchalance of I-don't-give-a-shit.

"We may not have a long history," I continued, "but you're forgetting that my entire career has been about rooting out lies. I've gotten very good at sensing when I'm being played."

"And how should the board react to your objection to developing a strategy?"

He looked at me with the hint of a smug smile lighting his eyes. He had me backed into a corner, exactly the way he wanted. If I refused to cooperate, the board would see me as self-serving and obstructionist even if we both knew what was going on. I matched his smugness with a smile of my own.

"I look forward to working with him," I said. Game on.

3

I was three moves into a chess match I hadn't even known I was playing. I rubbed the back of my neck and tossed the balance of my salad into the trash. Why eat this flaccid mess when I was meeting Cai at Nico in two hours?

The conversation with Ramelli had left me steaming and feeling manipulated. I had no doubt that this consultant was entirely Ramelli's doing. It was a ruse to justify a coup or an attempt at making my life at Link-Media so miserable that I would be the one begging to leave. The consultant was probably one of Ramelli's buddies hand-feeding him a desired outcome.

The legal realities of my ownership made it impossible for the board to fire me outright, but they could make it ugly. Did I want a life that included constant animosity from the people who were supposed to be my advisors?

It was a question I wasn't yet prepared to answer. I'd hoped, probably still did, that it wouldn't come to that. Ownership of Link-Media had been the last thing on my mind when Erik was killed. We'd been a few short months away from finalizing our divorce, and my thoughts had centered around cracking the sniper story well enough to prove myself as a journalist capable of being hired by someone other than my husband after the dust settled. Little did I know that the sniper story would bring about his death.

Still married in the eyes of Illinois law, I'd inherited Erik's business, installed Borkowski as the managing editor, and hoped that would suffice. In the eight months since, I'd had to wrestle with the overwhelming grief and guilt, my life in total upheaval, and I'd survived mainly by using work as an avoidance mechanism. But was I digging in over retaining control of Link-Media because I wanted to own this business or because selling it would be one more change I had to face?

I turned back to my notes on the embezzlement case. Somewhere in here was an angle I could work with. Nathan Sikora, the victim's son, and Wright's ex-wife, Elyse, both seemed majorly pissed off. Pissed off was good. Pissed off made people talk.

I started with Elyse. Given the couple's social standing, I'd start with a simple Google search then go deeper using Lexis-Nexis once I had a few parameters.

I pored over link after link outlining the couple's philanthropic pursuits and business accomplishments.

Elyse was highly accomplished in her own right. After completing her MBA at Northwestern, she had joined Jennus Creative as a copywriter, rising through the ranks to now hold the title of senior account executive. Her bio on the company website included references to Fortune 500 companies all over the country, describing her as focused and determined. I took that to mean hard-charging. In other words, qualities a man would be admired for and a woman suspicious of, at best. The woman I'd seen outside the courthouse wasn't someone who took crap from anyone. So how had Gavin Wright managed to hide his antics from his wife? Was she too busy with her own life? Or was he just a pro at burying secret accounts?

The pretrial investigation had absolved Elyse of all guilt, but like any good attorney, Gavin's counsel might be planning to shed doubt on her clearance if it looked like he would need someone to throw under the bus. Deflection anywhere you could find it could be helpful and would explain the personal PR campaign Elyse Wright seem to be waging. This wasn't a woman cowering in fear—this was a woman prepared to do anything to protect her reputation.

It must be one hell of a divorce proceeding. I changed the search parameters to see if I could find any scuttlebutt on their split. Bingo. A familiar name jumped out at me from a year-old article buried in the *Sun-Times* archive. I reached for my phone. Elyse Wright and I shared the same divorce attorney.

"Victor, it's Andrea Kellner."

"How nice to hear from you. You're not calling to ask for a rebate, are you? After all, we didn't bring our business to conclusion."

There was a faint chuckle on the other end of the phone. Well, as much of a chuckle as Victor could give me. Humor wasn't exactly a skill I knew him for, although I had come to appreciate his attempts.

"Of course not." I laughed.

"How are you managing your new life? I've been following your work at Link-Media. That story about the energy drink company was quite intriguing, although it had me questioning my caffeine consumption."

I didn't bother to fill him in on my current life challenges; after all, he wasn't my shrink or my contract attorney. "That's why I'm calling. I understand we have a mutual acquaintance— Elyse Wright."

"Please don't tell me you're calling me for dirt. You of all people understand attorney-client privilege." I could hear the exasperation in his voice. It was a rare moment for him to allow emotion to bubble to the surface.

"No, not dirt. An introduction. Elyse has been cleared. I thought she might like to tell her side of the story. She, too, has a reputation to protect."

There was silence on the other end of the phone. I knew I was pushing Victor into uncomfortable territory. I also knew that today's performance in Daley Plaza had probably not been Victor approved.

"Just ask her if she'll speak to me," I said. "Sooner or later she's going to want to talk to someone about this. Who better than someone who also understands what it's like to be on the innocent end of shitty male behavior?"

"Okay, I'll ask, but I gotta tell you that I think this is a bad idea. I'm only doing it because I know you'd be fair. My advice to my client will be to refuse the offer. At least until there is a final judgment."

I thanked him and reiterated my assurance of sensitivity. Given the complications, the Wright divorce could be in perpetual continuance. However, I was banking on Elyse Wright's self-interest taking precedent. I didn't see her as being comfortable in the role of silent victim.

"You got a minute?"

I looked up to see Brynn leaning against the doorframe, wearing her typical uniform of a striped button-down shirt and jeans. I motioned her in. As always, a large cup of strong java was welded to her hand. She took a sip and settled into the chair across from me, but her head stayed down and her eyes were focused on the top of the travel mug she gripped.

I waited for her to speak, sensing I wasn't going to like what came next. She'd joined me as an intern, becoming invaluable as a researcher. If there was an internet thread somewhere, she could find it.

"Please don't tell me you're quitting," I said, when the silence became unbearable.

She looked up, her eyes scrunched. "I don't want to but..." Her voice cracked. "It's my mom. She lost her job two months ago, and of course that meant her health insurance went down the tubes. She's diabetic and hasn't been taking her insulin. She can't afford it. I funnel money her way when I can, but it's not enough.

"We hoped she'd find a job with insurance right away, but the longer she's unemployed, the sicker she gets. Now she's basically too sick to work. Over the weekend she ended up in the hospital. Medicaid will cover some of the bill, but it's not enough. Somehow, it's now all on my shoulders." The words and tears tumbled out. Blotches of red dotted her dark skin. "I love this job, but I don't make enough to support her too. I know it's not your problem, but you've been so good to me, I wanted you to know what's going on. I'm going to have to do something, even if it's adding a part-time job."

"I'm so sorry, Brynn." My mind jumped back to my own family struggles as a young woman. I hadn't needed to shoulder financial responsibility after my mother died, but I understood at least some of the pressure a family crisis could bring. "Can you give me a few days to see what I can do? I can't promise anything, but you know I'll fight to keep you here."

She nodded and gave me a small smile. I got to my feet and walked around the desk to give her hug. "Don't commit to anything until you talk to me. I'll do what I can."

I plopped back in my seat when she left and leaned my elbows on the desk, rubbing my temples as a headache sprung fully grown behind my eyes. Was the universe trying to tell me this buyout idea was a good option?

4

I watched the snowflakes shimmer in the light of the streetlamps, pondering my new dilemmas as I headed north on Michigan Avenue in a cab to meet Cai for drinks. What had started as a productive day had morphed into a new set of problems. Hardly the worst day of my life, but these complications were likely to infiltrate everything in my business world for the foreseeable future. Luckily, Victor had acquiesced, phoning me back after speaking with Elyse Wright. That was one for the plus column. Now, would she return the phone message I'd left or make me call back twenty-five times to show me who was in charge?

Cai was waiting for me at the bar when I arrived. Her long dark hair was still clipped at the back of her head, and her navy blazer was draped over the seat beside her. She'd loosened the tie at the neck of her silk blouse, but her signature Louboutin stilettos hadn't even slipped the backs of her heels.

The staff plated dishes in front of her in the open kitchen, but she was oblivious, immersed in her phone. A half-finished martini sat on the counter in front of her as she deftly popped out a text, making faces at the screen as she did so.

"Good thing that's not video. You're not using your poker face right now."

She smiled and gave me a hug. "It's okay. My mood was properly transmitted in written form. Another idiotic brethren who is too stupid to see that his latest motion is contradictory to his case. Lucky for me, but unfortunately, I will have to inform my client that despite the weakness of the argument, it's going to mean another continuance. It will be our fourth." She rolled her eyes and set the phone aside.

"So that explains the martini." I looked at the menu, deciding on a Nebbiolo from Piemonte, while Cai held out her drink, tempting me. "I'm going to stick with wine. Michael is stopping by later and I'd prefer not to pass out before he shows up."

"You've become such a lightweight since you started seeing him," Cai teased, removing the clip and shaking loose her hair.

"What are you talking about? I've always been a lightweight. One martini leads to three, and that leads to regretting everything you did the night before."

We laughed, and Cai filled me in on the latest machinations of the case that was her current obsession. After graduating second in her class from the University of Chicago Law School, she had taken a position at Goodin and Wagstaffe, one of the top firms in the city and her cases were always an obsession. If she took a case, she was all in. There was no low-speed setting and her track record reflected it. Supernatural focus was one of her strengths as an attorney—or your nemesis, if you opposed her.

"And how's life in the media world today? I've been too buried in work to pay attention lately. What's the big scoop of the moment?" Cai asked.

"I've been sitting in on the Wright trial. You know, that guy who embezzled funds from his elderly client? He's out on bond, but there are a lot of hot-headed people in that room who'd like to see that change. Screw over an old guy and people get mad."

"Please tell me that that lizard is going to jail."

The vehemence in her voice caught me off guard. "You've been following the trial?"

"Hard not to. The whole city is pissed off about it." She looked down at her drink and fidgeted with the skewer of olives before she continued. "And Wright and I overlapped at Goodin for half a minute when I first joined the firm after law school. I can't stand the guy. Luckily, he left and went into solo practice a year or so later."

"And?"

"And what? We both worked at the same firm. He's an ass. End of story."

"And you look like you want to punch the guy." Perhaps it was the case she had just taken on or the martini, but I saw anger in the set of her jaw. "Is there some history there?"

"Stop fishing. You're just reading my irritation with men in general. It's always men doing stupid shit, isn't it?"

I wasn't sure I believed her but let it go. My phone vibrated in my bag. I pulled it out, expecting Michael to be checking in. Nope. Elyse Wright. I tapped and took the call. She agreed to meet, and we made an appointment for the next day at her—our —divorce attorney's office, which meant she felt the need for a chaperone or maybe was just making Victor happy.

"Thanks for the break," I said, finishing the last of my wine. "I should probably get to my apartment before Michael does."

"If he blows you off, call me. I'll have another glass waiting for you."

"Only if food is part of the deal." I smiled and gave her a hug. "You might want to order prosciutto before you have another one of those."

I walked the four blocks back to my co-op, past the now dark designer boutiques on Oak Street, the weather helping me to shake off the effects of the glass of wine. The temperature was dropping rapidly, and snow had moved from a light dusting to the early stages of accumulation. Walter, my Ragdoll cat, mewed at me and lunged for my legs as I opened the door. I scooped him up, tossed my bag on the sofa, and gave him some love. He insisted on being my first priority. Attention first, food second. I set him down long enough to get rid of my wet coat, then opened a new can of his favorite smelly, mushy fish.

Michael had promised to bring dinner, so the only prep I had to do was to change into something more alluring than the courtroom work garb I had thrown on that morning.

I'd met Michael several years ago, but I'd only known him slightly through my previous career. He was a detective with the Chicago Police Department and had worked a robbery case I'd prosecuted. We'd become reacquainted last summer after a highway sniper took out a driver in front of me on the Dan Ryan. A shooting that became the impetus for an investigation into what I eventually learned was a high-level real estate play and my first major story.

Both single at the time, or nearly so in my case, the relationship had inched into the romantic. Inched was my preference; sprint seemed to be Michael's. It was challenging, not just because I had gone from almost divorced to widowed in the blink of an eye but also because our careers were significant obstacles to a relationship, and we definitely hadn't figured out the boundaries.

Before I changed, I grabbed a Pellegrino and walked to the master bath. Boxes of Carrara marble sat stacked in the corner along with adhesive and trowels. A wet saw filled the space where a toilet would eventually be installed. Three rows of hexagon tile had been installed on the wall of the future shower. Good, my contractor had followed through on his commitment.

The apartment was a grand old sprawling mess of a place with vintage details like herringbone floors and marble mantles. It hadn't been updated since well before I was born and was substantially more space than one single chick needed. But I hadn't been single when I purchased it, imagining a life vastly different from the one I lived today. Despite the impracticality, I adored it, even if I had to renovate one room at a time for the next ten years. The kitchen had been completed not long after Erik was killed, and I was now midway through the number two priority, a decent bathroom. Seeing that the installer had made a good start, I changed into jeans and a cashmere sweater I knew hugged the right curves.

My phone buzzed. The doorman announcing Michael. I propped open the door, then returned to the kitchen to open wine. Walter eyed the open door suspiciously. The vestibule was a private space, but he knew the open access meant either contractors and their noisy equipment or a guest. Neither were particularly welcome. Walter's hiss and sprint underneath the coffee table told me Michael had arrived. I'd hoped that over time, the two of them would warm up to each other, but it didn't seem promising.

"In the kitchen," I called out.

A moment later, a paper bag appeared on the quartz counter beside me and an arm circled my waist.

"You smell good," Michael said, kissing my cheek.

I turned for a proper mouth to mouth. "I think you're confused by whatever is in that bag."

"Bag? What bag?" He nuzzled my neck.

"Are we eating or playing?"

"Do I have to choose?"

"Only what comes first..." I laughed, gave him a quick kiss, and reached for the food.

As I carried dishes and containers of Chinese takeout to the dining table, we began the chitchat of sharing our day. It felt comfortable. At times, too comfortable. Inevitably something would creep into my mind like a sharp stick in the eye and tell me to hold back. Warning me not to relax, not to make assumptions that I was safe. One failed marriage under your belt did that. Particularly when trust had been thrown in the wood chipper.

Would I ever again believe with certainty that I wouldn't be hurt again? Was that even possible? I knew it wasn't fair to Michael. He wasn't the lying, cheating bastard. Guilty simply because he possessed the appropriate appendage wasn't the recipe for a solid relationship, but I couldn't seem to let down my defenses fully—and Michael was showing signs of impatience.

But that was his issue, not mine. My care-taking days were behind me. As was any sense of wide-eyed innocence. At least that was something I could hold on to.

We settled into our meals and playful banter while I teased Michael over his struggle to use chopsticks. After several aborted attempts, he stabbed a shrimp shumai rather than picking it up and popped it in his mouth. Letting the ease of the conversation and good food take over, I shoved my insecurities back into the recesses of my mind, content to enjoy the moment.

"This is really nice," Michael said, reaching across the table and squeezing my hand. "We should do it more often. Maybe all the time."

Caught off guard, I forced down the stir-fried veggies I had just chewed, then sat, silent, struggling to interpret his message.

"No comment?"

I reached for my wine before responding. "What do you mean?" It was the least innocuous thing I could think of to say. But inside, my head was on fire, and my heart was racing toward an exit.

"This is nice, isn't it?"

I nodded, waiting for the kicker.

"Well, I was thinking how great it would be to have dinner together every night, to wake up next to you every morning. I was thinking that maybe we should live together."

Michael looked at me, his expression a mixture of nervousness and excitement, as I fought back hyperventilation. I looked at him, seeing the raw anxiety and emotion on his face and feeling like a schmuck for not being able to respond the way he deserved. He was an amazing guy, but my mind whirled in fear. Fear that had nothing to do with him. My throat clamped down, and words wouldn't come.

"I'm not sure I'm ready for that," I said, my voice a whisper. It was the only thing I could squeak out.

Rejection hardened his eyes. He looked away, then opened his mouth to say something more, but the trill of my phone broke the moment. I jumped up and grabbed it off the console table, the unknown caller suddenly my top priority. In reality, I didn't want to face Michael. Confusion and my flight reaction were all I could focus on.

"Ms. Kellner, this is Nathan Sikora. Isaac Sikora's son. You know, from the trial?"

"Yes, Mr. Sikora, I know who you are. What can I do for you?" I could feel Michael's eyes on the back of my head.

"Can we meet?" Sikora said. "I think there is information that isn't being presented well in court. Maybe you could do a story? Get our side out? My dad is being portrayed as a senile old kook, and that's not the man I knew. This guy Wright is an actor and a manipulator. That needs to be talked about."

"Of course I'm willing to listen to anything you have to say. I can't make promises on a story or what the content would be if I moved forward. If that's agreeable, I'm happy to talk."

"That's fair. And that's exactly why I called you instead of one of the other leeches in the media. You seem to understand balanced reporting. I remember that casino piece you did last year. You could have let your husband off the hook, but you didn't. That's what I need."

We discussed the details and ended the call. When I turned, Michael had cleared the table and was putting on his jacket.

"Forget I said anything." He walked out.

5

I walked into the Link-Media conference room with a foggy head and an unsettled heart. I'd phoned Michael after he'd left last night, hoping for an opportunity to explain myself and to try to smooth over his ruffled feathers, but he apparently wasn't in the mood to hear me and hadn't picked up. Throughout the evening I'd run back over the conversation in my mind. Had I been too abrupt? Too insensitive? Or was he just pissed because I'd allowed a phone call to change the subject? I wasn't sure of anything other than being a damn girl and feeling like I needed to be the one to apologize. Would he have taken a call from a suspect just as I wanted to have a sensitive talk? Yes. And he would expect me to understand, so why was I the one feeling like I'd slapped him in the face?

His question hadn't just surprised me, it had bumped my panic button. While I felt a great deal of affection for Michael, neither one of us had said the three magic words. Was I deeply "in like" with the man? Yes. In love? I couldn't even conceive of the emotion yet. But that wasn't about Michael. It was about me being damaged goods. I thought I had been transparent about my fragile emotions. Either I hadn't been as clear as I thought, he was choosing not to hear me, or he assumed he could change my point of view by sheer force of will. Regardless, the two of us had some serious talking to do.

The first to arrive, I placed my mug of Earl Grey on the table and settled into a chair. The judge in the Wright trial had apparently come down with some minor stomach bug, so I was in the office instead of the courtroom. Borkowski had sent out a note at 7:30 this morning asking for an impromptu meeting of the senior team, I assumed to break the news on the consultant who'd be interrupting our work days with requests for the next few weeks. The other members of our small crew started filtering in and inquiring about the reason for the morning powwow, but I just shrugged. Borkowski needed to handle this one.

Ten minutes later my hands were wrapped around the cup I'd lifted to my lips when Borkowski strolled in. By then the conversation in the room had moved to comparing notes on stories in process. Deep in discourse, the small group of journalists didn't give his entrance any additional import. Nor did they immediately notice his companion.

I, on the other hand, nearly spit out my tea.

Ryan Molina. Just as gorgeous as the last time I'd seen him. He strode to the head of the table alongside Borkowski. Catching my eyes, he gave me an innocuous smile before turning back to hang on to whatever words of bullshit Borkowski was spewing. I kept my cup at my mouth and sipped slowly, needing a moment to recover. And to find my poker face. My stomach, unfortunately, was sinking into the floor. What was he doing here?

RPM Consultants was the group that Borkowski had told me he'd hired, but he'd never mentioned the specific person assigned to work with us. Nor did I have any historic reference to a company by that name. Back in the early days of Link-

Media, Erik had worked with Ryan, bringing him in to set up his overall strategy for the company. They'd kept in touch, and periodically Erik would bring Ryan in when he felt the need for a reset or an objective pair of ears. But he had worked for a larger firm at the time. I searched back through my memory, trying to recall whether I'd heard that he'd gone out on his own, but as recently as two years ago, Ryan had very clearly been employed elsewhere.

I knew this because after I'd discovered Erik had been cheating on me, I'd slept with him.

How in the hell was this going to work? No one knew, not even Cai. She knew I'd indulged in a bit of payback in a moment of anger, but I'd never told her who it was. At the time, it hadn't felt that "the who" had mattered. It wasn't an affair—it was revenge. Now here I was, panicked, facing weeks or maybe even months working with the guy.

What had he told Borkowski?

"All right, you guys, let's stop the gossip. The quicker you shut up, the quicker we can all get back to working. You remember that, don't you?" Borkowski said, silencing the chatter. I looked longingly at the door.

The handful of us in the room shuffled in our seats and tried to pretend that we weren't being spoken to like ten-year-olds. Borkowski had an old newsroom style. I knew he wasn't consciously sexist, but he came from an era of gruff talk and real men, whatever that meant back in the day. The realities of today's workforce weren't about to change his delivery style, despite the number of times I'd had to calm down a female coworker with a bruised ego. He was just one of those guys who was a grizzly bear on the outside even if there was a gooey middle deep at his core. He meant nothing with his harsh tone; he simply had standards and, at this point, wasn't going to adapt. So the rest of us had to.

"I want to introduce you all to Ryan Molina. I've brought him in to help us take an objective look at the business. You've been hearing me say it for quite a while now: competition out there is tough. We need to be lean and mean if we expect to hold our own in the marketplace. I haven't been shy about telling you our readership numbers have taken a hit, and we can't survive long-term with that decline. So I want you all to give Ryan your full cooperation."

Suddenly all eyes in the room seemed to turn in my direction. Everyone was wondering the same things—did I know about this, and what wasn't Borkowski saying? I caught glances of fear and expectation, as if I were the one who was supposed to jump in and assure everyone that their jobs were safe. Unfortunately, that wasn't something I could do. I didn't even know if my own job was safe, and I owned the damn company.

It was a struggle, but I did what I could to keep the thoughts that were bouncing around in my head from showing on my face. The next question was, had Ryan said anything to Borkowski about how we knew each other? And if not, could I keep it that way?

"I'm happy to be here," Ryan said, his voice confident and welcoming. "I look forward to getting to know everyone. I've followed Link-Media for a number of years. Even did a little work for the company at its inception. It's an impressive organization, and I am honored to be part of the effort to make it even better. I promise I'll make this as painless as possible." He laughed and looked around the room, trying to make light of his presence. There were small chuckles of agreement. Trying to warm up his audience was the better way to think of it.

"To start, I'll be meeting with you all individually, just to understand who's part of this great team. Then we'll dig into process. I want to hear any ideas you have on how Link-Media could be improved, obstacles that are standing in your way. But for now, I just wanted to say hello, and we'll speak again soon."

"That's a wrap, guys. You have deadlines," Borkowski said.

I hung back, processing my thoughts as the crew vacated the room. I wasn't sure if I felt better or worse about knowing the consultant Borkowski had hired and that he had a history with the company. I guessed it would depend on what happened from here on out. When the room cleared, I stood and walked around the table. Ryan reached out a hand.

Borkowski jumped in to make an introduction.

"It's good to see you again," Ryan said. His hand held mine firmly, lingering a little too long. Noticing the confused look on Borkowski's face, he added, "Andrea and I met, briefly, several years ago when Erik first founded the business. I didn't think it relevant to mention. She probably doesn't even remember," he said casually, his eyes on Borkowski.

When he turned back to me, I could see by the new intensity in his eyes that he remembered every second of our encounter. I felt the heat of that look at my core, then mumbled something bland and welcoming and got the hell out of the room.

6

Ryan Molina. Of all the people who could have come back into my life, did it have to be him? Memories flashed into my brain, sultry and sweaty, and I escorted them right back out. Damn! Why him? Why now? And how in the hell was I going to make this work?

I wasn't normally prone to conspiracy theories, but the thought that Ramelli had somehow learned of our history and was intending to use it to shake my footing popped into my head. All the more reason to stay as far away from Ryan as I could. This was business and only business. Then why could I still feel the heat of his touch?

I sat in the back of a cab, thoughts tumbling. Victor Kirkland and Elyse Wright were waiting for me in Victor's office, and my head wasn't focused. I jumped out of the car at Monroe and Clark, and the wind tunnel off the lake nearly knocked me off balance. I rubbed the palm of my hand on my wool pants, shaking off Ryan's touch and went upstairs.

I didn't know what to make of Elyse Wright. Was she an innocent victim caught on the edges of her husband's deceit and trying to defend her reputation? Or as some were suggesting, happily pretending to have known nothing about her ex's shenanigans but now optimizing the moment for her own gain? Although the investigation had exonerated her of any involvement, the rumors still swirled. I did know that she was working the moment for a positive spin. After all, she was an advertising executive. Perception mattered.

But it also made her suspect. Not necessarily in the criminal sense, but how far would she go to create her own reality and protect her reputation?

I entered the reception area at Kirkland and McCullough, informed the receptionist of my appointment with Victor, then was led back to the large conference room. Elyse had already arrived. She wore a dove-gray architectural jacket and skirt, a white blouse, and fire-engine red lipstick. Arrogant ex-husbands weren't the only thing we shared. Boy, would I have fun pawing through her closet.

She and Victor sat nearly elbow to elbow huddled over a legal pad. Victor stood when I entered, puffing up to his full five foot seven. His dress shirt strained over his belly, a new development since the last time I'd seen him. He smiled and came around the table to clasp my hand.

"Andrea, let me introduce you to Elyse Wright."

She flashed me a brief smile and extended a hand. "Obviously, we know of each other, and it's nice to meet you formally. Although I have to say I wish we were here to talk about something else. Lord knows I'm tired of all this embezzlement mess."

"We should probably be meeting for drinks," I said. She chuckled and adjusted the gold bracelet on her left wrist. It held a charm of some kind, and the gesture seemed nothing more than a nervous tic.

"Please, ladies, have a seat. Andrea, I know you don't drink coffee, but I can have tea brought in."

"No, nothing for me," I said. "Thank you for meeting with

me, Elyse. I know this is a crazy time." She raised her eyebrows as if to say, "Really? That's the best you've got?" I brushed it aside, taking the response as a signal to be direct and opened my notebook.

"Courtroom testimony seems to be clear in exonerating you from any knowledge of or involvement in your husband's alleged crimes, yet suspicion seems to be under the surface in the public's perception. Why do you think that is?" I said.

"Finally, someone willing to ask a direct question." She nodded her approval and smiled. "I think you know exactly where that suspicion comes from. Flat-out sexism. Decades of people assuming 'wifey' is either some Stepford robot or a conniving bitch. Clearly we are not yet at a place in society where the majority can understand a woman whose career is as demanding, or even more so, than her partner's."

She shot a look at Victor, presumably to see if she was over-stepping. I didn't sense she cared about the decorum of her strong voice in most situations, but I was certain she had been advised repeatedly by her legal team to tone it down in public.

"Since I didn't hover over how he spent money," she contin-ued, "and didn't devote myself to house and home, the only stereotype left is that of a money-grubbing taker. People don't seem to understand where to place a successful, childless woman. I don't fill the slot, so in the absence of something better, I'm labeled to fit something they think they understand. Right or wrong, it seems irrelevant to most. Hard for me to say as an ad executive who takes part in the dumbing down of Amer-ican women, but here we are."

Her voice was filled with irritation, as if disappointed in society or maybe in herself. "How are you countering the suspi-cions?" I asked.

"The same way you did." She paused, and our eyes locked. She seemed to be daring me to challenge her or commiserate as if we had some sisterly bond over our ex-husbands' bad behavior. I couldn't sort out the message behind her eyes. Was I reading into her comment or just feeling paranoid?

When I didn't acknowledge her statement, she looked away, tugging again on the charm.

"I'm doing what strong women do everywhere," she said after a moment. "I'm telling my truth and reminding myself every day that I'd rather have the steel backbone of a woman than the spinelessness of three-quarters of the male population. Not all of us define marriage as two people joined at the hip. Gavin is an actor. Greedy, self-serving, hiding behind a facade. That doesn't make me guilty just because we shared a bed. What am I, his babysitter?" Her voice went up an octave.

Victor was looking uncomfortable again. He shifted in his chair and scribbled something on his legal pad. Notes about what not to say next time?

"When in the hell are men going to man up, grow up, stop pretending to be shocked when they're shown to be assholes?" Elyse continued. "And when is society going to stop making excuses for them? I am so damn tired of this 'boys-will-be-boys' attitude or 'he has a tough job, so he shouldn't be expected to do anything other than bring home a paycheck.' Don't even get me started on the double standard of women who can think for themselves without getting permission from the hubby. Who the hell has time to treat men like babies? Certainly not women who are interesting."

Again I had the feeling she was posturing or perhaps trying to bait me into offering an opinion, as if we were just two girls frustrated by male weaknesses. That could be a week-long conversation, but I wasn't going to get trapped in that rabbit hole.

Off the bat I didn't like her. There was something about her that came across as manipulative. I couldn't put my finger on what it was, but nothing about the conversation was shaking that impression. Maybe it was that she seemed to assume there was a commonality between us, a connection. Or maybe it was that her entire life seemed to be about appearances?

But I wasn't here to make friends, nor was I here to make judgments. She was understandably resentful of the situation her ex-husband had put her in, but so what. She was far from the only woman wronged. That didn't make it a story.

I held back and let her talk, hoping that some tidbit would move this conversation beyond angry ex-wife. The more she downloaded, the more Victor was getting agitated. I didn't blame him. If I'd been one of the tabloid hacks, my notebook would be full. The clock was ticking. Victor's patience for a client going off the rails could only be wearing thin. Time to up the pressure before he shut the conversation down.

"Elyse, is there anything the prosecution should have asked you but didn't? You seemed frustrated while you were on the stand. Or was I reading into the exchange?"

I was playing a hunch, remembering moments of what I perceived as impatience in her delivery when being questioned. She paused briefly and took a drink of her coffee, but I could see her eyes light up ever so slightly.

"They should have asked if he'd ever done anything like this before."

"What do you mean by that?" I pulled myself upright and jotted down her exact quote. This wasn't an answer I'd been prepared for. Nothing had come up at trial. Had he embezzled previous clients and simply not been caught?

"All right, that's enough," Victor interjected, concerned by where this was going. "I've got to stop you right here. We're getting into territory that is out of the scope of what we agreed to."

"It's on the table, so at least let Elyse explain what she meant.

Was there a prior investigation?" I asked, looking from Victor to
Elyse. She sat quietly, calm satisfaction on her face.

"No, this meeting is over. We're not turning this into a
sideshow." He looked straight at Elyse and glared. "Elyse was not
implying anything about Gavin's history or any other misdeeds.
Disregard her comment."

He stood. "Elyse, I'm sure you're needed back at the office."

"Yes, I'm sure I am." She gathered her purse and moved
toward the door. "Lovely to meet you, Andrea." She held out a
hand with a sly smile, and I half expected her to wink. She'd
accomplished what she set out to do. She'd sowed additional
doubt on her husband's reputation. But if she had knowledge of
another crime, it sowed doubt on her reputation as well.

With Elyse out of the room, Victor turned his attention back
to me.

"Don't you dare print that."

"Come on, Victor, you know me better than to suggest I'd
print something so flimsy. It was a vague accusation. I write
nothing I can't substantiate. But I'm all ears if you have something to say about Gavin's history. Elyse was hinting at something. Has she spoken to you about it?"

"I knew this was a bad idea," he grumbled, looked at his
watch, and moved toward the door. "It meant nothing. She's
been under considerable stress and misspoke."

"Okay, if that's the explanation you want to go with, but I'm
not going to promise I won't look into it."

Conversation over. I followed him, assuming he had only
stayed in the room with me long enough to make sure Elyse was
out of the building. We walked out of the conference room and
into the open area of office cubicles. As usual, the paralegals and
administrative staff had their heads down, many drowning out
distraction with headphones.

"She seems a bit hot-headed," I said as we walked. May as

well throw in a few more stabs while I had him alone. "Was their relationship volatile? Her and Gavin's? Off the record, of course."

"Don't push our friendship," he said, stopping to make sure we made eye contact.

"Okay, I got the message. Just doing my job."

"And I'm doing mine." He clasped my hand and shook his head before leaving me at the reception desk.

I pulled out my phone to check messages as I stepped out of the reception area into the hallway. Two male voices bounced back at me as I walked toward the elevator, but I couldn't see the bodies they were attached to.

"It's appalling. She's depriving a man of a job that's rightfully his. He has a family to support."

The comment made my chest tighten. Wanting the men to know I'd heard them, I continued making sure my feet were heavy. I saw them as soon as I rounded the corner. They stood inches from one another in front of the elevator doors, turning their heads toward me when I came into view. One of the men was familiar, a paralegal—if I remembered correctly—who worked for Victor's firm. He at least looked startled, even a bit embarrassed, probably wondering how much I'd heard. He nodded at me, then quickly looked down at the floor. His friend, however, showed no discomfort.

"It's Marcus, isn't it?" I said. "I think we spoke a few times during my divorce proceedings."

"Yes, ah, I think so. Good to see you."

He was a huge man, in girth—wide but not particularly tall, with a soft round body built for couch surfing. His cheeks splotched pink as he looked at his friend. I wondered if the buzz cut he wore was a holdover from Catholic grade school or the army.

I turned to his companion, who seemed even more unhappy

with the interruption. "Andrea Kellner." I held out a hand. "Are you with Kirkland and McCullough as well?"

"Leon Rutkowski. I'm a forensic account, independent. I get called in from time to time." He said the words but ignored my outstretched hand.

Whatever.

"Nice to meet you. Enjoy your day, gentlemen." They hustled out of my sight, this time silently.

As I waited for the elevator, I wondered if Victor knew of his employees' misogynistic leanings. It wasn't exactly a confidence builder for new clients. Elyse Wright's diatribe on sexism also floated back into my mind. But I shoved it aside. No need to torture myself further by dwelling on the obvious.

I was, however, interested in her comment suggesting that Gavin may have a history of embezzlement. If he did, that would change the story's trajectory. And possibly mine.

7

Was embezzlement a pattern of behavior for Gavin Wright or a one-off opportunistic crime? And if Elyse had known something, wouldn't that have come up at trial? It was far easier to convict if you could show a history. Perhaps Elyse was exaggerating? Looking to cast suspicion and hoping that I'd help deliver the final blow?

There were two things I knew to be true: whatever her motives, I doubted they had anything to do with being altruistic, and Victor had heard these allegations before.

I waved at Brynn as I returned to the office, immediately feeling guilty that I didn't have answers for her. Being a junior member of the team, she hadn't been included in today's meeting that dropped the consultant bombshell, and I'd been too busy to bring her under the tent. I tipped my head toward the door, inviting her in, then picked up the phone to see if I could get a minute with Borkowski. Voicemail. I left a quick message saying I needed to talk and was just finishing up as Brynn walked into my office. I could tell by the look on her face that the rumor mill was already running rampant.

"I'm guessing you've heard the news," I said, as she plopped into the chair and set her large mug of coffee on the edge of my desk. She nodded, but her face told me I'd screwed up. "How bad is it?"

"It's everything from the company is being bought out to you are being shown the door. Is it true?"

"I'm sorry I didn't get to you first. I figured it would be better if we weren't at the office, but I had a meeting with Elyse Wright and I forgot to call you. I apologize. You should've heard about the consultant from me." The hard line of her jaw softened slightly, and she took a drink of her coffee, but I could tell she was pissed.

"It's not as bad as everyone's making it out to be," I said. "At least I don't think it is. Borkowski is bringing in someone, a consultant named Ryan Molina, to help us be more efficient. What I've been told is that this will largely be a deep dive into process."

"What you've been told? You weren't in on this decision? How can he do that?" She jumped in her chair, nearly spilling her drink.

I hesitated, tucking my hair behind my ears as I gathered my thoughts. This was one of those moments where the line between my role and Borkowski's was confusing to everyone. The professional in me needed to back up Borkowski's right to make decisions about day-to-day operations as he saw fit, but I also felt an obligation to Brynn. She and I were more than coworkers—we were friends, and because of that, I owed her honesty, up to a point. We all had our secrets, and I, for instance, saw no reason to tell her or anyone else how great Ryan looked naked.

"You know I've always been straight with you, Brynn. No, I didn't believe this was a process or expense we needed, but it's his decision. I made him managing editor, and I can't micromanage how he does his job."

"Even if that means cutting heads?" Panic tinged her voice.

"Let's not jump the gun. All businesses need to be continually looking at how they operate. This isn't necessarily a bad thing."

"It isn't necessarily a good thing either."

"Let's let it play out. See where the conversations go. Nothing is going to change in a dramatic way without me weighing in. Look, you're doing a great job here. I know your personal situation is a little concerning right now, and I promise I'll do everything I can to keep you here with me for a very long time. Okay?"

She looked at me over the top of her coffee mug. The furrows in her brow had softened, but she didn't seem fully convinced. "Okay, but I don't have a lot of time for this to work out itself out on its own."

"Fair enough. I have a call in to Borkowski. In the meantime, I have a possible lead I want to work through. Care to give me a hand?"

"Any time. What do you need?"

"Gavin Wright. His wife, well, ex-wife, said something today I need to dig into. She insinuated that this embezzlement situation is not the first."

"Details?"

"No. Her divorce attorney was present and shut that down the minute she opened her mouth. But she was clear. She wants me to dig. What I don't know is whether something happened or if she just wants to create the appearance that it did."

"The classic, 'a woman scorned'?"

"Maybe. I get the sense this woman is a master at spin; she's in advertising, after all. But she also is not going down with his ship. She's fighting back."

"Got it. I assume if there'd been a prior conviction, that

would've come up in the trial, but I'll run his history. Maybe it was in another state."

"Or maybe charges were never filed. It doesn't make sense that a prior history wouldn't have been used if they had caught him in the past, so we'll probably have to do some digging. I'll work some of my contacts in the legal community and see if there are any rumors while you do what you do best. Let's touch base later."

I flipped open my laptop and quickly refreshed my knowledge of Gavin Wright's background. He'd graduated from the University of Wisconsin law school, then bounced around between a few of the smaller firms, trying to find his niche, before ending up at Goodin and Wagstaffe. He and Cai must have overlapped for less than a year. I thought back to her tone last night when Wright's name came up. She obviously disliked the man, which meant there was a reason, but it wasn't like her to hold back. I made a note to myself to call her later and ask what that was all about. After leaving Goodin and Wagstaffe, Wright had gone off on his own, becoming a solo practitioner. I pulled up my notes on the case, then logged in to Lexis-Nexis to see what else I could find.

Twenty-five minutes in, my phone pinged with a number I didn't recognize.

"Andrea, this is Elyse Wright. I'm sorry our conversation got cut short today. Can we meet?"

I stifled a laugh, beginning to understand why the woman was successful in advertising. But what did she really want? I paused for a moment, listening to my gut before responding.

"I'm happy to meet, but if this is about vague accusations and scoring points in your divorce, I'm not interested. I don't write a society column, and he-said-she-said isn't interesting to me. But, if you have information to flesh out what you hinted at, then of course we can talk. However, before we go any further, I have to say I'm confused why—if what you alluded to is true—there've been no allegations of previous embezzlement in this trial? I find it hard to believe it wouldn't have been covered extensively already."

"He never got caught," she said, her tone impatient. "But look, there's more to it. He's...he's not what he seems. I'll give you the information, and you'll check it out yourself. But there's something else. Something damaging. He threatened me last night."

"What do you mean? He threatened you? How?"

"My life! He threatened my life. He's been sending me emails. I can show you."

What in the hell kind of game was she playing now? My instinct again was that she was manipulating me, seeking attention, branding herself even further as the victim. It wasn't a role that suited her. Maybe that was why I was having trouble finding her credible?

"Elyse, if your life has been threatened, you need to call CPD. And Victor. Does he know?"

"Of course. I told him all about it, but he said the threats are too vague. That Gavin is just trying to rattle me. That it's just his frustration. That I should just save the emails and if it gets out of hand, he'll have a restraining order issued. Blah, blah, blah. What's a restraining order going to do? The man is out on bail!"

"And why are you telling *me*?"

"Because someone else has to know. I don't feel safe. Please, can we get together tonight? I'll tell you everything I know about his history. And I'll show you the emails he sent me. You can decide for yourself if they constitute a threat. And whether it changes anything about your story."

"I'm having a hard time here. First you say he's embezzled before, and now you say he's threatened your life. I'm struggling

to see why any of this would have been left out of a trial if there
was evidence."

"He's a master con man. He's lied to them all, me most of all.
And now I think the jury believes him. That they're going to let
him off. But if they know his past and how he's been communi-
cating with me, they can't let him go. Please, Andrea, I need to
show this to someone. All I'm asking is that you take a look. Can
you meet tonight? At my house in Lincoln Park?"

I heard desperation in her voice and agreed to meet her at
seven. But every fiber of my body said I was being manipulated.

8

Damn! A second text from Borkowski pushing me on a time frame for the Wright story and a phone message from Ryan asking to clear my schedule tomorrow for our first meeting. Why had I bothered to look at my phone?

I was in a cab on my way to speak with Nathan Sikora. After his outburst in court yesterday, I figured the pump was primed for some good dirt on Wright. Or at the very least, some colorful quotes that his attorney had cautioned against.

I tossed my phone back in my bag in disgust. The full day? Ryan had to be kidding. Was this what life under the thumb of a consultant would be like? Drop everything and jump? The Wright trial was slated to reconvene at 9:00 a.m., assuming the judge had worked through his stomach issues. Ryan would just have to find someone else to hassle. Or Borkowski and I would need to have a tough conversation on priorities.

But the more I rebelled against our involvement with Ryan's firm, the more likely it was that our history would come out. Ryan had played it cool yesterday, but I knew I couldn't count on that. Nor did I want to spend my work day worried about whether I was sending him the wrong message and appearing to reignite a personal relationship. This situation was annoying any way I looked at it.

"The blue awning ahead on the left," I said to the driver.

I paid, jumped out of the car, then sent a response to Ryan, politely telling him I would be in court in the morning and asking for another time slot.

Isaac Sikora had lived in a vintage co-op on Lincoln Park West, which meant lake views and old money. His son, Nathan, had suggested we meet at the apartment while he cleaned out the home before listing it for sale. Nothing like watching family members cry their eyes out while they packed up grandpa's china. But Nathan was biting mad and had been all too happy to take a break from the business of death.

I could relate. I still hadn't put Erik's condo on the market. The human desire to avoid pain was alive and well in my world, too.

I entered the grand lobby filled with dark wood paneling, mounds of fresh flowers, and upholstered wing chairs. It read rich, old, and conservative. The monthly HOAs could likely buy someone a nice used starter car. I announced myself to the uniformed doorman and, after a few moments, was sent up.

The elevator opened into a private paneled vestibule, flanked by double doors on each end. As I looked around for an apartment number, the doors to my right swung open, and a small gray Yorkie ran out and howled at me.

"Squeaky, get back in here." Nathan Sikora stood in the doorway, a look of disapproval on his face. "She's harmless," he said, motioning me in and shaking his head. "But she makes a hell of a lot of noise. She was my father's dog and hasn't settled into her new life. Not sure I have, either, to be honest. I bring her over here when I come, thinking it will calm her down. But the poor thing just howls no matter where she is."

"Pets mourn too. It takes time and love." I shook his hand,

then followed him into the apartment. Sunlight streamed in, and Lake Michigan gleamed cobalt blue through the row of tall windows that lined the living room. My decorating eye scanned the room in admiration. Tall coffered ceilings. A massive carved fireplace mantle. Inlaid wood floors. And from what I could guess, a floor plan that meandered nicely. I wasn't in the market, nor was I in the price range, but that didn't stop my remodeling lust from kicking in.

Sikora was pale with wiry hair and a body that hadn't seen the gym in probably a decade. Exhaustion had settled around his eyes. Was it the business of death or the business of justice that was weighing on him? Boxes were stacked willy-nilly around the room. Some sealed, many empty, awaiting their next treasure.

I felt the weight of the task. The decisions that needed to be made. Donate, sell, keep because it's too precious to discard. The reminder of the work I had yet to do with the last of Erik's things pressed on me as I looked around. I knew it was time for my own avoidance to end. It was the final tie to the memory of a life we'd shared. But that life was long gone, and my memories had turned out to be faulty.

"There is a system here, even if it's not readily apparent. I never thought of myself as a minimalist, but going through this experience makes me want to go home and throw out everything. Save someone from the task when I'm gone."

"Are you sure this is a good time to talk?" I asked, feeling a bit like a vulture waiting to prey on the man's vulnerability.

"Yeah, a break will do me good." He nodded, trying to smile. "Not to mention how it'll help me work off some of this anger. That son of a bitch Wright deserves to be exposed. And I'm more than happy for the world to know what he's done. Let me move a couple boxes and we can sit."

Sikora picked up the dog and set her on his lap as he sat in the floral chintz club chair. The pup wagged her tail enthusiastically, then rested her head on Sikora's knee.

"From the testimony, I understand that your father worked with Gavin Wright for the last eight years of his life," I said. "During that time did you ever have any suspicions or concerns about Mr. Wright's handling of your father's estate plan?"

"Not a clue." Sikora shook his head. "Dad loved the guy. Trusted him completely. When his memory started to get a little fuzzy, I was just grateful that it was one less thing I had to worry about. For the last year or so, we had a home health aide come in, one of those services you employ, but you know how that goes. You can never quite tell if old age and senility are popping up or if the aide who shows up that day is one of the better ones. Not that I'm bashing the service we used. They were great as far as I could tell, but when you're not there, it's hard to separate truth from fiction."

"Are you saying your father made accusations?"

"A little paranoia seems to be a common aspect to aging. Dad would tell me things, like a book had been stolen, when in fact he had removed it from the shelf and forgotten where he'd put it. I never took it seriously. Just an old man becoming forgetful. I didn't realize anything was amiss in his finances until after he died, but then you heard that in court. Dad had worked with Wright for years. It never crossed my mind that he was a lying scumbag."

"And you first learned of the problem when Wright's administrative assistant brought it to your attention?" The image of her hunched figure in the courtroom came to mind, and I wondered about her moral struggles.

He nodded, continuing to pet the dog now sleeping on his lap. "Of course, I was in touch with Wright's office as soon as Dad passed. As you know, my father had established a trust that held his assets. I'm the executor, so I called to set up a meeting with Wright to discuss the terms of the trust and how all that worked. He was out of the office for a couple days, so in advance of our meeting, I went in to drop off a copy of the death certificate for their records. That's when Jocelyn dropped the bad news."

"To be clear, you're talking about Jocelyn Lawrence, Wright's administrative assistant."

He nodded.

"And is that when she gave you copies of the bank transfers?"

"She didn't entirely know what she had. It was just bits and pieces that said something wasn't right. But there was enough data for us both to see some kind of scheme was probably underway. She had copies of invoices on my father's account for the year leading up to his death, and each invoice included a line item for miscellaneous fees."

"Was there something odd about that? Did she know what that covered?" Although Lawrence had testified that she hadn't been aware of what her boss had been up to, I found myself questioning the timing.

"It wasn't odd at all. There are always charges that get lumped together for postage and printing. Some of the research materials on funds go into that line item as well as a host of other things related to managing the assets. My father had a substantial portfolio, so the number was never large enough to cause him to question it. It was just part of doing business. However, when the invoices were laid out sequentially, we could see that that line item was increasing over time and always by a round number. Five hundred dollars, a thousand dollars, two thousand. Never enough that it was immediately obvious, but if you were to graph it, the upward trajectory would be clear."

"Something that confused me at the trial was why you believed the situation wasn't kosher. Your father's estate sounds complex. Was there something other than the dollar amounts increasing that gave you pause?"

"Yes, but I'm not able to discuss it."

I stopped writing my notes and looked at him. Had he withheld information from the legal team?

"You can relax. The prosecuting attorney knows everything. There is just a piece that, although related, isn't directly tied to Wright's crime. Let's leave it at that. After I brought my suspicions, and the documents Jocelyn retrieved, to the attention of the authorities, they were able to subpoena Wright's financial records, even the deep, dark hidden ones, and the rest, as they say, is history. Well, history playing out, and if all goes as it should, Wright himself will be history."

What was Sikora holding back? Or protecting? And was Lawrence connected?

"Wright testified that these charges were a result of the complexity of your father's accounts," I said. "But you immediately brought the authorities into the situation. Why didn't you question Wright first?"

"That jackass wasn't going to tell me the truth. The only reason to confront him would be to watch what he did after."

9

The sharp February wind swept the side of my face, throwing my hair over my eyes as I got out of my car. It was just after 7:00 p.m., and I was running a little late for my meeting with Elyse Wright. As always, parking in this neighborhood was a total bitch, and I'd been circling for twenty minutes waiting for a spot to open, finally wedging my Audi into a space that was more snowbank than pavement. Cai made fun of me for holding Uber in contempt; tonight she may have won the argument.

I scanned the street, looking around at the vintage brownstones in this quiet stretch of the Lincoln Park neighborhood. Soft lights lit the front stoops or glowed delicately behind curtains drawn for privacy on this lovely treelined street. I tapped open my phone to double-check the house number, looked around again to get my bearings, then walked six doors north on Cleveland Avenue.

The neighborhood was classic Chicago elegance. Single-family brick brownstones lined the street with small multifamily dwellings dotted in, but the overall mood was of history, wealth, elegance, and education. It was one of the most desirable neigh-

borhoods in the city. Lincoln Park itself stretched along the lake-
front a few blocks to the east, running for seven miles and
covering over 1,200 acres. It housed a zoo, a conservatory, two
museums, and every manner of recreational activity. In other
words, it was almost the heart of the city. Two of the city's top
private schools were nearby, attracting professional families and
pushing the price point of these homes well past the million-
dollar mark.

But tonight that was barely evident in the cold, the snow, and
the dark. Although I had agreed to the meeting, I expected it to
be another waste of time. Elyse had an agenda, and somehow I
was in the middle as we played a little game of tug-of-war to see
who got what she wanted first. Or who got what she wanted
without giving up everything. I had a suspicion most things were
a delicate negotiation with Elyse. The image of her one day
gracing the afternoon talk shows with a book tour, proudly
sharing her life story of female triumph over another sad, self-
centered man, wasn't hard to envision. But I guess there were a
few of us with that story. Perhaps her story would just be a little
more salacious in the tell.

The porch light was out at the top of the stoop when I
reached the front of her building, but light radiated through the
transom from somewhere inside. Like everything else on the
block, it was a vintage home, likely built in the late 1800s, in an
era of household help and horse-and-buggy transportation.
Today all signs of that life were long gone. The external shell of
these buildings hinted at history, but the interiors had long ago
been modernized.

I reached the top of the stairs, fumbling in the dark for a
doorbell. The stained-glass side panels along the heavy wood
door yielded inadequate light, so I turned on my flashlight app
to get my bearings. Broken glass glittered at my feet. A small
area of the sidelight appeared recently broken. I bent down to

inspect, finding it strange and feeling my body react. I didn't imagine Elyse Wright was the kind of person to leave something like that unattended to. My breath quickened as I found the buzzer, and I held it until I could hear the hollow ding inside. But I heard no footsteps. Pressing on the buzzer repeatedly, I peered through the hole in the sidelight, seeing even more glass on the floor inside.

"Elyse!" I shouted and raised my fist to the door. It swung open freely with my touch. Phone in hand, I pushed the door back, listening for sounds, running my eyes over the shimmer on the floor in front of me, looking for other signs of disturbance, listening for sounds of someone inside. And ready to dial 911.

"Elyse?" I called out. "It's Andrea. Is everything okay? Are you here?" Silence. I ran my eyes over the room. Beyond the glass the room was orderly—nothing overturned, nothing appeared disturbed. "Elyse," I called again. My heart thumped as I tried to imagine a reasonable explanation for the unlocked door and the broken glass, but nothing came. I stepped forward, avoiding the fragments on the floor as best I could. Entering a vestibule, then stepping into what would've been known as a front parlor, I saw a single lamp next to the fireplace softly lighting the room. I moved forward slowly, looking for some sign of what might have happened, listening for indications that someone was here.

"Elyse?" I called out again. A thump came from somewhere beyond my sight, somewhere down the hallway on my left. I moved quickly toward the sound. My eyes rushing ahead, trying to make sense of what my instincts were telling me. As I moved out of the parlor, down the hall, more lights radiated in the back of the house. I flitted from caution to fear as I crept along, then saw a bloody handprint smudged on the wall to my right and a single stiletto lying on its side a few feet in front of me.

Dialing 911, I raced forward frantically, once more yelling her name.

The hall opened into a large kitchen, warm, friendly, and spotted with blood. I heard her before I saw her on the backside of the island. She lay sprawled, one high-heeled leg kicking repeatedly against the floor. Her face and neck and chest were covered with blood. She was nearly unrecognizable.

I shouted the address into the phone, demanding an ambulance. Elyse was alive, but barely. As I gave the information to the emergency operator, I knelt down and grabbed Elyse's hand. Holding it firmly, I told her help was coming, begged her to hold on. After switching the phone to speaker, I threw it on the floor and pulled a kitchen towel off the counter, trying in vain to staunch the blood gushing from her chest. Tears streamed down my face, and I held Elyse's hand tight as I spoke to both her and the operator.

My eyes were locked with Elyse's. I could see the terror in hers, and likely she could see the horror in mine. We stayed that way for what seemed an eternity, me willing her to live, listening to the rattle of her breath, and knowing it was likely too late.

I heard the ambulance roar to a stop outside the brownstone and yelled to the EMTs that we were in the back as they entered the building. When I turned to let Elyse know help had arrived, she was gone. Her eyes stared blankly at me.

An EMT took me by the shoulders and pulled me up so he could get to Elyse. I leaned against the kitchen wall as the technicians worked, unable to look away, my body wracked with tremors of emotion, but there was nothing they could do for her.

"Ma'am?" a deep voice said. I turned my head away from Elyse to see two police officers standing at the entrance of the kitchen.

"Are you injured?" one of the men asked. I could only shake my head.

"Is this blood yours? Are you hurt?" he asked again. I looked at my hands, stained with the blood of a dying woman, as if I'd never seen them before. I felt my mouth open but couldn't find words within me to respond.

"Do you know this woman?" The younger officer addressed me, his voice low. I let my hands fall to my sides. "Her name is Elyse Wright," I squeaked out. "This is her home."

"Do you know what happened?"

"She asked me to come over. We—we had a meeting," I said, hearing my voice crack, not knowing where to begin or what to say about my reason for being here. My mind was too muddled. "When...when I got here, ah, the window was broken. I saw the window, the side window by the door, and so I came in. The door was ajar. I, ah, I called for her, and I saw the blood."

I sobbed at the horror of what was going on, struggling to collect my thoughts. All I could see in my mind was the look of panic in her eyes.

"Take a breath. Collect yourself," the officer said.

The other chimed in. "So after you saw the door was open and the glass, what did you do? Is that when you called us? Is that when you called 911?"

"No." I shook my head. "Not right away. I wasn't certain if something was wrong. I called out to see if anyone was here. Then I heard her. She signaled me by kicking the floor, so I...I followed the sound."

"So she was alive when you got here?"

"Yes, but I knew it wasn't good. I called 911 as soon as I saw her. I held her hand and tried to comfort her," I choked out. "I couldn't help. There was too much blood." I felt myself shake and my throat close up. My God, what had happened? I couldn't comprehend it. Nor could I let go of the fear I'd seen in her eyes.

10

I leaned against the back of the wing chair in the breakfast nook, eyes closed, hearing my heart thunder in my ears, smelling the acrid, metallic scent of blood. The officers, concerned about further contamination of the crime scene, had parked me here. I'd tried to focus my attention on the darkness of the rear garden outside the tall windows next to me, but the reflection in the glass of the activities around me made that impossible. So I closed my eyes and tried to shut down my mind until someone needed something from me. The din of the technicians just feet away faded as my mind and my body tried to come to grips with what I had witnessed. As voices blended into a low hum, images and sounds bombarded me, regardless.

Crime scene technicians filled the open kitchen as additional police officers busied themselves with speculation, reports, and initial projections, but I was only vaguely aware of their presence. Every ounce of my strength was allocated to either not curling into a ball or forcing my lungs to inflate. It was as if my body could no longer do these things on its own and I had to remind myself to breathe.

The sharp rip of the body bag zipper jolted me back to the

scene in front of me. Immediately my eyes were drawn to the black lump of plastic containing Elyse Wright's body as they lifted her onto a gurney. I looked away as she was rolled out of the kitchen, trying unsuccessfully to shut out my terror and fear. My eyes landed on something safe, the marble-topped kitchen island. An open bottle of merlot rested there, one glass of wine half-drunk, and another sat empty. Had the glass been intended for me? Or was Elyse expecting someone else? I forced myself to take in my surroundings—partly out of distraction from the body bag, partly because I needed to remember what, if anything else, I had seen. The officers would be wanting more details from me shortly.

The room was warm, cozy even, despite its expensive under-pinnings. Custom cabinets painted a creamy white outfitted the large room, and a warm glow filtered in from under-cabinet lighting, accenting the glass canisters and tall ceilings. The breakfast nook where I sat contained a round oak table and upholstered chairs nestled into a bay window. It was a family space. If I kept my eyes above counter level and ignored the cast of thousands, the room seemed unremarkable. Tasteful, expensive, but homey and loved. If I looked below, it was a scene out of a slasher movie.

I drew in a few breaths and tried to focus. Tried to remember my training. What else had I seen or heard that my mind might have brushed to the back recesses of my memory after the shock of discovering Elyse?

I was drawn to a technician dusting for fingerprints on a stool lying on its side on the floor. Knocked over in the struggle? Wait, the bloody handprint. I turned my head toward that first sign I had noticed inside the house. I looked at it hard, trying to memorize its shape and position. Left hand, small, the print low and clearly made by someone trying to leave the room. Elyse's? I burned the image into my memory and followed the blood trail back toward where I had found Elyse's body. I shuddered again. There was so much blood.

Gathering strength, I forced the image of her back into my mind. Forced myself to see, to remember the details I missed in my initial reaction. She had still been in her work clothes, the same silk blouse and gray pencil skirt she had worn earlier at our meeting with Victor. Only her jacket was missing. She hadn't even removed her shoes yet, so that suggested she hadn't been home long. A new question filled my mind, an even more terrifying one: How long before I arrived had the killer left?

Blood had covered Elyse's chest, her neck, her face, and her hands. Given the gusher at her chest, I could safely assume this was the primary wound site. A gunshot? No—it would have done even more damage, possibly killing her instantly. Perhaps a knife to the gut or the chest? There was no pool of blood at the back of her head, only blood that had dripped down the sides of her face and into her hair. The flesh of her face around her mouth had been exposed, cut, but I doubted that been the wound that killed her.

But what had been done to her mouth?

The questions formed in my mind instinctually. I looked around the room for signs of blood spatter, something to confirm my initial theory. The pattern of blood on the floor showed signs of a struggle, possibly a fall or marks suggesting she had been dragged—or had even dragged herself, trying to get away. Technicians were marking blood droplets on the sides of the island and the stools, but I saw nothing marking the upper cabinets. That meant her killer was close. He hadn't used broad, sweeping motions where blood would have flown or sprayed backward from the violence of his thrusts. He hadn't been frenzied. He'd been controlled and close, likely with a strong, direct jab or two.

The crime scene technicians would photograph the scene,

carefully documenting the shape of the blood droplets, calculating the angle of the trajectory to determine as best they could where Elyse might have first been attacked. Much could be learned from blood splatter that could determine the likely position of attack and defense. And bloody footprints could determine the dance between killer and victim as one of them fought to the death.

But why? Beyond the broken glass and the struggle in the kitchen, the home appeared normal. Elyse's purse sat on the countertop, seemingly untouched. How long had it taken her to die? Who would mourn her this evening? I knew nothing about her family other than Gavin.

A technician came over to take samples from my hands and to confiscate my shoes, questioning me again about whether I needed medical treatment.

"No, I'll be okay," I said, wondering if I was being honest or whether I'd be in dire need of a sedative hours from now. In reality, my only injuries were things that a bandage could not fix. An officer came over, this time the younger one, asking me for a formal statement. I reiterated what I had done and seen before the EMTs' arrival while a technician cleaned the blood from my hands.

As the officer grilled me, I felt a strong, tender grip on my shoulder. I turned my head to see Michael kneeling next to me. I let out a sob and fell into his chest, letting loose raw emotion yet again. I stayed there, allowing the trauma to wash through me and feeling Michael's embrace. He mumbled something to the officer, who then walked away. When the panic left my body, and I was able to control my breathing, I sat back. Michael's eyes were wracked with fear.

"I'm okay," I said, hoping to reassure him and myself. His eyes said he didn't believe me. But more than anything, I wanted to bury myself in his arms and not leave for days.

"You sure have a habit of being in the wrong place at the wrong time." Karl Janek stood behind Michael, looking down at me, his face expressionless, but his eyes held a hint of concern. Janek was Michael's partner and the detective who had saved my life nearly a year ago. Gruff and methodical on the exterior, a bulldog when he needed to be, there were no other men I'd rather have protecting me. I gave him a weak smile.

"What were you doing here?" Michael asked, his eyes not leaving mine.

"As you know, I'm covering Gavin Wright's trial," I said. "I met with Elyse earlier today. She said she had some information to show me. She implied that her ex-husband had been involved in a prior embezzlement scheme and asked me to come over tonight, said it was information I needed to see in person. And that he had threatened her. When I got here, it appeared someone had broken into the home. I found her bleeding to death on the floor."

"Did you see or hear anyone else? Maybe someone on the street before you walked in?" Janek asked. The look Michael shot his way told me exactly how close I might have come to walking in on the act. I shook my head, but the aftermath of the question chilled me.

"Did she indicate what she had to show you? Account statements? Maybe emails?" Janek asked.

"She told me Gavin had threatened her via email, but since her attorney didn't take the threats seriously, I assumed it was just more divorce anger and that she was exaggerating. As far as the embezzlement accusation—the prior incident, I mean—she was pretty evasive. To me, it sounded more like she wanted to get back at him. Maybe more concerned about her own reputation. She seemed more attention seeking or manipulative than anything else." I shuddered. "Anyway, I figured it was worth hearing what she had to say, even if it went nowhere. Oh, I have the email she sent me." I pulled my phone out of my coat pocket, pausing when I saw the blood staining my sleeve. Immediately I took off the coat, unable to tolerate the sight. The urge for a long, hot shower swept over me. I took a deep breath, opened my mail app, and scrolled down until I found Elyse's note. "I found it," I said, running my eyes over the text, refreshing my memory. The note she'd sent was communication about her address and the time we'd agreed to meet. But a single word jumped out at me in a way that hadn't had the same impact earlier. I read the note again, slowly this time.

"What is it?" Michael asked. He was still crouched at my side, his arm on my shoulder reassuringly but I could see the worry in his face.

"Something I guess I overlooked or didn't take seriously at first." I handed Michael my phone. "She said when we spoke on the phone that Gavin had threatened her physically. This is the second time she mentioned it. Could he have done this? Could he have murdered his wife?"

11

I walked into the Link-Media office midmorning, my head pounding. I'd been at Elyse Wright's home, speaking with CPD until nearly midnight, and then bumbled around my own home, unable to rest for hours after. It had been a night filled with more questions than I could count, and Elyse Wright's pleading eyes had burned an indelible image into my brain. I couldn't imagine the horror she had felt during those last moments of her life, sprawled on her kitchen floor and likely knowing she was about to die. Had she known her killer?

The cuts on her mouth suggested intimacy or a perhaps a threat. A metaphorical and physical silencing.

Try as I might, sleep had been impossible, and lying in bed, unproductive, left me feeling impotent, consumed with fear and grief. Not knowing what to do with myself, I'd spent much of the early hours of the morning pacing in my apartment helplessly, while Walter followed me from room to room, waiting for a moment when I would sit so he could curl next to me. Whether that was for my comfort or his—who knew what went on in that little brain—regardless, he knew something was wrong.

I finally found sleep around 6:00 a.m., just as daylight was breaking but only after physical and mental exhaustion took over. But the two and a half hours of rest had done nothing to rejuvenate me physically or emotionally.

Despite several attempts, I'd been unable to get ahold of Ryan this morning to move our ten o'clock meeting, so I'd forced myself into the office. Rescheduling again would not make him happy, but wasting half a day being grilled by the man on head count and job titles wasn't on my top ten list, either, after last night's ordeal.

All eyes in the newsroom turned my way as I walked through the large, open loft to my office. Faces full of shock and curiosity looked back at me. I prayed my coworkers would give me the space to compose myself before descending on me with questions. Borkowski had assigned someone to cover the new development, making me a source, but I needed a few minutes of breathing room first.

I had been checking my news feed for hours, listening for developments as CPD worked the case, but thus far, I knew more than the talking heads were revealing. I'd already put in two calls to Michael, one last night after they had allowed me to leave and again this morning before I left home, but unfortunately both calls had gone to voicemail. Already my impatience was building, having been the last person to see her alive. Having been the person who held her hand as she took her last breath, I needed to know what had happened to her. I needed—no, I *deserved* to know everything as the investigation unfolded. Somehow I was now entitled.

I nodded solemnly to my coworkers, flipped on the lights in my office, settled in, and then checked one more time for a response from Michael. Nothing. I sent him a quick text, then opened my laptop. I caught a flash of movement out of the corner of my eye as Brynn made a beeline for my office. Unfortunately, Ryan was three steps ahead of her, causing her to abort the trip.

"Good morning, Andrea. Why don't we meet in the conference room today?" He stood smiling in the doorway, his blue shirt open at the collar, showing off his tawny skin. A herringbone sport coat sat comfortably on his broad shoulders. An image of the well-defined muscles I knew were underneath popped into my head, and I quickly brushed it away.

"Would you mind if we rescheduled? I've got a lot of follow-up to do on the Elyse Wright story. I'm sure you've heard about last night's development," I said, hoping for a reprieve. How in the hell was I going to keep my mind on stats and org charts when all I could hear in my head was Elyse Wright's last dying breath?

"I'm afraid that doesn't work for me," he said, opening the calendar app on his phone and scrolling through. "I'm pretty backed up, and we've already rescheduled this once. Grab your tea and meet me in five." He turned and headed toward the conference room, shutting down any additional objections as I glowered at his back.

"Shit!" I said out loud, not meaning to, then grabbed a notebook.

"Are you okay?" Brynn stood in the doorway, her face creased with worry.

"I don't know how to describe how I feel," I said truthfully. "But apparently that doesn't matter right now. I get to go waste a couple hours with Mr. Molina." I stood and moved toward the door. "Ignore my mood. As you can imagine, I didn't sleep. We'll talk later," I said, squeezing her hand as I left.

Ryan was standing next to the conference table and typing something into his phone when I arrived. I closed the door and took a seat, trying not to be irritated, but this was the only mood I had at the moment.

"Just need to finish this text," he said, not looking up from the phone. Mine sat on the table in front of me, the ringer silenced, but I had a full view of the screen. Why was Michael taking so long to get back to me? Surely he understood how upset I was? Why in the world would he leave me hanging? I'd give him another hour, and if I hadn't heard from him by then, I'd call Janek directly.

"Sorry about that." Ryan came around and stopped next to my chair. He leaned back and sat on the edge of the table, his leg brushing mine. "Finally, I get you alone," he said. "It's great to see you, Andrea. You look fabulous. Being single agrees with you."

He smiled down at me with a look entirely inappropriate for the situation at hand. I had the sudden urge to turn around and see who might be watching through the glass-walled office. It took tremendous effort, but I kept my face neutral.

"I'm glad to see you're well," I said, ignoring his suggestive smile. It was far more difficult to ignore the nearness of his body. "So how did this happen? You being the guy Borkowski brought in, I mean?"

"Switching to business mode already?" He laughed. "I'm disappointed, but I will answer your question. Coincidence, really. I worked with one of your board members, Wade Ramelli, about six months ago. I guess he liked the work I did, so one thing led to another, and here I am. You don't mind, do you?" He leaned over, placing his palm flat on the table and tilting his head toward me and, in the process, allowing his leg to touch mine again.

I shifted in my seat, making sure I was being obvious about pulling away. "Ryan, let's be clear. What happened between us is in the past. It was a moment when I needed something, and you were there. That's all. We can't let that history influence the situation we find ourselves in now. I can handle myself in a strictly business manner, and I hope you can too. If not, then I would suggest this isn't quite the right assignment for you and you should consider withdrawing."

He crossed his arms and looked at me, a smile still dancing around his eyes as if pleased with the challenge. Not the reaction I was going for.

The last thing I wanted was Ryan Molina thinking of me as a challenge, because that inevitably meant questions about how he could use his charms to wear me down. I'd seen his competitive streak firsthand and had no interest in being his prize. But would his ego allow him to walk away from a job, particularly if Ramelli was the one who'd recommended him? Unlikely. There would be lots of uncomfortable questions if he took that route. Questions I didn't want asked or answered. Not that I wanted Ryan to know that, but how would he play this? My gut told me he'd prioritize his career and reputation and that he had as much to lose as I did if Borkowski and Ramelli found out about our previous relationship.

If Ramelli had made the recommendation, that meant he and Borkowski had been working together. A tingle of fear crawled up the back of my neck. Ramelli clearly wanted me out of the business. Was he using Borkowski to help him, or did Borkowski have his own agenda? It wasn't inconceivable to think that Borkowski might have been made a promise if I was out of the picture. Ramelli was certainly the type to play it that way.

I pinched the bridge of my nose and tried to focus. The lack of sleep was getting to me; I was probably just being paranoid.

"So, what do you say? Can we keep this a professional relationship?" I asked.

"You are quite irresistible, especially when you talk tough. But please, give me a little more credit than that."

He laughed again and took a seat, tapping on the notepad in front of him. "So much has changed at Link-Media since my early days working with Erik. I was really only around during its infancy. As you can imagine, I have dozens of questions, and Borkowski, well, he's only been in his current role for a few months. I'd like to get an overview of what has transpired, how the company has grown over the last few years. If we start there, I can better understand the structure and operations of the organization as it exists today. Given your relationship with Erik, you may know things that Borkowski wasn't privy to."

"That's fine," I said, feeling slightly relieved that the conversation had moved into business territory, although I knew full well that Borkowski could answer his questions just as easily. "I need to say before we get started that there are several developments on a story I'm working, and I may have to cut this short."

"Well, then, we'll just need to continue this conversation over dinner."

My mouth dropped open. I stepped right into that one. But before I could shoot back a response, my phone lit up. Michael.

"Sorry, I need to take this," I said, not waiting for an answer from Ryan.

"I apologize for being AWOL. It's been a long night," Michael said. "And I only have a minute, but I wanted to check in and see how you're doing."

"Like you, short on sleep. But other than that, I'll be okay. Do you have the cause of death? Any leads on the killer?"

Ryan cleared his throat, irritated with the interruption. Out of the corner of my eye, I saw him tug on a shirt sleeve, exposing a flash of gold watch at his wrist. Gold. Elyse's bracelet. My mind was drawn back to my meeting with Elyse the day before while Michael gave me the standard lines about too soon to comment, still investigating, blah, blah, blah.

"Did you find a bracelet?" I asked, interrupting him.

"What? What bracelet?"

"When I met with Elyse yesterday afternoon, she was

wearing a gold bangle. Thin. It had a little bauble, a single charm hanging from a jump-ring. I think it was a pearl caged in gold wire. She wasn't wearing it last night when I found her."

"Maybe she took it off?"

"Maybe. But she hadn't changed her clothes yet. She hadn't even taken off her shoes. Her jacket was on the dining chair. Why would the bracelet be the only thing she took off? Did she take it off, or does her killer have it?"

12

"If you're finished with your calls, perhaps we can get back to the task at hand?" Ryan gave me an irritated stare.

What did the man expect? That the news was supposed to stop because this was the moment he needed to ask a bunch of questions that Borkowski could answer just as easily? Obviously, I wasn't going to be able to shut the whole thing down, but he needed to understand that the business of running Link-Media came first. If we didn't prioritize news content, there was no point to any of this.

"I'll do what I can to give you my full attention," I said. "But surely you understand that stories don't break according to your meeting schedule." My comment was a little sniping, but I didn't care. That was the news business. His other consulting clients may have the luxury of clearing their schedules; we didn't. If the staff saw me sitting in a conference room all day rather than out pounding the pavement, they would make assumptions and follow my lead. A moment of paranoia popped back. Was that part of Ramelli's plan? To bury us in consulting meetings so that new leads would slip through our fingers? If you wanted to get rid of someone, one of the best ways to do it was to throw obstacles in their way so they couldn't be successful.

"Why don't we start with an overview of the last few years?" Ryan said, ignoring my chastisement. "I've gone over the financials, and it looks like the business began to soften about a year and a half, maybe two years ago. That's right around the time Borkowski was brought on board. Can you give me any context for what was going on in the company at that point?"

My stomach knotted immediately. Ryan knew exactly what was going on back then. Perhaps not the inner workings of Link-Media, but he knew the basics of what was going on in my personal life. Our night together had been the aftermath. And he had deliberately asked as a way to remind me. What was he trying to do? Rattle me? Instill some kind of misplaced guilt? Or was this some weird "Hey, why not pick up where we left off" comment? Well, I wasn't taking the bait.

"Yes, Borkowski came on about two years ago, and I was about five months behind him. At the time, the board was pressuring Erik to think more conventionally about the staff. Subscriptions were soft, and their answer to those problems was to bring in some star power from the print world. Hence Borkowski. A respected *Tribune* journalist was an idea Ramelli and the others understood. Erik needed their backing, so he went along with it. One of his investors had just withdrawn, so things were tough. Borkowski quieted them down for a while."

"And then there was the distraction of his marital problems." Ryan looked at me, all sorts of accusations in his eyes.

"The only distractions were the ones Erik created himself," I shot back, not bothering to control my tone. I wasn't going to let Ryan turn this into some armchair therapy session. I'd done that work and felt no responsibility for Erik's bad choices.

A text popped up on my phone. Michael letting me know there would be a press conference outside of Gavin Wright's apartment in thirty minutes. Wright? Had Wright killed his wife?

"Sorry, Ryan," I said, picking up my phone. "There's been a development in one of my stories. I need to run." I didn't wait for a response, my mind jumping ahead, trying to fill in the blanks. A press conference likely meant they were arresting Wright. The man was out on bond over the embezzlement charges, so if any halfway credible information existed, the man would be under lock and key in a heartbeat. And if that was the case, then CPD had gotten lucky or had done some kick-ass police work overnight.

I returned to my office, grabbed my coat and my bag, then moved toward the hallway. Brynn flagged me near the elevator. "What's going on with this consultant thing?" she asked. "I know you're in the middle of everything and it's a crazy time to ask, but I'm kinda going nuts myself. When can we talk?"

"I'm sorry. I owe you a more detailed conversation, but it sounds like they've just arrested Gavin Wright. I have to run. I'll be back as soon as I can." The look on her face told me I was skating on thin ice, but this couldn't wait.

I grabbed a cab, jumping out on Michigan Avenue at the Wrigley Building. In a strange bit of a coincidence, Gavin Wright had leased an apartment in Erik's condo building after moving out of the Lincoln Park home he'd shared with Elyse. A shiny glass-and-steel high-rise, it was nestled in a courtyard behind the iconic landmark.

Clad in white terra-cotta, the two towers of the Wrigley Building had been the star of Chicago architecture since their completion in 1924. Influenced by the White City of the Columbian Exposition, William Wrigley Jr. had commissioned the building for his chewing gum company. Situated on the north shore of the Chicago River, the clock tower of the south building rose to thirty stories with a face in each direction, making it instantly recognizable. As I walked under the arch created by the walkways connecting the two parts of the building, I was struck as I always was by the stunning architecture. The foresight and beauty created by the city planners and visionaries of the late 1800s and early 1900s never grew tiring.

Although the new glass structure immediately to the west did nothing to inspire awe in me, I loved the dichotomy of old against new. The wind was too raw off the lake for the tourists who would fill this plaza and the neighboring Riverwalk in warmer months, but the sun glinting off the accumulated ice and snow made it beautiful nonetheless.

I tightened my scarf around my neck as I stepped out from between the buildings, then pulled out my gloves. Camera crews were setting up at the base of the multi-use tower wedged between the river and Wabash Street. Housing a hotel and a Michelin-rated restaurant in addition to condos, it had become yet another marker on the Chicago skyline, but that also meant pedestrian traffic.

With the building's main entrance on Wabash, it appeared the cops were pushing the reporters over toward the east side of the building, trying to keep residents and hotel guests out of sight of the cameras. The last thing owners in this price point wanted was a camera shoved in their faces. The press conference may have been set up in the plaza, but Gavin Wright would not be paraded in this direction.

I stood at the edge of the press corps for a moment nodding at a few of the familiar faces and wondering how CPD had narrowed in on Wright so quickly. I also knew I wanted a shot of Wright doing the perp walk, and this throng wasn't going to give me a proper vantage point.

But where would he exit? His attorney wouldn't want the image of him handcuffed and escorted out of the front door by men in blue playing on all the news networks for the next five days. Nor would the hotel management.

If I were Wright's attorney, I'd be pushing to have him slipped quietly out one of the service entrances.

Having an inside track on the layout of the building, maybe I could circumvent the crowd.

My colleagues seemed to be hedging their bets; many were stationed patiently at the side of the building waiting on the official word, but others were making backup plans and directing their attention to the front door.

The service entrance was on the west side of the building, but the path over had its own obstacles. A half-dozen news trucks sat double parked in front of the hotel, and four burly security guards in matching gray overcoats kept nonresidents at bay, drawing even more attention to the situation. Even people who didn't know what was happening stood waiting at the fringes, aware that the cameras and the guards meant something big was going on.

A cluster of men blocked the sidewalk as I tried to make my way to the far side. I paused, debating whether to push through or to jump the snowbank and try to go around. Glancing around the perimeter, I wondered if I had a shot of getting past the throng elsewhere. The group seemed to be riled up, arguing with the two guards obstructing their path. I recognized one of the security guys who normally worked the night shift from my previous visits to clean out Erik's apartment. If I could convince him to let me into the lobby, I could catch Wright coming out of the elevator.

I moved forward to the edge of the group of men and shimmied around the support columns. The group was about twenty strong and seemed to all be white men in their thirties. As I eased forward, angry rhetoric filled my ears.

"That bitch deserves what she got" seemed to be the

prevailing sentiment. The comments made my blood run hot, and I looked at the men with a growing sense of unease. Who were these guys? Elyse Wright's outspoken behavior surrounding the trial hadn't earned her many fans, but this language was outrageous. It was another ugly reminder that chauvinism was still alive and well and that the lunatic fringe felt emboldened.

I made it to the front as the guys argued with the guard. As soon as I could catch his attention, I flagged him over.

"Hi, Joe. You've sure got your hands full today," I said. "Any chance I can run upstairs?"

"Not a good idea, Ms. Kellner. Can you come back later? Cops want us to keep everybody out that isn't essential staff."

The group of men on my right changed their tack, shouting versions of "You letting *her* in and not us?" All eyes turned my way. I could see that the more I pushed my point, the more volatile the situation might become.

"No problem. Another time."

I backed off, leaving Joe to hold his own as the men sneered at me. Now what?

As I removed myself from the friction, an unmarked door flew open in front of me. Two cops marched out, trailed by Gavin Wright, cuffed, with two more officers at his flanks. I whipped out my phone, immediately tapping on the video camera. CPD was hoping to hustle him into a waiting SUV before the crowd knew what was happening. No such luck.

The men behind me caught sight of Wright and readjusted, flocking toward the car. One officer assisted his charge into the back seat of the vehicle while the other three blocked the advance.

Angry chants of "Free Wright" and "He's innocent" swirled around me as the men pushed forward toward the cops. Luckily for all of us, the vehicle sped off before anything other than ugly words could be exchanged. Feeling uncomfortable around the riled-up men, I lowered my camera and continued around the side of the building.

The majority of the camera crew had missed Wright's departure. I typed out a quick text to Borkowski and sent him the video, letting him know CPD would issue a statement momentarily. He could figure out how to edit the clip. The story was Gavin Wright being charged with the murder of his wife, the group of overzealous chauvinistic supporters simply added texture.

A short while later, Detectives Janek and Hewitt rounded the corner and walked to the microphone that had been set up between two pillars next to the building. Apparently Janek had drawn the short straw today. He cast a disapproving eye, waiting for the reporters to settle down.

He was tall and lean with close-cropped hair and a runner's body, and every time I saw him I thought FBI, not cop. Michael stood by his side, playing the sidekick role where I could watch him surreptitiously. Despite the occasional friction, the men had a strong bond, and I had no doubt each would take a bullet for the other. But where did I fit in the loyalty hierarchy? Where did I want to fit?

"Moments ago," Janek began, "CPD arrested Gavin Wright for the murder of his estranged wife, Elyse. We have obtained emails that indicate Ms. Wright's murder was a contract hit, arranged for by Gavin Wright. Although we have not yet identified the individual, we have every confidence that this person will be arrested as well. While the murderer has not yet been apprehended, we have no reason to believe this situation was anything other than a direct threat to Elyse Wright individually and that the public is not at risk. We will update you as additional information becomes available."

Wright had ordered a hit on his own wife? Although the

tension between the couple had been palpable, a hired hit was a bold move. It was one additional set of potentially loose lips. And how had CPD gotten into Wright's email so quickly?

I jotted notes to myself with the immediate unanswered questions while Janek turned away from the microphone, ignoring the journalists firing questions at him. Michael followed, so I moved to cut them off before they got to their waiting SUV.

As I did so, the reporters around me became aware that another aspect of this story was right beside them, me as the person who'd stumbled on Elyse's dying body. Suddenly cameras and microphones were in my face, with journalists pushing me for comment just as hard as they were pushing Janek. I caught Michael's eye, and without missing a beat, he stepped toward me, grabbing my arm and ushering me out of the crowd with him.

"The things I have to do to get your attention," I said, smiling at him.

13

"Guys, when do I get to see the email?" I directed the question at Janek largely to make sure it was clear I wasn't trying to work around him.

I'd followed Michael and Janek out of range of the other journalists, and we stood in the alley next to Janek's unmarked Chevy Tahoe. Although our relationship had improved since the sniper story, Janek wasn't a fan of reporters, and he certainly wasn't a fan of pillow talk between his partner and a reporter. I didn't know for certain what conversations had gone on between Michael and Janek about my role in Michael's life, but I was convinced there had been a fair amount of "It's none of your damn business" on Michael's end.

But that didn't mean Janek was wrong to object. The optics were hard to ignore for anyone other than Michael, it seemed. I couldn't imagine that he had run this latest idea of us living together past Janek. Although Michael was the one pushing for a commitment, he kept his feelings for me close to the vest at work. In my way of thinking, that meant he was as conflicted as I was, but apparently I was the only one noticing.

"You aren't getting the emails," Janek replied, "at least not before it's made public to everyone. So you can just stop the sales pitch right there. Ain't happening." He slipped his sunglasses back on his nose and scanned the street behind me. One eye on your subject, one assessing for threats. Cop habits never died.

"So we're supposed to believe Wright paid off some thug to get his wife out of the way?" I asked. "Why? Maybe I should say, why do it now? Their divorce was nearly final. She'd already testified against him. The timing makes no sense."

"Sounds like a classic case of revenge to me. Maybe he thought the missus would stand by her man and keep her big mouth shut, but she surprised him."

"That's funny, Janek. Anybody who'd ever met Elyse Wright knew keeping quiet and standing on the sidelines were two things she never did."

I wasn't ready to concede to Janek, but his theory fit with the slash wounds to her mouth. Someone wanted her quiet. I turned up the collar on my coat and looked at Michael, but he wasn't going to contradict his partner.

I was also thinking about Elyse's comment that Gavin had threatened her the day before she'd died. An accusation I hadn't taken seriously. Would it have mattered if I had?

"Unless you're telling me these emails are a year old, it doesn't make sense. Timing, I mean. And how would killing her now help Wright? There's a big difference between trying to get yourself out of an embezzlement rap and conspiracy to commit murder. I don't buy it. There's more to this."

"I just catch them," Janek replied. "It's up to your friends in the state's attorney's office to figure out why."

"So is that confirmation that these emails were generated recently?" I slid in the question hoping he'd budge.

Janek shot me an irritated glare. "No comment."

I looked back at Michael, who just gave me an amused

shrug. "Come on, you know you're gonna release this information anyway, and it had to be something pretty easy to find. The woman hasn't even been dead twenty-four hours. What am I missing?"

I was stuck on the logistics—both the timing of when Gavin might have made the threat and how CPD had come up with evidence so quickly. Scouring his computer thoroughly for a hidden threat would have likely taken a few days, if not longer, in my experience. So how had they struck pay dirt so fast?

Janek just shook his head and let out a breath. He had no patience for the fine art of negotiation, preferring silence or a bulldozer. Typical cop.

"Wait a minute," I said, a new thought popping into my mind. "It wasn't Gavin's computer. It was Elyse's. Or the family desktop sitting right there for the taking. He communicated with the hit man before he moved out. That was about four months ago, if memory serves," I said, recreating a timeline in my head. The men said nothing, but I caught Michael stifling a smile.

"You may as well fess up," I said. "After all, you do want me posting accurate information, don't you?"

"I'm going to give you a pass based on what you went through last night, but as usual, you are pushing your luck."

"Come on, Janek. Just tell me if the email exchanges started before or after they charged Wright with embezzlement?"

"After he was charged and after he moved out of the house. The missus obviously didn't trust the man for some reason before they split up. Somewhere along the way, she hacked his account or had someone else do it. Then she installed software that allowed her to monitor his text messages, his email, and his phone. We got into her iPad, and that was our way into his."

"Sounds like handy software," I said, wondering how long the monitoring had gone on for and what Elyse really knew about the threats. "These emails, are they direct threats leveled at Elyse or vague communication between Gavin and the person he hired? Did Gavin say to flat-out 'get rid of her'? Have you identified the other party?" Questions were flying through my head faster than I could get them out, not that Janek was going to suddenly tell all.

If Elyse had shared any of this with Victor and he'd been able to brush it aside, that meant the language had been vague. Or that Elyse hadn't recognized the emails between Gavin and the killer for what they were, instead staying focused on Gavin's words to her.

"That's all I'm gonna say. Forensics is still working through the data. You've got enough for now."

"Never," I said, smiling at the men. "But thank you for the tidbit." Then to Michael: "I guess we'll talk later." Michael gave me a wink before he and Janek got into the SUV.

I headed back toward Michigan Avenue. It was time to ask Victor what he knew of any threats Gavin Wright had made against his wife.

As I made the short cab ride to the Loop, I found myself fixated on why Elyse Wright would have been secretly monitoring her husband's communication. Had she suspected an affair? Or was this related to the embezzlement case? In her communication with me, she'd been vague about the threat. But Elyse had trusted me, or thought she could trust me enough to make her information public. The guilt I felt being dismissive of her claims was now hard to shake. I could only assume that part of what CPD had discovered were the very same emails she had intended to show me.

I jumped out of the cab at Wabash and Monroe and headed upstairs to speak to Victor. When I walked through the heavy double doors of the law firm, I immediately sensed an office frozen with shock. A group of three employees stood in a cluster on the far side of the reception area, speaking in low tones instead of hunkered down in their cubicles, eyes on computer screens or heads buried in briefs as they typically were.

"The hell with being politically correct. She was a first-class bitch."

Marcus Bennett, one of the firm's paralegals, stood at the center. His round face flushed red when he realized I'd heard his remark. Caught in the act. He sniffed, his eyes went to the floor, and he mumbled something to the men he was with before slinking off to his desk.

On any other day, this group would have known better than to speak within earshot of a client.

"I need to see him," I said to Nancy, the long-term receptionist. She seemed confused, then answered robotically, mumbling something about checking his schedule. "Tell him I'll be in the small conference room." I strode past her, confident that whatever Victor had going on right now could be moved lower on the priority list. Nancy didn't bother to argue.

I removed my coat and scarf and settled into a chair. Moments later, Nancy came in carrying a cup of tea for me. "He needs about five minutes," she said before leaving.

As I waited, I fielded a text from Borkowski about the video clip I'd sent, then checked my Twitter feed. I'd posted a few brief updates earlier in the day, and as usual, the comments surrounding Elyse Wright's murder were a crazy mix of vitriol interspersed with brief moments of thoughtful dialogue. It seemed there was nothing that made the Twitter trolls come out in force more than political commentary or an opinionated woman. Throw a wealthy interracial couple into the mix, and the racists and chauvinists alike were now spouting their ugly rhetoric. I turned it off, disgusted. Victor came into the room, his face as somber as I'd ever seen. He rushed over and pulled me into a hug, then stepped back, embarrassed by his own behavior.

"I'm sorry," he said. "I probably shouldn't have done that. Not exactly kosher these days." He turned as if he'd forgotten something, then turned back toward me and took a seat at the table. His face had that pasty look as if he were at the tail end of a week-long stomach flu. I knew the feeling.

I sat beside him and squeezed his hand. "We're all in shock. I certainly didn't sleep last night."

"I can't imagine you did. I've heard lots of nasty things over the years in this business, but this?" He shook his head. "I can't wrap my head around how anyone could do this."

"Did she tell you we were meeting last night?"

"No, and if she had, I would have strongly advised against it. What did she want?" He looked at me as if afraid to hear the answer.

"She told me that Gavin had embezzled from others before Isaac Sikora. And that he had made threats against her. I don't have any details. She was intending to show me something last night. Did she discuss any of that with you?"

Victor let out a breath and ran his hand over his mouth.

"When Gavin's misdeeds were exposed, she, of course, needed to have other counsel represent her interests. My understanding is that during that time, she found some information that seemed suspicious and caused her to believe there may have been a previous embezzlement incident. This was after the initial charges were made. The information was shared with the prosecutor, but nothing came of it. Apparently, they couldn't corroborate her statements and felt they had enough evidence against him already. But trust me, if they'd been able to prove additional allegations, that would have come out."

"How did she take that?" I asked, remembering the vehemence of her assertion.

"Elyse fixated on it, couldn't let it go. She was furious that Gavin had gotten her into this mess. But the information she presented, well, it just wasn't enough. No one was going to go to court and make themselves look like an idiot. And if the prosecution had been unable to prove history, it could have damaged the case Sikora put forward. So, bottom line, she told me about it, but no one other than Elyse really thought it worth pursuing."

"I don't imagine that sat well with her."

"No, it didn't." He let out a wimpy chuckle.

"Do you know what she meant by 'threats'? Did Gavin threaten her in some way?"

"There were a lot of emails, some vaguely threatening. But she took everything to a fevered pitch in this divorce. My read of them was that Gavin was blowing off steam. These two had an explosive relationship. She was just as fiery as he was, and they both said things in the heat of the moment. I guess I didn't take it seriously because she was right back at him every time with something equally demeaning. I certainly didn't think he'd harm her. Would he cheat? Would he steal? Would he lie? Sure. Kill her? Never in a million years did that cross my mind. Elyse could be a bit—I guess you could say they were both a little high-strung. Yelling at each other was how they handled conflict. You know, some couples are just like that."

He paused, looked at his hands for a moment before continuing. "I got the news early this morning, and it's all I've been able to think about. Was I wrong to downplay it?"

I was struggling with those very thoughts. There was no walking away from "What if?" Victor and I would both question our decision for quite some time.

"And you have copies of these notes?"

He looked at me and nodded. "What are you asking, Andrea?"

"CPD will be here soon, I imagine, wanting to talk to you," I said.

"Yes, of course. I assumed as much." He ran his hand over his forehead. "I can't help but second-guess myself. I'm just sick over this. Would she still be alive if we'd shared these emails with the police?"

"Victor, I doubted her too. I agreed to see her, but I'd already made up my mind that it was just some melodrama I was getting pulled into." I leaned forward in the chair, my elbows on the table as I rehashed my response to Elyse and once again saw her pleading eyes. "Can I see them? I know you'll need to turn your notes over to CPD, but could I see them before you do that?"

Victor let out a breath and templed his fingers in front of his mouth, debating. "Obviously Elyse had intended to show you everything last night, so I don't see why not?" He reached over and picked up the phone.

Moments later, Marcus Bennett entered the conference room, a file in his hand. He laid it on the table, and Victor flipped through the file briefly before tossing back at him. "What is this? These are not the correct documents. It's not even the correct case file. Surely you can handle something this rudimentary." His tone reminded me of a particularly cantankerous professor I'd had back in law school and was out of character for the Victor I knew.

"If there's a mistake, talk to Nancy. I don't organize the database. Perhaps her female brain isn't wired for complex thought."

Victor scowled at Bennett but held back on chastising him further, presumably because I was in the room. "Here." He jotted something on a notepad and handed it to him.

As Bennett left, I turned to Victor. "What's his story? That's the second time I've heard him shoot out a sexist comment."

"I'm sorry about that. Marcus isn't my most progressive-thinking employee, but he knows better than to make snide remarks in front of clients. I'm sorry you heard that. And I know better than to embarrass an employee publicly. We're all a bit on edge today."

I let it go, but when I added in what I'd heard the other day, this guy would have a hard time spelling *progressive*. When he put down the file, I'd noticed the wedding ring on his finger and immediately wondered whether he tempered his chauvinism at home or treated his wife like dirt. Regardless, Victor would likely remind him he'd be better served by watching his tongue.

Bennett returned a few minutes later. Victor confirmed the contents, then handed me the file.

As he'd indicated, there was a plethora of email exchanges that put even the most contentious of divorces to shame. My chest tightened at the ugliness and my own memories of divorce. Well into the pile, one line caught my eye.

"'You hateful bitch. I hope you die,'" I read aloud from one of the notes. "Hard to not look at that statement in light of what happened last night and think he wasn't serious."

14

I *hope you die.* The words were now engraved into my head, permanently associated with the horror that had been Elyse Wright's last few minutes on earth.

As I left Victor's office, I pulled my hat and gloves out of my bag and turned up the collar on my shearling. The sky had grown dark while I'd been inside, but luckily the wind had quieted. Under most circumstances I would have hailed a cab, but tonight I needed the crispness of the evening air to wash away the demons circling my mind.

Cai and I had made plans to meet this evening at Erik's condo. I'd been stalling on sorting through the last remaining items. Most of the furniture was gone, as was anything that lacked emotional value, but I'd been unable to finish, my mind and body fighting the finality.

So after months of being deep in avoidance mode, I'd committed to getting his condo listed for sale by the end of next week. Apparently, a kick in the backside was the only way I would get this done, so like it or not, last night's trauma could not be the source of another delay. The place needed to be cleaned and then staged to soften the slick masculine finishes, then photographed in less than a week.

Selling the condo was the last task in settling Erik's estate. I knew I would feel better once it was over, but until then, my mind rebelled at the task. To counter the pain, Cai had committed to providing moral support and liquid courage.

As I walked north on Wabash toward the river, my head filled with images of Elyse, thoughts about her husband, and the thorny overlap between our lives. Two men governed by ego and greed, both experts at lying. And two women left with the shock of their betrayals and obligations to clean up their messes. Erik hadn't been the one to try to have me killed; in fact, in the end, he had tried to save me. But somehow Elyse Wright and I both had ended up in situations where someone thought we were better off dead because of our husbands' misdeeds. I shivered at the thought, flashing back to the evening on my terrace when Erik's business partner tried to silence me.

There was too much pain wrapped up in those thoughts for me to deal with right now, and I wasn't sure how I would get through the evening. The likely answer was to cry it out and try to move forward. It wasn't as if I had a choice. Sorting through your ex-husband's memorabilia was not a task I could hire out.

I let the lights of the city and the cool air do their best to clear my head as I walked north, past office buildings clearing out for the night, random retail stores, and fast-food restaurants now empty without their lunchtime patrons.

I paused at the Wabash Avenue Bridge, admiring the beauty of the Chicago River reflecting back the lights of the high-rises. The DuSable Bridge to the east, with its four decorative bridge houses and double-decker roadway, glowed over the water. I turned, looking up at Erik's condo building, instinctively trying to figure out which blackened windows were his, dread in my heart. But avoidance was no longer an option.

Continuing north, I arrived at the condo tower, signs of the

commotion from earlier that day now long gone. It was after six
o'clock, and the TV news would be blasting their video feeds of
Gavin Wright's arrest. The desire to check my phone, curious
about how others would slant today's development, came and
went. It could wait.

I said hello to the doorman, asked him to send up Cai when
she arrived, and took the elevator to the thirty-fifth floor. My
hand shook as I put the key in the lock. Despite the number of
times I'd been here since Erik's death, my emotions were always
in turmoil. One part of me expected to see him, alive and well,
and another felt I was intruding in someone else's home.
Another was still stung by the pain that had been part of our
marriage.

I didn't immediately turn on the lights when I entered the
apartment, captured as always by the beauty of the Chicago
skyline at night. The sweeping view included a partial view of
the lake and panned south over the river, Millennium Park, and
the iconic diamond shaped roofline of the Crain Communication Building.

Erik had purchased the condo almost immediately after we
separated, pissing off his attorney with the new complication in
our financial settlement. At the time, it had been the last thing I
cared about. As I stood in the dark, the space was both foreign
and familiar. Foreign with its hard edges and slick surfaces,
familiar because now and then I swore I could still smell Erik's
cologne. It always made me turn, expecting to see him or maybe
expecting an apparition, one refusing to let go of the life he had
led with vigor.

Time to chase away the ghosts. I flipped on every light in the
apartment. There was nothing to be gained by allowing my
thoughts to wallow in pain or in what might have been. Making
my way to the kitchen, I opened the wine fridge, hoping that I'd
had the forethought to leave a bottle handy for this last task. No

such luck. I'd have to wait for reinforcements. Packing materials were already stacked in the dining room, so I kicked off my shoes and distributed boxes between the rooms, trying to figure out where to start. Certainly not the bedroom. I would need far more alcohol to get through that task. Instead, I returned to the kitchen and began wrapping the small number of remaining items in paper. Cai knocked fifteen minutes later.

"Martinis or wine?" she said the minute I opened the door, handing me a brown paper bag.

"Love it. A girl who thinks of everything. Tonight, martinis. Definitely martinis."

Cai barreled in, tossing her coat onto the island in the kitchen as I emptied the contents of the bag.

"Are there any glasses left, or shall we make do with the plastic cups I brought?"

"We're stuck with plastic."

"Well, it wouldn't be the first time." She laughed, pulling her long dark hair up into a clip. "Let's get drinks made. I brought a change of clothes, then you can put me to work."

"You even brought olives. And where did you get chilled vodka?" I asked, thrilled with Cai's resourcefulness.

"The market in my office building keeps a stash on hand behind the counter. You'd be surprised how many attorneys need a good stiff drink in the middle of the day. I take that back —I guess you wouldn't be surprised. I forgot who I was talking to for a moment." She laughed.

As Cai mixed the drinks, I looked around, feeling overwhelmed again.

"Hey, are you getting weepy on me already?" She handed me a cup.

"Sorry, it's going to be one of those nights. Just ignore my blubbering, and keep tissues nearby."

"You mean keep your glass filled." She raised a brow and

gave me an amused smile. "Are you really going to give this listing to Lane? Do you think she can sell it?"

My sister, Lane, was a Realtor, and in the eight months since Erik's death, she'd alternated between hounding me about this listing and pushing me to downsize, with her as the agent for both transactions, of course. We had a relationship that could only be described as complex. I disapproved of her life choices, she disapproved of mine, and money was often a touchy subject because she never had any.

We'd healed a few of our old wounds the previous fall after she nearly died of poisoning, and now I was feeling sorry for her.

"It's a bit above her normal price range, but she's motivated. After losing so much time while she was ill, it's been hard for her to rebuild momentum. The holidays didn't help. But I told her if we're not in contract by the first of June, I'm taking it to the competition."

"You're a better person than I am. I hope you don't regret it." Cai lifted an eyebrow. She knew our history, and if history repeated itself, this moment of empathy would be another one I'd regret.

"Cheers." I lifted my plastic cup. "Cai, thanks for being here. I know this is no fun, but I'm glad you're doing it with me."

She leaned over and gave me a hug. "Are you kidding me? I've been looking forward to this for months. I want to see you box up all this man's shit and light a match to it." I laughed, knowing she meant every word.

I took another drink and let out a breath. "Okay. I think I'm ready. Let's pull the Band-Aid off quickly. Grab your drink, and follow me to the bedroom."

"Are you having it fumigated after?"

We laughed again and headed down the hall. "Why don't you start with his closet, and I'll do the dresser," I said, carrying a dozen boxes over to the walk-in closet. Cai saluted and winked. After tossing her pumps in the corner, she slipped into jeans and a sweater, then removed suits from hangers and folded them into boxes. We worked for about an hour, mostly silent, boxing and bagging Erik's clothes, sorting those for donation and those that just needed to go into the trash.

Drawers emptied and closet nearly done, I moved to the nightstand. My heart suddenly pounded in my chest. I sat on the edge of the bare mattress, clenching my hands and trying to wipe away the emotion.

Cai sat next to me, her arm around my shoulder. "Cold feet? Do you want me to do this?"

"No." I shook my head. "I'm just expecting to find something that breaks my heart again."

"Like I said earlier, I'm happy to research dumps that still allow burning." She smiled and squeezed my hand. I nodded, let out a breath, and opened the drawer. With a trash bag at my feet, I glanced at the assortment of receipts and odd papers it contained, then began tossing everything in the trash. At the bottom of the pile was a small silver picture frame, a photo of me inside. Happy, smiling at the camera, caught in a moment of carefree laughter. The tears flowed freely as I looked at the image, trying to remember when it had been taken. And why Erik had kept it.

Cai looked at me, compassion in her eyes. I smiled back, opened the back of the frame, pulled out the photograph, and ripped it in two, depositing the pieces in the trash bag.

"I will not let this man make me feel like shit after he's dead," I announced and picked up my pace, doing everything I could to suppress any misplaced sentimentality from the process at hand.

"Talk about work," I said after a moment, wiping away tears. "Give me something else to focus on."

"I don't have anything fun to talk about. Just sorting through the mess of a case I told you about the other day. You, on the other hand, seem smack dab in the middle of another interesting story. I see that jackass Gavin has been returned to jail. Did he really kill her?"

Again, I heard an odd tone in her voice. I looked at her, trying to sort through what was behind the attitude but couldn't place it. "I don't know if he killed her, but CPD thinks he did. So what gives? This is the second time you've said something about Gavin Wright that makes me think you had some kind of personal run-in with him. Am I wrong?"

Cai stopped what she was doing and looked at me. "No, I don't like the guy. We had an incident, but it was years ago. No big deal. We all have stories."

"Are you forgetting who you're talking to? An incident? What kind?"

"Oh, all right." She shrugged and took another drink. "The guy made a move on me. I was working late one night. So was Wright. I went into his office to ask him a question. I can't for the life of me remember what it was, but he used the opportunity to pin me to the wall and put his hands under my skirt. I kneed him in the balls and pushed him away, then got the hell out of there. But not before he threatened to end my career. I was a kid, just out of law school, and Wright, he was tight with a couple of the partners. I knew he could take me down. So I've kept my mouth shut."

"Oh, my God, Cai. What a pig!"

"Look, it was a long time ago. We've all had run-ins with assholes like Gavin Wright. Women are used to playing defense and moving on with our lives. That's what we do, isn't it?"

Cai was right. Nearly every woman I knew had had an experience she looked back on with disgust.

"What if Gavin Wright never changed?" I said, my thoughts

running in a new direction. "Or if he became even more aggressive over the years?"

"You mean, is he still a lecherous bastard? So what if he is? Or are you suggesting that this is tied in somehow to his wife's murder?"

"Maybe? I found out that Elyse Wright was secretly monitoring his communication. She obviously thought he was hiding something. What if this was a pattern? What if he went further than copping a feel?"

15

No sign of Brynn. Good. I was feeling guilty for having pushed her off so much lately and wanted to get in to see Borkowski first thing this morning. It was unfair to have kept her hanging because I'd been too busy, and I was certain the delay was only adding to her anxiety. The last thing I wanted was for her to take another job before I had an opportunity to make this work.

I tossed my coat and bag on my desk, then went looking for him. It had been a late and emotional night, so I'd steeped my tea extra long this morning, needing a jolt of caffeine, but my head was still fuzzy. Last night's martinis weren't helping.

Physically and emotionally drained, a tough conversation with Borkowski wasn't a pleasant thought at 8:30 a.m., but Brynn was counting on me. When I neared his office, I saw him and Ryan standing just inside the door, speaking in low tones, their conversation seemingly intense. He caught sight of me, and their conversation stopped. I looked from one to the other, wondering what I had interrupted.

"Yes?" Borkowski said, a flash of irritation crossing his eyes.

"I need a few minutes with you."

"Give me five. I'll meet you in the conference room."

I nodded, trying to read their faces, but I didn't like the vibe. Whatever was going on between them was not making me comfortable. I poured another cup of tea and went to the conference room. For the second time, I had the feeling that some secret activity was going on behind my back.

As I waited, I shot Lane a text letting her know we were on track with the listing. The boxes for donation would be picked up later today, cleaners would follow tomorrow morning, and the stagers would be ready to come in on Monday. With any luck, by next Wednesday, any bad mojo that still existed in the condo would've been eradicated and Lane could bring in her photographer. After that, it was in her hands to market; I had done my job.

Borkowski strutted into the room, his reading glasses bouncing on a leather cord around his neck, and he took a seat next to me at the head of the table. "You got any more on the Gavin Wright case? Hey, you got real lucky on that video. Doesn't look like anybody else has the same footage. Nice job. Cops got any idea who the hit man was?"

He launched questions at me, not giving me time to respond. "No leads yet." I held off on telling him about Elyse's use of tracking software. I wasn't sure how it fit in yet and didn't want him to get excited before I knew what it meant. "Actually, I wanted to talk to you about Brynn. I want to give her a raise. There's some stuff going on in her personal life, and we're at risk of losing her. You know she's doing great work, and she's paid well below her peers here in the office."

"It's a crappy time to be bringing this up," he said, pulling his glasses back up to his nose and glancing at his phone. "We need to work through any restructuring before I start thinking about pay. Yes, she's doing a fine job, but the timing sucks. We'll take care of her at review time, just like everybody else."

"That's months away. I know the timing isn't ideal, but she isn't going to be here if something comes along that pays better. I don't want to lose her."

Borkowski and I had yet to have our first disagreement on a personnel issue, but I could feel a showdown coming.

"Then maybe we should put more effort into getting through this evaluation project. I understand you've, ah, struggled to be available." He cocked his head and looked at me, a scowl forming on his face.

"Stories don't work around meetings, and they don't come at prearranged times. Perhaps you should explain that to Ryan. He doesn't seem to want to hear it from me."

I felt the headache of last night's intense emotion creep back up my temples. I didn't have the bandwidth to deal with anyone else's fragile ego right now. I got to my feet.

"Please give some thought to this situation with Brynn. It'd be a shame for her to jump ship and go to the competition just because we couldn't be flexible with our timing."

I didn't have any confidence I'd made my case with Borkowski but knew I'd been heard. I also knew I'd pushed the limits of where I could take the argument, at least for today. I'd let him sit with the idea for a couple days. I left the conference room, and Brynn caught up with me just outside my office.

"Please tell me you have some good news," she said, hope etched on her face.

I sighed and said, "Not yet, but I'm not done with him."

Her body slumped. I took her by the arm and led her inside, not wanting our conversation to be overheard. "Listen, Brynn, you know how he is. He needs to think it's his idea. Don't make any decisions yet. I'm going to go back at this. I'll figure it out. Trust me." She nodded but didn't look convinced, then turned and closed the door.

"I need to tell you something," she said. "It's about this guy,

Molina. I've been checking him out, and I get the impression he's got a game plan that isn't obvious."

"What do you mean?"

She scrunched her face, pausing as if about to tell me bad news.

"I have a friend at Midwest Regional Bank. He works in commercial lending. Molina has approached them for cash, millions of dollars in cash. It's some new partnership he runs called Synthesis Group. My friend didn't know what that money was for, just that it was some big deal the bank is excited about."

The pit in my stomach got deeper. "And you think this cash is connected to his work here?"

"Well, his partner in Synthesis Group is a name you're familiar with. Wade Ramelli."

I dug my nails into my hands reflexively. This whole thing was a charade, a goddamn setup. Ramelli had been telling me all along that he wanted to buy me out. Now, apparently, he had a partner. My initial instinct was to reach for the phone to call my attorney, but first I needed to keep Brynn from panicking. Who was I kidding? I needed to keep myself from panicking.

"Thank you for telling me," I said slowly.

"What are you going to do?"

"Fight like hell. Please, don't leave. Let me figure out how to fix this. Give me time to speak with my attorney and see what options I have. Okay?" I looked at her hopefully, feeling like I was begging. But I didn't care. I was begging. Brynn looked at me warily.

"I'll try. I'm sorry, Andrea. They're complete assholes."

That son of a bitch Ramelli. Apparently he wanted a fight. Well, he was going to get one.

16

W hy the spy software? I couldn't let go of it. Elyse had suspected her husband of something or was trying to gather evidence of other embezzlement scenarios, but was the spying related to her murder or simply incidental? One thing I did know, if Elyse Wright had concerns about her husband, it was likely she had talked to someone about it—a friend, a sister, a colleague, or, at the very least, maybe even the person she'd hired to set up the spyware.

First on the list, Julian Metz. Pushing her family so soon after her death was the height of rude; her employer, on the other hand, he was fair game.

Hidden in a nondescript office tower on Clinton Street in the West Loop, across from the French Market and walking distance to a dozen fabulous restaurants on Randolph Street, Jennus Creative occupied nearly half of the fifteenth floor. Frosted glass doors opened to cool gray terrazzo flooring. The reception area was open and bright with a video slide show of the firm's ad campaigns playing on a huge screen.

I announced myself to the receptionist and asked to speak

with Elyse Wright's boss. She flinched but asked me to have a seat as she picked up the phone.

The advertising agency was a midsize firm with an international client base and a focus largely in the consumer product category. According to her website bio, Elyse had started with the organization as a copy editor directly out of college, rising to the position of senior account executive three years ago. It was a notable achievement for a woman in her early thirties. I thumbed through the company's marketing material as I waited, impressed by the breadth and depth of the work they had done.

"Ms. Kellner?"

I looked up to see a man in his early fifties: hair slicked back, lightly spray tanned, and wearing an intricately printed open-collared shirt. I recognized the pattern from one of the designer boutiques on Oak Street and was well aware of its five-hundred-dollar price tag. He extended a hand. "I'm Julian Metz. I can't tell you how broken up we are about Elyse. We're all utterly stunned."

I stood and shook his hand. "As am I."

"I'm sorry you came all the way over here, but I'm not sure now is the right time for us to be speaking to reporters. I'm sure you understand." He smiled at me condescendingly, as if quite used to getting what he wanted.

"I realize that the timing may seem a little, shall we say, inappropriate, but you might not be aware that I'm the one who found her."

He looked at me blankly, the information catching him off guard. "No, I wasn't. How horrific. Please, let's go to my office."

I followed him out of the reception area and into another large room lined with windows and a direct view west over the Kennedy Expressway. Here the firm's employees sat ensconced behind huge computer monitors, with many desks supporting two or three. Metz's office was in the far corner space, another glass-walled office, this time a corner view with floor-to-ceiling windows. The furnishings were sleek, modern, ridiculously expensive—if my last trip to the Merchandise Mart was any indication—and also looked horribly uncomfortable. Long on show, light on function. It was an interesting metaphor for the advertising industry. I was directed to a seat at a boxy, mirrored conference table. My first thought was to wonder how many times a day someone had to whip out the Windex to keep this piece free of fingerprints.

Metz cleared his throat. "I read that she didn't die right away."

I nodded. "That's correct. She was still alive when I got to her house, but in bad shape. I was there with her, holding her hand when she died. But she was gone before the EMTs arrived."

He looked at the ceiling and let out a breath. "At least she wasn't alone. At the end, I mean. I can't understand how this happened? And now to hear Gavin's been charged, it's unthinkable. I knew both of them. We had dinner together, company functions. I can't understand any of this madness."

"I know this is awkward, but did Elyse ever say anything about difficulties in their marriage? I mean, prior to the embezzlement charges being brought against Gavin?"

"Look, I'm not sure she would have shared anything like that with me. And quite frankly, I don't think it's something our firm should comment on."

The slight hint of a smile around his eyes told me he knew exactly what I was talking about, even if he didn't want to discuss it publicly. Office rumors? Or had he and Elyse dated?

"Were you aware of any threats she might have received?" I asked, deciding to unsettle him a bit. "Any problems she might be having with other people, coworkers? Clients, perhaps?" It was a long shot, but perhaps getting him to talk about his business would loosen him up.

"Oh no, of course not, everybody loved Elyse."

For a brief second, a shadow crossed his face, then he moved quickly back into sales mode, his natural state. I couldn't blame him. He'd probably been spending his time calculating how Elyse's murder might affect his business and fielding calls from clients ever since he'd heard the news.

A young woman rapped lightly on the door and entered. "I'm sorry to interrupt. You said you wanted this immediately." She looked at Metz expectantly. He motioned her in.

She walked in and handed him a file. Her eyes were bloodshot, and she held a tissue tightly in her other hand.

"Stacy, this is Andrea Kellner. She's the one who found Elyse."

She drew in a breath and brought a hand to her mouth, her eyes wide, and a tear spilled onto her round cheek.

Metz turned to me. "Stacy was Elyse's assistant." Stacy and I nodded solemnly at each other. The mention of Elyse's name unleashing another torrent of emotion.

"I'm so sorry about what happened," I said to her. "Had you worked for her for long?"

"About four years," the young woman mumbled, fighting the urge to collapse in grief. What was she doing at work?

"Ms. Kellner was asking about difficult cases, conflicts that Elyse might have had with clients. I was just telling her how everyone loved Elyse. She was amazing, and her clients adored her. I don't know how we'll fill her shoes. Obviously, we have no insight into the intricacies of her marriage, but there can't possibly be any other explanation."

End of story. The message to me, and to Stacy, was that the problem wasn't here. It's all good. I looked again at Metz, his office, his dress, his grooming. This was a man to whom appearance meant everything. I had the sense he would proclaim record growth numbers even if the firm had just filed for bankruptcy. But then again, illusion was the job of advertising.

How did illusion infiltrate Elyse Wright's life?

Stacy sniffed, dabbed at her eyes, and nodded weakly. "It's nice to meet you," she said.

I watched her leave the room, wondering if she was as practiced at fiction as Metz was.

"Are you sure there's nothing that comes to mind about any tensions in Elyse's life?" I asked, then for good measure added, "I'm certain CPD will want to speak with you shortly about this same issue."

"I'm sorry I don't have more information for you. Of course we knew Elyse was going through the trial. It was in all the papers, for God's sake. But she was a pro. She kept her personal life out of the office, so I really can't speculate about what might have been going on. I wish I could be more helpful." He stood and gave me a practiced smile. Nothing more to say.

"Again, I'm sorry for your loss." I extended my hand. "I'm sure it's just devastating to the staff. I can find my way out."

He nodded solemnly but didn't object as I left. The moment his office door closed behind me, I pulled a business card out of my bag and scribbled on the back: "I'll be in the French Market for the next hour, back seating area." I caught Stacy's eye and slipped the card onto her desk as I passed.

Once in the Market, I headed straight to Vanille Patisserie and ordered an Earl Grey and an almond croissant, resisting the luscious and more elaborate French treats, then slid into a seat at a table facing the main aisle. But would Stacy show? I answered emails and returned phone calls for forty-five minutes, thinking I had miscalculated her grief.

It was nearing the lunch hour, and the early diners had begun to fill the tables. The smells of donuts and Cajun food and grilled onions mingled in the air, reminding me that the croissant had been the only thing I'd eaten that day. I looked at my watch. I'd give her another twenty minutes, then succumb to the urge to eat something more substantial. The only question was banh mi from Saigon Sisters or empanadas from Lito's?

Moments later I saw her in the smoothie line at Raw, a scarf wrapped around her neck but no sign of a jacket. I left my coat at the table and grabbed my wallet, then caught her at the counter.

"Can I buy?"

"Okay, sure," she said. "Sorry, this was the soonest I could get away. I only have a couple minutes."

I paid for her drink, something pink that I wasn't familiar with, and we returned to the table.

"I'm glad you came down," I said, watching her scan the nearby diners for familiar faces. "I had a feeling it wasn't the best time to talk upstairs."

"Did you really see her dead?" Stacy asked, after assuring herself that no coworkers were within earshot. Her pale skin was blotched pink from the cold and the tears.

I nodded solemnly. "She was nearly gone when I found her. I called 911 and tried to stop the bleeding, but there wasn't anything more I could do. It was too late."

"Is it true that she was all cut up? I read that online." Her voice held the fear of someone who wanted to know the truth but wasn't sure she could handle it.

"Yes, her face had been cut, just her mouth."

Stacy stared at me, reeling, covering her mouth with her hand and letting the tears flow again. "Why?" It was the only word she could get out.

"I don't know. CPD hasn't released anything yet, but it's hard not to wonder if the cuts to her mouth were a message, or punishment, or perhaps even retaliation?"

"You mean he killed her because of something she said?"

"I don't know why she was killed, but the slashing of her mouth wasn't what killed her. It was a message. At least that's what I find myself wondering about."

Stacy sat quietly, wiping her tears and letting that possibility sink in. As did I. Had Gavin Wright orchestrated her manner of death? Or had the killer gotten creative, leaving his own message? Although I had no reason to believe it, in some ways the cut marks to her mouth suggested a warning.

"Did Elyse ever speak to you about problems in her marriage?"

"A little bit. I guess they fought a lot."

"Fought how? Was he physical? Did he hit her?"

"No." She shook her head vehemently at first, then seemed to reconsider. "At least I don't think so. She never talked about it. I didn't see bruises or anything."

"But they argued a lot?"

"I think they were both just that way. Hot-headed. Emotional. Big egos. They'd have a fight, and a day later everything would be fine."

"I know this is an awkward question, but did Elyse ever say anything about Gavin having an affair?" I asked, thinking about the tracking software.

"No, I don't think it was anything like that. That's just how they were."

"Do you know if she ever felt threatened? Did she mention that?"

"By her husband?"

"Yes. Or by anyone else." I left the question open, wondering if the man Gavin had hired had ever contacted her prior to breaking into her home.

"I don't know. I can't really think right now. My brain hasn't wanted to work since I heard about Elyse."

"Was there a client who was angry?" I prodded. "A coworker

she had pissed off? A stranger who left messages? I know I'm grasping, but this stuff just doesn't happen out of the blue, and I'm trying to figure out if there were any signs of someone wanting to hurt her. Anyone who was angry with her, other than her husband."

"She pissed a lot of people off along the way, but usually it was just a fleeting thing. Sexist, really, because the men around here are the real ballbusters. Elyse had high standards and she could be tough, but everyone in the office was cool with that. It's not like anybody held a grudge or took it personally."

"How about clients?"

"Well, the biggest scandal, if you can call it that, was a campaign we did a few months ago. It was for one of the heart associations. They wanted to get the message out about how women are underdiagnosed, or more often called 'hormonal' and just flat-out ignored by their doctors. Elyse did a thirty-second spot that got a little controversial."

"In what way?"

"Well, the image showed a woman in a doctor's office, and she's talking about these symptoms she's having that could be signs of heart disease or a mild heart attack. Anyway, the doctor in the spot is like a total chauvinist and tells her she needs to get a hobby or agree to have sex more often. Totally downplayed the seriousness of her concerns. They intended it to be a little infuriating. But that's the reality—women are often treated dismissively. Elyse loved the ad. Thought it was right on point. But she had to work pretty hard to convince the heart association to run it. In the end they agreed. It was active for about two weeks all across prime-time cable. And the minute it started, the social media idiots just blew up over it." She shook her head, disgusted by the outcome. Her voice had strengthened in recounting the incident, and I had the sense it had been a big blow.

"What do you mean? What happened?"

"Doctors were mad because they thought *they* looked dumb. The crazy sexists on Twitter started making a fuss. The association got calls, we got calls, it got pretty ugly, so they yanked it. You know how those lunatics are on social media. When a woman doesn't stay in her lane, suddenly she's a lesbian bitch who needs to die. Elyse got the brunt of that. Julian was mad at her. After that the client dumped us. Said their reputation had suffered."

"Needs to die? Did someone say that? Were there threats on her life?" I asked, keeping my tone light, but inside my blood pressure was jumping.

"Yeah, but it's Twitter. You can't take any of that seriously. It's just a bunch of lonely, emotionally stunted pigs who blame the world for their unhappiness. Maybe if these guys got a life, they wouldn't have to spend their time fabricating hate about why women won't date them."

Funny, Julian Metz hadn't mentioned the incident. I guess it didn't meet the image he wanted for his firm.

"Look, I really need to go. They'll be wondering what happened to me. Thanks for the drink."

"Call me if you think of anything else I should know," I said. She nodded and headed back upstairs.

I turned back to my phone and began scrolling Jennus Creative's social media accounts.

17

Social media was the ultimate Band-Aid rip. It had a way of yanking away or building up the reputation of companies and individuals alike, usually in unexpected ways. The Jennus Creative accounts had largely been scrubbed clean. I didn't blame them; few companies would want that hate speech attached to their brand, certainly not an ad agency where image is what they sold. But they couldn't suppress what they didn't control.

A chicken banh mi, also known as The Hen House at Saigon Sisters, under my belt, and eyes fuzzy from staring at my phone, I packed up my things. I'd found some of the hateful rhetoric online that Stacy had referenced, but Brynn had skills in technology deeper than anything I possessed.

As I walked out to the street, I put in a call and asked her to use her magic to do a deep dive into the social media accounts. If she couldn't find it, we'd have to figure out how to hire a Russian hacker.

Jocelyn Lawrence seemed the next logical target. Although she'd been the one to bring Wright's financial shenanigans to the surface, she'd seemed reticent. I'd gotten the feeling during her testimony that while she appeared to answer questions directed to her, she wasn't completely forthcoming. Was she holding back because she knew more, or was she concerned about her own vulnerability?

Not a cab in sight. I walked to the corner, stood in front of the Jennus Creative building, and scanned the street, hoping for better luck. As I waited for the taxi gods to smile on me, I adjusted the scarf around my neck, then checked my phone for messages, blinking away the eye fatigue. A text from Ryan about rescheduling our meeting had just come through. I popped the phone back in my bag without answering. He could wait until I was out of the biting wind.

A black SUV pulled up to the curb, spattering dirty, melted snow up to my knees. As I looked up to growl at the driver, Michael stepped out of the vehicle with Janek right behind him.

I put my hands on my hips and gave Janek The Glare. "I hope that wasn't intentional."

He looked at my soiled legs and shrugged. "Have you thought about wearing boots?"

I shook my head and sighed. "Let me guess, you're heading upstairs for a chat with Elyse Wright's employer. Well, you're getting a late start on the day, gentlemen."

Janek huffed. "As if our job isn't hard enough, we have to battle reporters for face time with subjects. Do you wanna tell us who you've already spoken to? Did you learn anything relevant?"

"Quid pro quo. Tell me the cause of death, and I'll consider sharing." As much as Janek loathed our ongoing dance of wills, I found it amusing. It reminded me of my days as a prosecutor, when "give, give, get" was something of a mantra. No reason for me to give up anything for free. I hadn't learned much from Metz, but Janek didn't know that. Would he be a little looser with his tongue when he had a cop in front of him instead of a reporter? In my experience, a cop in your face either scared you so much you spilled every minor childhood secret or it shut you up. I was betting Metz was an experienced bullshitter and Janek would hear the same nonsense I had.

"There were two stab wounds just below the breastbone. Deep. Big honkin' knife. She basically bled out," Janek said.

"And the slashes to her face?"

"Superficial wounds. Didn't help slow down the bleeding, but that didn't kill her either," he added.

"The mouth wound was inflicted after she was stabbed in the gut and probably already down," Michael said.

"Why do you think he bothered?" I asked. "If she was already down and bleeding to death, why cut her face?" I saw it purely as a message. As far as I could tell, there was no other way to interpret it. Although the official CPD statement had mentioned wounds to the face, they had withheld the details. That meant they thought it was important. Withholding information was one of the useful little interrogation tricks they could pull out later when they needed to up the heat on a suspect.

Michael looked as Janek, then back at me. "It's hard to tell. Maybe she was making too much noise? An impulse in the heat of the moment? I don't think we know enough yet to speculate."

"Or this is what happens when a woman talks," I said, wrapping my mind around that particular horror. I shuddered, again imagining Elyse Wright's final moments. How could a husband hate his wife that much?

The men stayed silent but didn't contradict me. We stood awkwardly, reflecting, none of us wanting to tip our hands.

I broke the silence. "I met with her boss, Julian Metz. According to him, everyone loved her, they know nothing about her personal life, yada yada. But I don't think he's being honest. He's slick and a salesman. He doesn't want this to in any way reflect on his firm. But if I were you, I'd ask him about the heart association campaign."

"What about it?" Janek asked.

"You should be able to take it from here," I said, raising my arm to flag a passing cab.

———

JOCELYN LAWRENCE LIVED IN LAKEVIEW, just a half a block off Halstead on Roscoe. From the looks of it, the building was a classic brick three-flat. Railroad layout, one unit per floor, vintage charm, a sunroom in the front, and an exterior stairway out the back. I entered the vestibule, found a mailbox nameplate for unit two, and headed up the stairs.

A wreath of lavender decorated her red painted door, and a coir doormat printed with "Welcome" sat in front. I knocked, listening for footsteps. A moment later, the door opened several inches, and I could see Jocelyn peer at me through the crack. Her hair was pulled back into a ponytail, and she wore no makeup, giving me the impression she was under the weather or hiding from the world.

"Ms. Lawrence, my name is Andrea Kellner. I'm a reporter with Link-Media. I'd like to speak to you for a few minutes about the Gavin Wright trial." I held out my business card.

"I don't have anything to say." She began to close the door.

"Were you aware that Elyse Wright was murdered earlier this week?" The door stopped its momentum, and I saw what little color that had been there drain from her face.

"No, I...oh, my God." Her hands went to her chest, and her breathing became rapid.

"It looks like you should sit down," I said, getting worried that she was about to hyperventilate. "May I come in?" She nodded and opened the door the rest of the way. I followed her into a sunny living room. Wood floors, crown molding, plants dotting the space everywhere. It was warm, inviting and utterly feminine.

"If you point me toward the kitchen, I can get you a glass of water," I said, fearful that she would pass out. She nodded and fluttered her hands toward the back, then took a seat on a love seat in the sunroom.

The vintage kitchen was painted a sunny yellow, with glass-doored cabinets that looked original to the space filling one wall. Shelves had been added to the window over the sink, and small pots of herbs grew there, scenting the room with rosemary. I found a glass and opened the tap till the water ran cold, then returned to Jocelyn.

"Here you go. Are you feeling any better?"

She took the cup, mumbled her thanks, then took a big sip. "Yes, a little better."

"May I sit down?" She nodded. Her skin was still looking a little pasty, and her hand was trembling when she drank.

I sat across from her in an oak Windsor chair while she regained her composure, removing my coat as the sun beat down on me.

"I haven't been watching the news," she said. "It's been too much for me. The trial was so awful. I couldn't listen to it anymore. You were there, weren't you? I think I remember seeing you."

I nodded. Her voice was sounding a little stronger, but the woman was clearly shaken.

"What happened?" she asked.

"Elyse was stabbed in the chest. In her home." I paused to see if she was ready to hear the rest. "They have arrested Gavin for her murder."

She gripped the arm of her chair as if it were the only thing keeping her from collapsing. "Oh, my God. Oh, my God. Oh, my

God." She stared at the floor, repeating the words as if unable to comprehend what I had said.

"Are they sure it was Gavin?" she asked, once able to catch her breath.

"Sure enough to arrest him. CPD says he hired someone. That he didn't do it himself."

"At least that makes more sense," she said, crossing her arms over her chest. Her voice was icy.

"What do you mean by that?"

"Just that stabbing is messy, too easy to pin on someone. Gavin isn't the type who likes to get his hands dirty. He keeps his misdeeds behind closed doors. But you never really know about people. What they show to the world is often a big, fat lie."

Her jaw was set, and she stared out the window. I had the feeling that we were talking around something. Was I sensing her general dislike of Gavin, or was there something else?

"I know that you worked for Gavin for quite some time— eight years, wasn't it? Would I be correct in assuming that you'd met Elyse, maybe had contact with her occasionally?"

"We'd met." She didn't elaborate. Interesting.

"Did she come into the office often? Or did you meet at social functions? I assume there were Christmas parties, company picnics, perhaps?"

"No, we didn't do much of the social stuff as a group outside of work. There were only a handful of us. But even then, Gavin was too cheap to buy us a meal. You'd think he could have parted with a couple hundred bucks for a little morale building, but no, he had other priorities. Himself."

This time the edge in her voice was unmistakable. Resentment? It was also obvious that she hadn't expanded on her interactions with Elyse.

"It sounds like Gavin was a difficult boss." The trial had touched on procedural aspects of reporting and money management and Gavin's strict managerial style. But I didn't know how Jocelyn felt about the man prior to the embezzlement charges.

"He wasn't afraid to raise his voice, if that's what you're asking, and the pay was pathetic, but most of the time he let me do my work and didn't hassle me, so I put up with his ranting. No job is perfect."

She took another drink of water and pushed a stray strand of hair off of her forehead.

"Frankly, I wasn't sure where else I could go. I don't have a degree or anything. A couple of times I tried to find another job, but I never got anywhere with it. There was always somebody else with the right degree or more experience. All I had on my resume was my time at Gavin's firm. My title may have been administrative assistant, but basically I ran the office. Employers would rarely get past my title, especially with all the screening software that's used these days."

She shrugged, apparently feeling the need to explain her long tenure.

"Did Gavin ever direct some of his hostility toward you?" I watched her face closely for a response, hoping I could read what was being left unsaid.

She looked at the floor, chewing on the inside of her lip for a moment.

"I suppose if he's in jail, there's no reason I can't talk about it anymore. Gavin Wright is an awful man. I just didn't know how awful for a long time."

"What happened?"

"He started coming on to me. He'd say things, inappropriate, suggestive things. At first it started out innocent. He'd tell me I looked pretty or would compliment my dress, stuff like that. Then he moved into talking about my body and blatantly staring at my chest. Then one day it went further than that. He touched me. He reached over and grabbed one of my breasts. No pretense, no mistaking it as an accidental brush."

"And how did you react?" I asked, my voice soft and measured. She pulled her legs up underneath her and wrapped her arms around herself, responding to the memory.

"I swatted him away. Told him to cut it out."

"Did he stop?" I asked, Cai's revelation of her assault fresh in my mind.

"For a while, maybe a couple weeks. Then one day I was working late. Everyone else had gone home, or so I thought. I was sorting through old documents in the conference room, trying to get caught up on a backlog. I had all these papers and files stacked on the conference room table. I never heard him come in. The next thing I knew he was behind me, pushing me forward on the table, grinding his pelvis into me."

"What happened from there?" I asked, feeling her anxiety, my own body tensing. Her face had taken on a masklike quality as she spoke, as if shutting off emotion was the only way to get through the telling.

"I managed to turn around and jab my elbow into his throat. It gave me enough time to push his hands off me and get the hell out of there."

"Did you report it to anyone?"

"Who would I tell? The cops? What would they do? I took a couple days off. Hoping to avoid him, hoping that it was some moment of insanity and that bruising his windpipe would shock him into reality and make him understand that I wasn't interested."

"How did he respond?"

She lifted her eyes up from the spot on the floor she'd been staring at and looked at me directly. "That's when he started threatening me. As you know from the trial, I'd made a few of the financial transfers for him, as I often did. They were into his personal accounts, but I didn't think anything of it at the time. When he attacked me, I was just beginning to have suspicions that he was stealing from Mr. Sikora, but I hadn't connected everything. Maybe he knew I was figuring it out, I'm not sure, but he told me that if I didn't stay quiet about the attack, he would make it look like I was stealing from the firm. Even fabricate a paper trail, if he had to."

"And you believed him?"

"Damn right I did. After that, I kept quiet, and Gavin kept his hands to himself. What he didn't know was that I had started making copies of everything. Mr. Sikora passed away not long after, so I felt I could speak freely with his son and then made a deal with the prosecutor to turn over the evidence. But you knew that part."

"Why didn't you speak about the sexual assault at trial?"

"Because it would look like retaliation. He attacked me, so I wanted revenge, blah, blah, blah. You know how that goes. Anyway, I didn't stay quiet because I cared that anyone knew Gavin had attacked me. What I cared about was the man going to jail for stealing, and I didn't want to muddy the waters with other things."

"Did Elyse ever know?" The surveillance software popped back into my mind.

"She called *me*. Asked me if I'd meet with her attorney, give a deposition about the assault. I'm not sure of the timing, but this must have been when she was just starting divorce proceedings. The thing is, I don't know how she knew about the attack. I've never told anyone until today."

nd I thought my marriage had been complicated.

Jocelyn's revelation weighed on me as I returned to the office. In addition to being an embezzler, Gavin Wright was also a sexual predator and a hot-headed prick. No wonder his wife was spying on him. But how had Elyse known of the assault? If she figured out how to track his digital communications, it was possible she'd figured out a way to listen in at the office as well. I didn't know enough about the possibilities of the technology to answer that.

But Michael and Janek would need to know. Wisely, Jocelyn had consented to my request, giving me permission to share the details of the assault with them. Back in my office, I picked up the phone and dialed Michael.

"Calling to gloat over what a waste of time talking to Julian Metz is?" he asked, chuckling on the other end of the phone.

"No one could accuse that man of not being a natural salesman. I guess that means he didn't lose any of his hot air between our conversations."

"To what do I owe the honor of the phone call? Dinner

tonight, perhaps?" The expectation in his voice punched my guilt button.

"Actually, I was calling because I had information on the case for you. A little tidbit about your buddy Gavin Wright."

"You have my full attention."

"I spoke to Jocelyn Lawrence, Wright's former administrative assistant. As you probably know, she's basically the one responsible for exposing the embezzlement. Well, it turns out there's some history there that didn't make it into the court proceedings."

"What happened?"

"Turns out that in addition to being a thief, Gavin committed sexual assault. He tried to force himself on Jocelyn one night in the office. After she fought him off, he threatened to falsify records to make her look guilty of financial shenanigans if she exposed him. Basically, he blackmailed her."

"Why didn't she talk?"

"Do you have to ask?" Although I knew it was a standard response, it always stunned me when men simplified assault to such black-and-white terms. "We've both seen how women are treated when they bring forward accusations of assault without proof. It's her word against his, and the man's is always the voice that gets listened to—while she gets ripped to shreds, I might add."

I could hear myself moving into soapbox territory, but Michael wasn't being judgmental with his question.

"She also didn't want to muddy the waters on the embezzlement charges," I said. "Didn't want anyone to think this was fabricated or retaliatory. So she kept quiet. She reasoned that it was better to keep the focus on the primary issue."

"I know it happens, but it never sits right with me when women feel no one believes them."

"Well, hopefully that'll change, the more men who are jack-asses get prosecuted. And more guys in your position help make that happen. Anyway, she gave me the authorization to speak to you about it. Use it as you will. I don't know if it plays into Elyse Wright's murder case directly, but as a prosecutor, I would have wanted to know about prior history of aggression toward women."

"Absolutely. I wonder if Wright's society buddies have any clue what a creep he is?"

"Would they care if they did know?"

"Good question. I guess that's reality."

"So, when am I going to get copies of the emails between Wright and the hit man? I did just volunteer information."

"It's not volunteering if there's a price attached. You'll get the emails when and if CPD releases them, just like any other journalist."

His voice was softer than his words, so I didn't give him a hard time. There were usually other ways to get what I needed, with a little persistence, if the direct method wasn't going to work.

"Have you gotten any closer to identifying him?" I asked, trying another tack.

"The situation remains under investigation, but thanks for the tip."

"More stonewalling. Interesting. Janek must be within earshot."

He laughed. "So what about my earlier question—dinner?"

Our little dance continued. Not that I was mad at him. A little verbal jousting was appropriate under the circumstances.

"I need to see how the rest of my afternoon plays out. Can I get back to you later?"

"Okay, send me a text. We can do something simple, like takeout, if you want."

I went back to my notes from the trial, wanting to review

Jocelyn's testimony. I understood her rationale for keeping the assault out of the proceedings, but as a former prosecutor, it left me uncomfortable. I could only imagine what the legal teams would be up against given the complications of overlapping legal actions. Embezzlement, conspiracy to commit murder, and divorce. Divorce was off the table, but there were several attorneys who would be thrilled with their billing hours despite the indigestion these new wrinkles caused.

"What the hell is up with you and Molina?"

I looked up to see Borkowski standing in the door of my office, his brows scrunched and his mouth a thin, hard line. Shit. Had he found out about my history with Ryan?

"What are you talking about?" I said, deciding on the "play innocent" strategy. No sense fessing up before I knew what I was being accused of.

"What is your problem over meeting with him? I know you don't want to do this, but dammit, throwing obstacles in the path and avoiding him doesn't help any of us. So get over it and just do what you're supposed to do already. An hour of your time so the man can do his job is not an imposition. I don't want to hear one more time that you've blown him off. Meet with the guy, answers his questions, and move on. In other words, man up. I'm done with this teenage temper tantrum."

I opened my mouth, intending to correct the record and remind Borkowski of the story I was working, but anything I said would just prove his point.

"I'll take care of it."

Borkowski shot me a scowl, lingering a moment as if expecting a rebuttal before leaving my office. I picked up my phone, feeling like the thirteen-year-old I'd been accused of modeling, and responded to Ryan's text: *When would you like to meet?*

"What did you do to piss off Borkowski? The way he stormed

out of here, I expected one of you would need medical attention." Brynn walked into my office and parked herself in the
chair opposite mine.

"You know how he is, always finding new ways to show his
appreciation for the work I do."

"You mean you're in the doghouse." She shook her head and
raised a brow. "I found something I thought you'd want to see."
She handed me a printout. "It's a screenshot of something origi-
nally posted on the Jennus Creative Twitter account."

I looked at the image and felt my breath catch. Elyse
Wright's professional headshot with a bull's-eye overlaid. "This
was on their Twitter feed?"

"It was at some point. No surprise that they wiped the post,
but at least for some period of time, it was live for the world to
see. They were sloppy when they deleted it, probably left it to
some intern to take care of. I found it in the cache. I'll need to
piece a few more things together to see if I can figure out how
long it was up and whether this Twitter handle is still active.
Creeps like this just change their profile names to bury crap
when they're outed. Anyway, under the circumstances, I figured
you'd want to see it immediately."

"Send me the digital version. I'm going to need to pass this
on to CPD. Maybe Gavin Wright wasn't the only one threatening
his wife?"

"Usually guys like this are all talk, no action." She shrugged
as if having personal experience. "However, since the woman's
just been murdered, someone with subpoena power will want to
look into this Twitter handle."

"Thanks, Brynn. Nicely done."

A response from Ryan popped up on my screen as Brynn left
my office. *Dinner. 7 o'clock. Fig and Olive.* Shit. I grit my teeth and
sent back, *See you tonight.* So much for dinner with Michael.

———

I WAS BACK in front of Victor's office building. I knew I was on the verge of abusing our relationship, but no one outside of the marriage between Gavin and Elyse Wright knew the complexities better than the divorce attorney who was charged with ending their ordeal. Divorce had a way of turning over every little stone full of ugly. Particularly when the uncoupling was as contentious as I imagined this one was. Victor was also my secret weapon. He'd share information with me that the police might not think to pursue.

The building was a warren of bland, carpeted hallways, with dated wallpaper and fluorescent lighting that made everyone look jaundiced. It seemed appropriate mood lighting, given the number of law firms. As I moved toward the office, I heard voices around the corner ahead of me. A man chastising someone I assumed to be his wife for showing up unannounced. Marital tension didn't strike me as odd considering where I was; what did strike a chord was his patronizing tone. The couple was choosing to have their dispute in what they knew was a public hallway, so I hesitated for only a second before continuing around the corner.

As I came into view, both heads turned in my direction, suspending the quarrel, at least for the moment. I stood face-to-face with Marcus Bennett, the paralegal from Victor's office. Red faced and sweaty, he towered over the woman receiving the brunt of his anger. She was average in size but looked diminutive compared to her husband. But the stranger thing was her wardrobe.

She looked straight out of central casting for some 1950s *Leave It to Beaver* movie. A long-sleeved, white cotton blouse with a Peter Pan collar and a strand of pearls. A floral circle skirt that fell to mid-calf. Nylon stockings, the real kind, not some fun fashion statement. Sensible pumps. Her chin-length brown hair was tucked behind her ears with a headband. She held a dark coat in her arms and stood facing him, eyes now downcast.

I nodded at Bennett and continued toward the law office. As the saying went, there was someone for everyone, but theirs was a relationship I had no interest in analyzing.

"Hi, Nancy. I need to see Victor again."

"I'll see if he is free."

After a few moments he appeared in the reception area. "I'm starting to think I need to ask you for a retainer," he said, only half joking. "Come on." He nodded, and I followed him to the small conference room.

"What now?" Victor asked as we both took a seat.

"I know I'm being a pest, but I'm sure you want to find Elyse's killer even more than I do."

"I do, but we have things to do for paying customers." He smiled, then reached over and squeezed my hand. "Go ahead. I know you're just doing your job."

"Aside from the embezzlement charges, were there other issues in the marriage?" I asked, leaning my elbows on the table. If Elyse had known about her husband's attack on Jocelyn, I found it hard to imagine she hadn't told Victor. I was also still stuck on the timing.

"Is there a marriage that doesn't have issues?" He laughed. "That's what keeps people like me in business. Did you have something specific in mind? I know you're not just looking for dirt."

"Given the charges against Gavin, I assumed their financial situation was put under a magnifying glass. Was there anything unusual? Any particular point of contention financially outside of Gavin's embezzlement?"

"It wasn't terribly complicated. Elyse came into the marriage with substantial assets, and there was a prenup. The family home belonged to Elyse, so defining marital assets was fairly uncomplicated, as these things go. Not that Gavin was in much of a position to fight it."

"So money could have been a motive?"

He paused. "For her death? I hadn't gone there yet. But yes, as you know, those assets will now pass to Gavin. She had no living family."

Unfortunately, that was a subject I had firsthand knowledge of, but if Gavin were after money, money he couldn't access because it was excluded as premarital assets, why wouldn't he have done the deed before she filed? Killing her after only highlighted the big red bull's-eye a prosecutor would place on his chest.

"That inheritance doesn't help him much if he spends the rest of his life in jail. He'd need to be pretty certain he was going to clear the embezzlement charges," I said. Gavin was arrogant enough to underestimate his legal jeopardy, but why chance it? Their financial situation added an interesting element to the case, but the timing still didn't sit well, and I didn't have an explanation for why Elyse might have been spying on her husband.

"I assume you brought in your forensic accountant. Were there any unusual expenditures as you looked at Gavin's finances?"

"If you mean, did we see any evidence of the embezzled monies in his personal assets, no, we did not. He'd firewalled that pretty well in secret accounts. In terms of other expenses, nothing is coming to mind, but let me get Marcus in here. He got a little deeper into the weeds than I did."

Victor reached for the phone and called Bennett into the conference room while I wondered if he was done treating his wife like an eight-year-old.

"Were there any suspicions of infidelity?" I asked while we

waited. My mind was wrapped around the idea that Elyse did not trust her husband. Something had triggered that, something outside of the testimony she'd given, was my guess. May as well start with the obvious.

"Nothing that Elyse indicated. Of course, that's always one of the first things we talk about. We brought in a private investigator, but our focus was financial. We wanted to know where his assets were hidden."

Bennett came into the room, a legal pad in hand. He looked at me sheepishly, clearly embarrassed that I had walked in on his argument with his wife. Given the comments I'd heard and the manner in which he'd spoken to his wife, my impression of him had moved from neutral to boy-was-he-an-ass. I knew it wasn't my place to be judgmental over how people conducted their relationships, but I couldn't stomach the demeaning sexism and outright male superiority I'd heard come out of his mouth. To see that tolerated made me nauseous and angry.

"Marcus, Ms. Kellner has questions about the Elyse Wright case. Since you were the liaison with our forensic accountant, I thought it best that you answer her questions."

"Happy to, sir."

Bennett took a seat, settling his squishy body into the chair. He looked at me, pen poised over the legal pad, and sniffed, giving me the impression he thought he was here to take notes. It had been interesting to see him behave so aggressively with his wife. It was a side I hadn't seen. My encounters with him in the past had suggested a mild-mannered, kind of dweebie guy. Maybe that was one of the reasons he'd chosen such a mousy mate? A way for him to feel in charge of something when he wasn't in other aspects of his life. I wondered if being a paralegal had been a choice or a fallback when he didn't pass the bar and now had a chip on his shoulder.

"Let's start with the private investigator," I said. "I understand from Victor that a private investigator had been hired to look at any financial entanglements between Gavin's embezzled funds and family money, is that correct? And that no obvious entanglements were visible. Is that also correct?"

"Yes, it is. Any money that Mr. Wright appropriated stayed separate from marital funds."

"In the course of that investigation, were there any unusual payouts or reoccurring expenditures that couldn't be explained?"

"Our forensic accountant, Leon Rutkowski, looked into everything quite thoroughly, I assure you. He found that Mrs. Wright lived a lavish lifestyle, spending significant funds on clothing and the like. Entertainment, such as dining out, also appeared to be substantial line items in the monthly budget."

I looked at the man, feeling the puzzlement etching my eyebrows. Interesting, I'd asked about Gavin. Why had he focused on Elyse? And his statement sounded judgmental. Judgmental because he thought her frivolous? Or their lifestyle frivolous? But if that were the case, why had he singled out Elyse? I jotted a note before continuing.

"And what about Gavin Wright? From what I could tell, he was a man who enjoyed nice things himself. Custom suits, for example, at five grand a pop."

Before Bennett could answer my question, the phone in the conference room beeped. Victor picked up the call.

"I'm afraid I have to step out," he said. "I'm sure the two of you can manage without me from here." He reached over and squeezed my hand. "I'll speak to you soon."

"Thank you, Victor. I appreciate everything you're doing."

"Where were we?" I said, turning back to Bennett. "Gavin Wright's wardrobe. Are you suggesting that Elyse spent significantly more, or are you making a comment about the fact that she maintained her marital lifestyle after they separated?"

Bennett shifted in his chair and pulled a tissue out of his pocket, then dabbed at his nose. I couldn't tell if I'd made him uncomfortable or if he was just battling a cold.

"You asked about *unusual* expenditures," he said, this time with a little attitude in his voice. Perhaps I'd misread his body language. "Mr. Wright had an image to uphold. His expenditures in that area were necessary for his position. Women don't have that same pressure. It seemed unusual to me. I figured she was one of those women who shop a lot."

It took everything I had to bite my tongue and not tell this man what I thought of his comments. You could play out that little-woman-as-second-class-citizen fantasy in your home life, buddy, but it had no place in a divorce attorney's office, particularly when your clients were often female. I didn't know if the guy was any good at his job, but if I were in Victor's position, I'd be keeping him away from clients or finding someone whose views on gender roles weren't embedded in a previous century.

"Okay, they had a lavish lifestyle," I said, putting emphasis on *they*. "Did you see any evidence that Gavin had been supporting a mistress?"

"We were looking at their finances. I don't know how you expect me to answer that." He tinged red around the collar and set his jaw.

He was either embarrassed by the question or playing dumb. Okay, we'd try it his way. Treating grown men like they were children was never my idea of fun, but it was a skill I could whip out if I needed to. I launched into a barrage of questions.

"Were there expenditures at jewelry stores? Were there reoccurring payments for an apartment outside of the home that Mr. and Ms. Wright shared? Were there expenditures by Elyse on a private investigator or a technology expert prior to the discovery of embezzlement charges? All of those financial scenarios could be suggestive of infidelity. It's quite common, as I'm sure you know, for forensic accountants to be used when there are suspicions of adultery in a marriage. I'm sure this isn't the first case you've been involved in here at Kirkland and McCullough where that situation may have come up."

I was certain I sounded like some fuddy-duddy law professor chastising a first-year student on day one, but give me a break, this wasn't the first divorce case the guy had been associated with.

"That is not my area of responsibility. I'm not sure why anyone would think buying a piece of jewelry means a man is committing adultery?"

I wasn't here to lecture the man, so I let the insanity of his statements go and moved into prosecutor mode. "Let me rephrase the question. Did you or did you not discover expenditures that indicated housing, other than the family home, was being maintained?"

"No, we did not."

"Did you discover any large lump-sum payments to individuals?"

"No, we did not."

"Did you discover any payments by Elyse to private investigators or technology firms prior to charges being filed against Gavin?"

"None that I recall."

"Great. Would I be correct in assuming that Gavin did not report the embezzled funds when he submitted the required financial disclosure documents related to his divorce?"

"Mr. Wright did not include those funds in his disclosures related."

"And where was the money parked?"

It was a question I already knew the answer to from the trial, but this guy was pushing my buttons, and I didn't want to let up on him.

"Mr. Wright had opened an account in the Cayman Islands. But we didn't know that information at the time Mrs. Wright initiated her action. That only came to light as the embezzlement charges were brought forward."

What? I sat up in my chair.

"Wait a minute. Let me clarify something. Are you saying that Elyse Wright initiated her divorce proceedings prior to the embezzlement charges being filed?"

"Yes, that's correct. We learned of the embezzlement charges roughly three months after Mrs. Wright filed, and that's when our forensic accountant was brought into the case."

I stared at the wall, processing. If Elyse filed for divorce before the embezzlement charges, then two things were true. Their marriage was already in trouble, and Gavin had gone to great lengths to keep that money secret. The timing was not what I thought it was, or perhaps I had just assumed the charges were the final straw that broke the marriage. Did it matter? Depending on the conditions of the prenup, it was possible that Gavin would have walked away from the marriage with nothing. Was that part of his motivation for embezzling the funds? Or part of his motivation for killing Elyse?

19

L ike it or not, my work on the Wright story was magnifying the chauvinism I saw in the world around me, sensitizing my intolerance of it in the process. Even in this day and age, with the progress women had made in business and in government, sexism was still alive and well, although the message was more blunted now than it was in the past.

Narrow-minded men were still forcing us to contain the boundaries of our lives. It was a power struggle and an ego play. The more insecure the man, the harder he fought when old-world order was challenged.

These were the thoughts rumbling through my mind as I walked from my apartment over to meet Ryan for dinner at Fig and Olive. I tucked my hands into my coat pockets as a harsh wind whipped down Oak Street off the lake. Luckily the snow was staying away.

I'd managed to get home for a few minutes after my conversation with Bennett, just long enough to feed Walter, send Michael a text letting him know I couldn't make dinner, and then change into something more appropriate for my meeting with Ryan. But I'd agonized over what to wear. Looking too much like a banker wasn't appropriate, but this wasn't a date, and I didn't want Ryan confused about my intent. I'd settled on a silk blouse and a skirt, ran a brush through my hair, freshened my lipstick, and then decided that walking the handful of blocks from my co-op over to the restaurant would help adjust my mood.

Arriving pissed off wasn't the most prudent idea under the circumstances, but I couldn't seem to let go. Even the crisp night wasn't doing the job. The situation at work with Ramelli and Borkowski seemed to meld into the societal chauvinism of the Wright case, and I was in the middle of both.

I would also need to figure out how to have a conversation with Victor about Marcus Bennett. While his sexism was not as overt as some, it was a huge turnoff nonetheless and, if allowed to continue, could only harm Victor's practice. Perhaps Bennett had been on his best behavior in front of his boss, but the man had a front-facing role, and that kind of attitude could not be tolerated. Women got the short end of the stick in most divorce cases anyway; they certainly didn't need to be dealing with an employee who viewed them as second-class citizens, too.

Stepping off the elevator and into the restaurant, I ran my gaze along the bar centered in the room. Soft jazz emanated from a live piano player near the window, setting a relaxed mood. Ryan sat nursing a drink. Lights glowed around him, highlighting the tree that anchored the bar and extended up into a skylight. Waiting for the hostess, I watched him, fighting memories of another night in a darkened room. His white shirt, open at the collar, and navy sport coat showed off his tawny skin and sun-kissed hair. Despite myself, I had to admit that the man distracted me in a way that could leave me conflicted, if I allowed it to. But there was nothing positive to come out of reigniting a romantic attraction, for me or for my relationship with Michael. I just had to keep reminding myself of that.

I checked my coat, took a deep breath, and walked over to join him. He stood when I approached, and the light from the overhead bottle storage danced against his jaw. I extended a hand, which he took, but then he pulled me in close, giving me a kiss on the cheek. His cologne lingered as I stepped back and extricated my hand. Not exactly the way one greeted most business associates. Ryan grabbed his drink.

"Shall we go to our table? That way we can hear each other talk." He flagged the hostess, and we were led away from the noise of the bar toward a private table in the back. Suddenly I had the feeling he'd scoped out the seating accommodations and put in a request before I arrived.

I slid into the corner booth, adjusted the pillows at my back, then ordered a Cabernet, painfully aware of Ryan's legs brushing mine. He exuded the quiet confidence of a man who knew what he wanted and nearly always got it. A devastating combination. And what was it he wanted tonight?

But then, did I know what *I* wanted? I'd thought so before I'd walked in the door, but sitting here next to the man, was I sure? The urge to flee washed over me, vulnerability and fear and memories were all tangled, and I couldn't separate them. Couldn't separate the business decisions I needed to make from the personal decisions, leaving avoidance as the most attractive option.

I suppressed my anxiety as we busied ourselves with choices from the menu and common courtesies. This was a business meeting, and the anxiety was of my own making, a result of too little sleep and the trauma of the week. "Get a grip," I said to myself.

"Why are we here, Ryan?" I said after our waiter left, laying what I thought to be obvious on the table.

"What do you mean? You don't like the restaurant?" Although he appeared to consider my question, a smile played around his eyes.

I lifted my glass and played along. "The restaurant is fine. A nice meal, just the two of us alone in the back corner booth. Is this a work conversation?"

"Since you've been too busy to meet with me during the day, I thought I'd try something else. We both need to eat. This way we can talk over a drink." He smiled at me, teasing, pretending I was somehow responsible for the circumstances.

"All right, if you're here to talk about work, let's cut to the chase. What is your intent with Link-Media? I understand that you and Wade Ramelli have a history. Ramelli wants me out. How do you fit into that?"

Ryan twirled his glass, took a drink, then shot a look at me that I felt in the pit of my stomach.

"You and I have a history as well. How does that fit in?" he said.

"Our history is irrelevant, and I'm not the one using it to try to accomplish something. You and Ramelli, on the other hand, that's what I'm not sure about."

He laughed. "Still the prosecutor, I see. You are so suspicious. Not everyone has an ulterior motive."

"Yes, they do. And I don't believe for a moment it's just coincidence, you stumbling into this gig."

I tucked my hair behind my ear and lifted my glass while I watched his face, waiting for a response.

"And what is it you think is going on, Andrea? And how can you say our history is irrelevant? I'm offended. I've thought of that night, and you, often. My memories are quite vivid." He trailed a finger along my wrist, his touch searing my flesh in the process.

I pulled back, trying to push the thoughts of that evening—

and the memory of where else he had traced his fingers—out of my mind as best I could. But the nearness of him, the maleness of him, the sliver of chest exposed at the neck of his shirt all made that impossible.

Our server returned and set appetizers in front of us, thankfully dulling the moment and giving me time to adjust.

"I think Ramelli is going to get exactly the result he bought and paid for," I said. "That he, that the two of you, have a plan and that this consulting scenario exists to accomplish two things. It will deliver the results that Ramelli wants it to deliver, to justify what comes next, and it will give you enough information about where we're vulnerable to close off my options."

"My dear, I love your directness, but you're getting paranoid." He grinned and leaned back against the banquette, slowly sipping a little more of the amber liquid in his glass. "You think the two of us are conspiring against you? For what purpose? A takeover? Are you that insecure about your performance that you can't handle a little outside evaluation?"

"I think you and Ramelli are going to make a run at the business and that I'm just one of the obstacles you've been sent in to eliminate." His smugness was beginning to grate on me, but I wasn't going to learn anything if I didn't control my temper. I quietly let out a breath and tried to modulate my reaction.

"That's so very James Bond of you," he said. "I didn't realize you had such an imagination. I like it. It's quite sexy."

"Can you be serious?"

"I'm completely serious." He smiled. "You've given me a great idea for dessert."

I crossed my arms on the table and leaned forward. "Are we here to talk business, or shall I leave you to finish the mushroom crostini on your own?"

"They are good, but I'd prefer your company." He paused, still smiling, then sipped his bourbon. "I really have only one question, Andrea. What do you want? What are you trying to prove by hanging on to Link-Media? You don't need the money. Erik may have been your husband, but he didn't treat you very well. Is this some misplaced loyalty to him? Are you trying to prove you're worthy? Or are you just hanging on because more change is too overwhelming to contemplate?"

20

I buried my head deeper into the pillow and pulled the down comforter up around my chin. Through closed lids I was aware of the light in my bedroom, so I knew it was past sunrise, but I was too content in my wrappings to move. I breathed slowly, letting myself become conscious but I was still too groggy to be fully awake.

A furry paw tapped the side of my face.

I opened one eye and blinked. Walter sat next to me on the bed, purring, patiently waiting for me to show signs of life. I petted the top of his head, blinked the sleep out of my eyes, and looked at the clock. 8:30. No wonder he was serving as my alarm clock. Breakfast should have been served an hour ago.

I threw back the comforter, then grabbed my robe from the end of the bed. Walter jumped down from his perch and moved toward the door. I let him lead me into the kitchen, where I refreshed the kibble in his bowl, topping it off with a dollop of coveted stinky, wet fish mush. His priorities satisfied, I attended to my own and turned on the water for tea.

As I pulled out a mug and the accompanying accoutrement, my thoughts went back to my dinner with Ryan. His question about what I wanted had thrown me. I hadn't been prepared, at least not to hear it from him. I'd blathered on with some nonsense about being thrown into the situation unexpectedly and now feeling that it was the best choice for my life and my skills. Even to me, my response had sounded political.

But the question Ryan asked, whether he knew it or not, was far deeper than the answer I gave him and deeper than any question I had asked myself. It came down to what was I trying to prove? In my gut, I knew that question was at the heart of how I saw my future and the future of Link-Media.

But I still didn't know how to answer it. Was I fighting to prove I was capable because Ramelli had a preconceived idea that I was in over my head? Was this about me, or was this about the business? Like it or not, that was indeed a question I would have to answer, if not for Ryan, then certainly for myself.

I finished assembling the contents of my morning ritual, Earl Grey with lemon and honey, then headed off to the shower. My master bath had weeks of remodeling to go before it would be useable, so I'd moved the essential grooming products to the funky old guest bath and boxed the rest. The shower head gave me a wobbly trickle and the cracked and stained tiles surrounding the tub made my germ meter swing, but it was better than decamping to a hotel or sleeping on my sister's sofa.

Cai and I had arranged to meet for brunch at 11:00, and I wanted to spend some time outlining my thoughts on the Elyse Wright story before I left. Every news outlet, including my own, had covered the surface details of the case. I was becoming known for the deep-dive story, investigating the why and the how and the motivations behind the cases. Although CPD had Gavin in custody, there were still too many plot holes. And in my mind, many of them centered on the timing of the attack.

As I dried my hair, I shifted my thoughts away from my own situation to Gavin and Elyse Wright. Someone knew what had been going on in their marriage prior to Elyse filing for divorce. My takeaway from the trial and discussions with Victor had been that the embezzlement charges were the wedge issue in ending the marriage, but his paralegal Bennett indicated Elyse had filed before his embezzlement was known. Perhaps the timing of events was not as cut and dried as they seemed today, and if so, what other assumptions did I need to question?

The sky outside was dismal. Gray, windy, and looked biting cold. I threw on jeans and a chunky wool fisherman's sweater, refreshed the hot water in my tea, then moved to my office. The room was functional, although I was still waiting for some furniture that was supposedly on a boat from Italy—likely a row boat, given how many times I'd heard the same non-answer update.

I grabbed a Sharpie and a pad of Post-its, then began filling a large custom linen tack board I'd recently hung with dates and events. Working back and forth between my notes and various reference material online, I began to lay out a timeline. I stepped back, absorbing the data and jotting down questions or additional issues that needed verification on a yellow legal pad.

As I looked at the information, my cell phone rang. Victor Kirkland. It wasn't like him to call me on a Saturday. It wasn't like him to work on a Saturday at all, given the seventy hours he put in between Monday and Friday.

"Andrea, I'm sorry to call you on the weekend," he said, sounding breathless and nervous. "The police just phoned me. It's happened again!"

"Slow down, Victor. What has happened?"

"Sorry, I just don't know. I wasn't sure what to do. I'm rattled. Another client has been murdered. Just this morning. The police tell me I'm just panicking, that Elyse's killer is in jail, but her mouth was cut and they won't listen to me. I didn't know what to do. I thought you could help figure this out."

The fear and shock tumbled out of his mouth while I

listened, my mind racing, trying to put together the pieces of what he was telling me. Another client had been murdered? This couldn't possibly be the same killer.

"Go back to the beginning," I said, keeping my voice as measured as I could manage. "Who was killed? Why don't you start with that? And then tell me what the police said."

"Oh, yes, of course. Her name is Skylar Hayes. They found her this morning, dead on the ground next to her car. The police said they think it was an attempted carjacking. She's a sales rep for a jewelry company and had some very expensive product in her car. She must've been taking her sample case to appointments. So of course they think robbery. Her car, the jewelry, probably both."

"Tell me about her mouth. You said her mouth had been cut."

"The police wouldn't say anything more, but of course I couldn't help but go there. First Elyse, now Skylar, two women going through nasty divorces, both having their mouths slashed, how in the world could I not make that connection?"

"Try to calm down," I said, panic rising in my own chest. "I'll see what I can find out. Give me her address."

As he read off the address, a new thought crossed my mind.

"How did the police know to call you?"

"She was going to drop off some documents at the office this morning. Apparently the envelope was on the front seat of her car with the papers, and my card was stapled to the outside with a note. So they called me."

"Thanks for letting me know, Victor. I'll find out what I can."

I hung up the phone, picked up the piece of paper with Skylar Hayes's address, grabbed a coat, boots, and texted Cai as I headed for my car. Brunch would have to wait.

I parked in a metered spot on Ashland Avenue five blocks west of Skylar Hayes's Lakeview home, knowing it was as close as I could likely get to the crime scene. Pulling on a cap and gloves, I threw my bag across my chest and headed west, picking my way around the slick, snow-covered spots on the sidewalks. The street in front of the Hayeses' home was blocked on both ends by squad cars. Lights flashed off the snowbanks as confused neighbors tried to determine what was going on.

Like much of Chicago, the homes were a mix of multistory single family and converted three-flats. Largely Greystone construction, although because of looser historic zoning obstacles, many of the old wood-frame buildings were being torn down to make way for a developer's idea of a modern box. The treelined streets and frequent front porches attracted those who wanted a family feel at a price more affordable than Lincoln Park—or diehard Cubs fans, as Wrigley Field was just blocks away.

As I rushed to join the crowd pushed back from the ambulance and the crime scene tape, I scanned the scene. The press had been corralled off to the opposite side of the street. There, a familiar face guarded the southern edge of the perimeter. A beat cop I knew from my years as a prosecutor. I snaked my way in.

"Hey, Tom, what dragged you out of bed on a cold, miserable Saturday morning?" I asked when I got close, already feeling the chill seep into my body.

"Looks like another crazy attacked a woman. Probably some dumbass addict seeing an opportunity to fund his habit. I hear she had a case full of gemstones. The guy probably thought she was easy pickings on an early Saturday morning. Who else would be out here in this weather?"

"I heard it was a carjacking?" I said, working him a little.

"I think he jumped her when she was getting into her car. Her keys were on the ground, not in the ignition, so he probably thought he had perfect timing. Took advantage of the moment.

Ain't clear if he knew she had twenty grand worth of baubles in her hand or if it was just dumb luck."

"Doesn't look so lucky for her. How did it go from jacking her car to her dead on the ground?"

He shrugged, then wiped away some ice crystals that were forming on his mustache. "Does anyone really know how these things escalate? Maybe she resisted? She's pretty cut up, so something went to shit."

"How do you know she had jewelry?" I asked, assuming the case was long gone. From where I stood I could see the burgundy Camry in the narrow driveway, parked alongside the well-kept Victorian home. The front door was only about twenty feet from the car, but to get to it meant walking down the steps from the front porch, through the gate, and along the wrought-iron fencing to get to the driveway. She hadn't snuck up on him. So if stealing the car had been his main objective, why he hadn't succeeded?

"This ain't official, but I'd say the job got interrupted. Car door was open when we got here and the jewelry case was lying in the snowbank."

That meant something had interrupted him and he ran off, or he had no idea the case held anything of value, which seemed unlikely. But why kill her? She had the car keys out. One good shove and he could have knocked her down, swiped the keys, and sped off.

"You said she was cut up. Any sign of the knife?"

"Not yet. But we'll find it."

"Thanks, Tom. Stay warm out here."

"No kidding. I could sure use a coffee right about now." He stomped his feet and rubbed his hands together.

"I'll bring one over before I leave."

I was about twenty-five feet away from the main action and couldn't see much through the throng of police personnel.

Ambulance, crime scene unit, and more cops than I could count swarmed the street around the vehicle. I scanned the barricade, looking for a better vantage point, and spotted Michael talking with an EMT. He was typing notes into his phone as they spoke. I maneuvered closer, hoping I could get into position to catch his attention and have a better line of sight to the activities.

Neither waving nor calling his name accomplished anything, so I pulled out my phone and sent him a text, knowing he would at least glance at it. Sure enough, he lifted his head and ran his eyes over the crowd. I raised my hand. He said something to the EMT, then headed my way.

"Do you have a secret police band radio at home I don't know about?" he asked when he got close, giving me a small smile.

"Better. Lots of connections."

"I don't think I want to know."

I leaned forward and whispered, "I heard her mouth was slashed."

He lifted his eyebrows.

"Like Elyse Wright's?"

He said nothing at first, conscious of the ears around us.

"I can't confirm any of the details right now," he said.

Hearing the clack of the gurney snapping into position, we both turned as the EMTs lifted Skylar's body and moved her to the waiting ambulance. The slam of the doors and firing of the siren put a hush in the crowd. I felt myself choke up, jolted by the finality of the sound. As the ambulance sped off, I could make out some of the markers the crime scene team had placed around the vehicle and noted their position. A flatbed tow truck would be here later in the day to transport the car for processing.

"Michael, she was also one of Victor Kirkland's clients. Does she have the same cuts to her mouth?" I asked again, watching his eyes as thoughts shifted in his head.

He looked at me, holding my gaze for a moment, then nodded. "We'll talk later."

A cold, harsh wind slapped me in the face as he walked away, and in that instant, I knew the same set of hands had murdered both women.

21

I'd spent hours at the crime scene, pressing anyone I could for additional details. Learning from a chatty neighbor that the victim was thirty-four, a sales rep for a New York-based line of fine jewelry, and traveled the entire Midwest as her territory, selling primarily to boutiques and other small mom-and-pop retailers. She and her husband, Oliver, had been married for about eight years, only two of which sounded happy. They had no children, and she'd filed for divorce nearly a year earlier after finding his cocaine stash and a $10,000 credit card bill for his hooker habit. As a senior VP at a major accounting firm, he was none too happy with the idea that his reputation might be damaged.

Having exhausted the resources at the scene, I was now so cold that my fingers refused to bend and my toes were a vague memory somewhere inside my boots. I returned to my car, cranked the heat up to the highest setting, and turned on the butt warmer. Then I phoned Cai and asked if she could meet me for a late bite to eat. I needed a sane ear to listen to me vent and a steady heart to keep me grounded in reality.

My head was racing. There was no question in my mind that

the same person had killed Elyse Wright and Skylar Hayes. Less clear was who and why. The women were linked in two obvious ways: they shared an attorney, and both had husbands who had misbehaved badly. Was it conceivable that the hired killer Gavin Wright had paid to take out his wife had also been hired to kill Hayes? I made a mental note to identify the opposing legal teams in both divorces.

As I drove back to the Gold Coast to meet Cai, I turned over options in my head. If the two murders were committed by the same hired killer, it seemed logical that the men would have had to have known each other and exchanged information. What was this, an Angie's List for hit men?

Although I was only a few blocks from my apartment, I left my car in a paid lot a block from the restaurant, afraid that one more unnecessary moment out in the cold would lead to frostbite. At three o'clock in the afternoon, Le Colonial, my favorite Vietnamese restaurant, was sparsely populated, and Cai was waiting at a table in the window. Her long dark hair fell loose around her face as she scrolled through her phone.

She stood to give me a hug. "Your cheeks are so red that if I didn't know better, I'd say you'd gotten sunburn."

"Careful, I think I could give you frostbite on contact." I took off my hat and coat but left the scarf wrapped tightly around my neck, grateful to be out of the wind. "I'm frozen to the bone. Thanks for rearranging your day for me."

A waiter arrived at our table. Cai had already ordered a glass of wine. I asked for a pot of Jasmine tea and told him he could bring me a Cabernet chaser in about ten minutes.

"So what crisis popped up and undid your plans for the day?" Cai asked.

"Another woman has been murdered," I said, grabbing the handle of the teapot that had just appeared and pouring a cup.

"Let me get some of this down. I'll order soup so I can thaw out, then I'll tell you all about it."

I ordered the canh hoanh ton, a seafood dumpling soup, and Cai got the banh cuon, an amazing chicken ravioli appetizer. I wrapped both of my hands around the porcelain cup and took a drink of the tea, feeling the steaming liquid spread warmth through my body. A second sip and I started to feel my hands again.

"So, are you ready to talk? Who was murdered? This is like a movie teaser."

"Another woman going through a nasty divorce."

"What? Oh God, that confirms it. I'm never getting married. The benefits don't outweigh all the icky bits. Let me guess, the husband did it. It's always the husband." She pushed up the sleeves on her turtleneck and shook her head.

"I'm not sure yet, but here's the odd thing. This victim shared a divorce attorney with Elyse Wright."

Cai crossed her arms on the table, her face registering the questions I was already asking myself. "You think they're related?"

I shrugged, glanced around for potential eavesdroppers, then leaned in a little closer. "It's not the only similarity. The killer slashed her mouth."

"I thought CPD believed Wright hired a hit man, so you're saying two guys ordered the same hit man who killed these women in the same manner? How could that happen?"

"That's one possibility. The only other I can think of is that their legal connection is coincidental and there's some kind of serial killer going after women." I threw out the theory, but the whole thing seemed too shaky to define yet.

"As ugly as it is, I think I like the first possibility better," Cai said. "A killer cutting up random women would have the whole city freaked out, me included. What has CPD said about the hit man? They obviously have some kind of evidence that convinces them Gavin Wright had taken steps toward a murder-for-hire. Do they have any handle on this hit man's identity or confirmation that Wright did anything more than initiate dialogue? I don't know what the going rate is for wife killing, but fantasizing about it and paying for it are two different things."

"So far, all I know is that Gavin had an email exchange with someone and that the dialogue was specific enough for CPD to bring him in. Granted, he was out on bond for the embezzlement, so getting him back behind bars wouldn't take much. I have no idea if they've discovered a payment trail. It's not the kind of thing that will show up on your Amex bill."

"Sounds to me like you need to work your inside connections a little harder," Cai said, winking at me.

Too bad it wasn't that easy.

My phone buzzed. Victor. "Have you learned anything else?" he asked immediately. I'd given him an update while I was still at the scene, but clearly he was just as obsessed with this as I was.

"Nothing I didn't share with you on our earlier call. I promise to let you know as soon as I hear anything more. Can you send me the names of opposing counsel in both divorce cases?" I asked. "I'm curious about any other connections between the women. Is there anything you can think of? Was Skylar threatened by her husband in any way?"

"I'm afraid my head's a little fuzzy right now. I'll need to take another look at the files, but nothing's coming to mind at the moment. The husbands did not use the same counsel. That I'm certain of. I'll send you a text later with the names, and I'll go over their files with a fine-tooth comb. If anything looks unusual, I'll let you know right away. And you do the same, please."

"I sure will. Speak to you soon."

Before I could reach for my wine, a news alert popped up on my phone. I read the brief story and shook my head in disgust. Wanting to be the first out of the gate, the *Tribune* was reporting the incident as a carjacking, quoting CPD's press liaison in the process.

"You're making faces. What is it?"

"For the moment, anyway, it seems CPD is trying to pass this off as a carjacking."

"Sounds like a great way to make women all over the city terrified to drive alone."

Ordering second glasses of wine, Cai and I tossed around all the bad divorce stories either one of us had ever heard. It wasn't fair, but like Cai said, these were the stories that gave marriage a bad name. Once burned, twice shy, but on ridiculous steroids. Very few divorces devolved to the point of one partner murdering the other, but given the heightened emotion, marital problems were usually law enforcement's first line of questioning.

Cai and I ended our late lunch just shy of either one of us vowing off relationships forever, said our good-byes, then returned to our respective apartments. I didn't imagine it had been the most productive conversation for Cai, given the date she had scheduled for later that evening. It wasn't as if she were going to give up men for the rest of her life, and neither was I, but marriage, that was a story left unwritten. Luckily, neither one of us had to put that thought to the test. Michael's live-together idea notwithstanding.

Walter was in his usual place just inside the door when I got home. He stretched and yawned, then rubbed against my legs, clearly having spent the day napping.

Despite the tea, the soup, and the wine, I still had a chill I couldn't shake. Was it the cold or the additional murder? A bath and a quiet evening in front of the fire sounded ideal.

I filled the tub, poured in some Epsom salts, added a few drops of essential oil, and climbed in, allowing the heat to radiate through me while Walter did guard duty. Bathing was a task that both confused and fascinated him. He made a habit of sitting on the ledge, mesmerized as the water shimmered and swirled. I soaked for fifteen minutes, my mind processing unsuccessfully the possible connections between the murders. If not the husbands, then who?

I toweled off before the water got cold, dressed in a sweater and leggings, then lit a fire.

Needing a distraction, I sat on the sofa with my legs up, the latest thriller from my favorite author on the coffee table next to me, but I couldn't clear my head. What were the odds that two men in the middle of a messy divorce had both hired the same hit man? It wasn't as if this was the kind of thing you placed a Craigslist ad for. Well, at least not in an obvious way. How would they have found a hit man to hire? The only scenario that made sense was that the husbands had some other connection. I got up from the couch and went to my office, grabbing a legal pad, Post-its, and pens. My technique for problem solving ever since law school had been lists, notes, and what-if scenarios. By writing everything down and organizing my thoughts in some kind of visual manner, I could begin to see patterns.

Had the men known each other? Were there common clubs or membership organizations they both belonged to? Each question went on the legal pad as I brainstormed.

A text popped up on my phone. Victor, with the names of the two divorce attorneys. I thanked him, then settled back on the couch, opening a browser window. Both men had hired well-respected attorneys, male attorneys with reputations for aggressive negotiations. I wasn't surprised.

These were exactly the types of attorneys that any individual in the middle of something this messy would need to have. If you didn't come to this type of legal showdown with your A team, there'd likely be nothing left at the end, even if you won. And under the circumstances, these guys would have been fighting for every scrap they could possibly get. Whether winning meant saving their finances or reducing the damage to their reputations, neither one of these husbands would have come out of their divorces feeling victorious. But with skilled legal representation, they might have had a shot of rebuilding after.

The choice of legal teams was also not surprising given that both were well-positioned career men. They were smart enough and financially solvent enough to afford quality legal talent.

Regardless, the connection between the men was not legal, and neither of these firms were sleazy enough to have relationships with this level of unsavory characters. I moved from the legal teams to doing a dive into Oliver Hayes's background, looking for any internet references I could find to previous employers, association memberships, evidence of similar social circles. The Wrights had been active in the world of charitable giving, perhaps the Hayeses had been as well. I opened Google Images, looking for photos of charity benefits, galas, golf outings, and any other place where wealthy, civic-conscious individuals might be enticed to give their time or their money.

After nearly three hours, my eyes were strained and my neck was stiff from hunching over the keyboard, but I'd found nothing that looked like a connection. I set my legal pad aside, moved Walter off of my feet, and went to the kitchen for a Pellegrino. My phone was ringing when I returned.

"You're still awake," Michael said on the other end of the phone.

"It's only nine o'clock. Tonight will be an early evening, but this is a bit much for Saturday night. Have you wrapped this case up yet?" I said, laughing.

"If only it were that easy. We're doing our best, but no leads yet."

"Come on, Michael, I don't believe that. Someone on your side is already speaking to the *Tribune*, calling this a carjacking. What about the similarities with Elyse Wright's murder? Two women, both in the middle of nasty divorces, both stabbed and then their mouths slashed? You've said Wright communicated with the killer. Hired him to do in his wife. Are you telling me you can't trace that email address? Have you found a financial trail?" I peppered him with questions. "If you've got a lead on Elyse Wright's killer, then you've got a lead on Skylar Hayes's killer. Seems pretty obvious."

"You're getting ahead of yourself. Granted, there are strong similarities, but it's too early to make a direct connection. Hayes had an unlocked car and a big haul of jewelry in her possession. That's an attractive motive."

"It might be too early to make a connection between the killer and the husbands, or that the husbands conspired together to have their wives knocked off, but you can't tell me the manner of death in both cases isn't identical."

"What I'm telling you is that you need to slow down. You're always rushing to a conclusion. Let us do what we do. Let the evidence speak for itself before you go off and convict someone."

"What it sounds like is that you've been muzzled by Janek."

22

S aturday's crappy weather turned into six inches of snow by Sunday, which suited me fine. I'd holed up in my apartment diving into as much deep background on the Hayes and Wright families as my skills allowed, amassing a lot of material but not knowing what, if any of it, was useful. Grudgingly, I'd left my apartment only to confirm Erik's place was ready for the stagers, who were scheduled to bring in their stash of furniture in a few hours.

Woven in between the research, I'd written a short piece on Skylar's murder but had danced around the connections between Elyse Wright and Skylar Hayes. I couldn't do the story without mentioning similarities but also couldn't link them on gut instinct alone. I'd sent it in, letting Borkowski do his tweaks, and the story had been loaded to the landing page early this morning.

But I'd only scratched the surface. In my gut I believed that how the women had died wasn't the real story; why they died was. However, with Michael and Janek shutting me out, I needed to nail down as many commonalities as I could, so what better way than to go straight to the source: the medical examiner.

As I drove south, swinging from Lake Shore Drive to the westbound Eisenhower, I listened to WXRT and debated with myself about how to deal with Michael. He was being evasive about the cases, which pissed me off. Was that about caution, Janek, or my reaction to his suggestion about our living arrangements?

I'd volunteered information that the dead women shared a divorce attorney, but even that hadn't been enough to get him to talk. One thing these murders had made clear was the complications of a relationship between a cop and journalist. If there was going to be a future for us, we'd have to figure out how to talk about the boundaries between work and our personal lives. Hardly an easy task for two headstrong professionals.

I was also keenly aware that I hadn't told Michael about my dinner with Ryan Friday evening. In the moment, it hadn't occurred to me. I didn't intend to hide the information from him; it was just a work meeting. But in light of Ryan's obvious interest in me, I was reassessing. Had my silence been intentional? And if so, what did that say about my feelings for Michael?

For the moment, avoidance of the subject seemed the better strategy. I was in no rush to sort that out, even if both of them seemed ready, willing, and able. I wasn't there.

I pushed both men out of my head as I pulled up to the squat hulk of a building on West Harrison that housed the medical examiner's office. Once again, my history as a prosecutor was coming in handy, and I was calling in a favor. Visitor parking was empty, so I pulled into a spot near the front door, walked inside, and told the receptionist I was here to see Samar Patel.

Patel was a pathologist who worked for the Cook County's chief medical examiner. I'd gotten to know him professionally through a couple of murder trials I had worked a few years back. He didn't realize it yet, but he owed me.

Knowing he started each morning by reviewing case files and test results, I'd arrived early. Catching him before he donned his protective gear gave me a fighting shot to get a few minutes of his time before he locked himself in the autopsy suite.

I waited for about fifteen minutes alone in a reception room, listening to bland music and trying to forget where I was, before I saw Patel's round face appear next to the reception desk. He paused, adjusted his glasses higher on his nose, and looked around. I stood and met him near the desk.

"This is a surprise," he said. "Don't tell me you were just in the neighborhood, because I wouldn't believe you."

"Nope, I drove out here to see you. Is there somewhere we can talk for a few minutes?"

Significant arm-twisting would be necessary, and I didn't want to discuss the details of my visit in public. Although the visiting room was empty at the moment, I knew that could change. The priority of the men and women who worked in this establishment was to protect the humanity of the dead and to not cause undue harm on the families forced to identify remains.

He looked at me quizzically but tipped his head toward the back. I followed him down a wide hallway to a small conference room, noticing the twenty pounds he'd put on since I'd last seen him.

"I'm afraid I don't have coffee or anything to offer you," he said, motioning me into a seat and immediately checking his watch.

"No, that's not necessary, but thank you. I've had my fill already today."

"So, Andrea, what's this all about?"

"The Skylar Hayes murder," I said. "She came in yesterday. Caucasian, early thirties, stab wounds." I recited enough of the details to jog his memory.

"I wasn't in yesterday. It's not my case. I'm not sure I can help you." He seemed to relax a little.

"I believe she's already in the case archive. At least that's what appears on Data Lens. I can give you the case number, if you need it."

He looked at me and scowled, correctly interpreting the dig. The medical examiner's office had started an online database of cases processed through this office. The database had started back in 2014 and was intended to provide more transparency to a department that had been embattled in political ugliness for quite some time and more than a few lawsuits.

He stood and walked to a computer, where he logged in a few keystrokes. "Okay, I think this is the case you are referring to. It's status is pending. I'm not sure I can tell you anything more than what you already knew. It's too early to have determined the cause of death. I'm afraid you've wasted a trip."

"Yes, I'm aware this is a pending case. But I believe not only is this a murder that isn't going to take your greatest medical minds to figure out but that it's also related to a similar case of a woman murdered just a few days ago. I want to see the preliminary files."

Patel drew back, crossing his arms over his chest and giving me a look that said I may as well have called his mother a whore. "Have you lost your mind? I can't show that information to nonofficial personnel. It's an outrageous request. And, if I must say, quite brazen. The fact that we know each other does not entitle you to walk into my office and demand information. There is a procedure and a protocol in place for sharing information, and you are well aware of that."

I looked at him and held my gaze. "Interesting choice of

words. Procedure and protocol in cases of suspicious death require an investigator from the medical examiner's office to come to the scene. No one from this office was at the scene yesterday. She was transported by ambulance. Nor was anyone from this office at the scene of the previous death. And I know this because I *was* at the scene. Both of them. I found the first victim."

The office had been in the middle of a political shit storm for over a year. Accusations had been flying related to lazy pathologists, incorrect identification of cause of death, flawed autopsies, all of it coming together in FBI investigations and lawsuits. It hadn't been Patel's fault; he was competent, but internal pressures could only be intense. And if I had to add to the pile to get what I needed, so be it.

"How many stories have been reported related to mismanagement in the medical examiner's office? We both know that procedure in suspicious deaths is for this office to be on the scene," I said, feeling only a little guilty for the tactics I was using. "How do you think your superiors will react when I publish a story giving firsthand knowledge of your failure to show up, as required by law, to the scene of these crimes? This office is already under the microscope. I'm convinced that the manner of death for both of these women, and the marks on their bodies, will be nearly identical. What I want you to do is to open the preliminary files and look at them. Tell me if I'm right."

Patel wasn't the one who screwed this up, and I felt bad about blackmailing him to get information, but I had to work the angles available even if it meant losing him as a source in the future.

He pinched the bridge of his nose and shook his head, irritated to be placed in this position. I knew his work was beyond reproach and he likely hated being drawn into the mismanagement, but I also suspected he had aspirations for the top job, and raking the office further into the muck wouldn't help him get there.

"I promise no one will know I got the information from you," I said, hoping to seal his decision.

"Fine!" he huffed, then went back to the computer and tapped into another database, this one internal. "Okay, here's yesterday's victim."

"Print it for me."

He clenched his jaw, but a second later the printer whirled.

"And the earlier victim?"

I gave him the details, and moments later, the printer whirled for a second time. After pulling the printouts out of the machine, he laid both sets of documents on the conference table, and together we went through them. The first thing that got my attention was the markings made to indicate the locations of the stab wounds on the bodies.

"Okay, we have primary stab wounds just below the corpus sternum, puncturing the right lobe of the liver and the gallbladder. Likely the cause of death. And secondary superficial wounds across the mouth," he said, pointing to the drawing.

"What can you tell from this about the weapon or the assailant?"

He flipped back and forth between the documents, comparing the details. "A knife. Large, serrated, possibly a hunting knife. Based on the angle of the wound, I'd say the assailant was directly in front of his victim when he struck, and the motion was a direct forward thrust. Like this." He simulated the stabbing motion. "That's relevant because it tells us he was close and quick." He turned back to the docs. "Hmm. Both victims were close in height, around five foot five to five foot seven. I'd speculate they were standing face-to-face with the assailant, and based on the angle of motion, I'd say he is no more than a couple inches taller. Again, this is preliminary, so don't hold me to it. First impression only."

"May I see the photos," I asked hesitantly. The images of death were hard to observe, tending to sear into one's brain unwillingly, but I felt I had no choice. He turned back to the computer, clicking back several pages until two pasty faces appeared. The waxy skin of death had been cleaned of all traces of blood, and the branding of the knife over the women's mouths screamed words they could no longer utter.

Patel and I looked at each other as tears streamed down my face.

23

C old, lifeless flesh now branded with knife cuts to the mouth.

I'd seen many photos of death as a prosecutor, but somehow the images of these two women unnerved me as few had. Was it my interaction with Elyse or my own similarities to the victims? Despite Michael's attempt at withholding details, I now knew without a doubt the same man had killed both women. Whatever reasons Michael had for holding back likely had more to do with Janek and department policy than with me.

Although CPD had withheld information about wounds to the mouth from the public, the similarities in the manner of death hadn't stopped local news outlets from speculating, increasing the number of wild hypotheses. Already this morning I'd heard conjecture that the murders were the work of a jilted lover lurking on an online dating site. The longer CPD kept silent, the more fantastical the stories were likely to become.

Arriving back in the Loop, I pulled into a parking garage on Wabash, intending to make a visit to Skylar Hayes's office. Since she was a road rep, I didn't have great expectations for a large staff of coworkers to speak with, but nonetheless, it was worth a visit.

The office was in a nondescript vintage high-rise facing the L, and I could hear the rumble of the train as I stepped off the elevator even though I was on the sixth floor. Mudra Imports, the door said. Lights shone through the textured glass, and country music streamed faintly in the background, so I knocked and opened the door. The space looked to be no more than two rooms. Four desks, just as many file cabinets, and boxes and boxes of accessories filled the space, their contents overflowing onto the surrounding surfaces.

"Can I help you?" A woman who'd been crouched down, pawing through the entangled merchandise, now stood. Barefoot and looking a little disheveled, she tugged at her skirt and peered at me quizzically. Her eyes were swollen and red.

"My name is Andrea Kellner. I'm with Link-Media. I'd like to speak to you about Skylar Hayes."

Her eyes got wider, but she didn't ask me to leave, although she seemed dazed.

"Most people wandering in here are either lost or trying to sell me something. Link-Media? What's that?"

"We're a digital news agency." I handed her my card.

"Reporter." She shrugged. "I wondered how long it would take somebody to show up. I've had the phone off all day in anticipation." She let out a breath. "You're the only one who's had the guts to walk in the door. I guess I should be grateful for that," she said, dabbing at her nose with a tissue. "I'm having trouble believing it's real. I just saw her on Friday." Tears brimmed in her eyes. "Sorry about the blubbering. It's going to be tough to get through the week."

A photo of Skylar surrounded by a small group of women, who I assumed were coworkers, rested on the bookcase beside her. I wasn't sure where to begin. Skylar's morgue photo was unmistakably fresh in my mind, yet just days ago she'd been the woman in this photo, a vibrant individual with friends and family and dreams.

"Can you tell me about her? Did she spend much time in the office?"

"I'll tell you. You get points for initiative. I suppose I can't avoid this indefinitely. Let me find a chair, and then we can talk." She moved boxes off a folding chair, placing them on the floor, and then offered me the seat while she settled behind the first desk.

"Sorry, I haven't introduced myself. I'm Tanya, the office manager." We exchanged half-hearted smiles.

"There's a lot of merchandise in here," I said, unbuttoning my coat and looking at the overflowing boxes of belts and hand-bags. Pieces of costume jewelry and swatches of different leathers and braids haphazardly covered the desks while walls were embellished with color cards taped to the surface. It wasn't the image I'd had of a jewelry showroom. "Do you sell out of this location?" I asked, not familiar with how the industry operated.

"No, these are just samples. There are four different reps who work out of this office, about eighteen lines between them. Everyone is independent, so they formed a mini-collective, each one pitching in to pay a percentage of the rent. And my salary."

"How does that work? The sales process, I mean."

"Skylar, and everyone else who works out of this location, is a road rep. So that means they take their sample lines directly to the retailers for consideration. They show them the product, the color swatches, and leave catalogues, if necessary. If they're lucky, they'll take orders on the spot. If not, the stores send in orders via email or fax. A few people will call in, but that's usually the old guys who don't trust electronics or know how to use a scanner."

She grabbed another tissue and wiped her eyes.

"Orders then get sent to the corporate office, then product ships from the warehouse when it's available. Some merchandise is in stock and ships whenever the store wants it. Other product is only made once minimums are met. So, Skylar didn't spend a lot of time here. None of them do, really. It's a place to keep samples, sales catalogues, do some of the office work, but mostly just a place to make it sound official. Nobody thinks you're big enough if you list your home address. And then, as we're learning, you gotta worry about the crazies. Poor Skylar. I know I keep saying that." She shook her head.

"How long have you known her?"

"Around five years, I think." She pinched the bridge of her nose and shot a look at the photo I'd noticed earlier. Reaching over, she picked up the frame.

"This is the crew. We had gone out for Skylar's birthday. It was two years ago, I think," she said, her eyes filling again.

"She looks happy here," I said, feeling the inadequacy of my words. "My understanding is that she sold fine jewelry. I assume that meant she was carrying valuables around frequently." If the merchandise here in the office was any indication, I wasn't seeing much of value.

"Her line was what we'd classify as an entry price point item. Gold hoops, lower-quality gemstones, some cocktail rings and chains. She wasn't walking around with the three-carat engagement rings or anything like that. We'd have to have serious security for those price points. After all, you walked in, right?" She shrugged and looked around the office. "The other reps handle what you see around the office, strictly the costume stuff, base metal, stampings, beading. Lots of belts and small leather goods. Skylar kept her product in locked jewelry suitcases. It's safer, and the delicate items don't get tangled and dinged that way."

"Was it common for her to have the merchandise—I mean, the samples—with her?" I asked, wondering how obvious it might have been to the killer that she traveled with valuables. Perhaps he'd been watching her? Knew her habits?

"She has a safe here at the office, but when you're on the road, there's not much way around having samples in your possession. It wouldn't be practical to come back here all the time. It's a balance, depends on how many appointments she had lined up. I'm not sure, but I think she had a safe at home, too, but it was always one of those things she worried about. But primarily, you worry about your own safety. Product can be replaced, but you never know how far some whacko is going to take things. A lot of the female reps will carry Mace or pepper spray. They lock the cases in their trunks so if they leave the car for a few minutes, it's not obvious there's something of value inside."

She picked up her cell phone as a message popped up.

"As you can imagine, the other sales gals are freaking out. I don't know what to tell them. It's not good when people know you walk around with sapphires in your bag. Do the cops really think this was a robbery?"

"It isn't clear yet," I said. No need to share any of my own theories. "I understand that she was in the middle of a divorce. Were you aware?"

"Yeah, we all knew she was married to an asshole, but none of us knew how big of an ass he was. She probably would have kicked him out a long time ago if she'd been home more to catch him. But when a guy wants to be a jerk, he's generally going to do it whether or not there's someone around." Her tone suggested she'd had firsthand experience.

"You said he was a jerk. In what way?" As I always did, I was trying to keep the tone of my questions open, leaving an opportunity for her to add her own commentary about Oliver Hayes's bad habits.

"The guy was a cokehead, for one," she said, shaking her

head in disgust. "I could tell that the first time I met him. I have no idea when Skylar knew or when she began to care. We didn't talk about stuff like that."

"Did she ever indicate there was any physical altercation between them?"

"You mean, did he hit her? Sounds like they fought a lot, but if he ever got physical, I didn't know about it. If I had to bet, between the two of them, I'd say she was the one more likely to punch his lights out." She let out a small laugh. "She was feisty. No one pushed her around. But then again, who knows what the guy did after he had a few snorts."

"How about money problems? Did she talk about anything?" If I had to guess, I'd say the large Victorian home they'd shared clocked in at a cool two million, maybe more, and it probably wasn't cheap to maintain.

"As far as I know, things were pretty good. They have a really nice house, take vacations. Skylar was one of the company's top salespeople. She was very focused, pulled in serious dough, beat her sales targets every year I've known her. Even got a healthy bonus annually. And her husband is in a big job, something in accounting, but I think she made more than he did. Not sure how that sat with him. Some guys are competitive. But she never said anything. I'm not sure how we're going to handle her accounts now. I guess corporate will work that out."

I stood. "Thank you for speaking with me, Tanya. I know it's a rough day. Call me if you think of anything you think I'd want to know."

"I will. And here's my card." She scribbled her cell number on the back. "Best to call me on the mobile. That, I always pick up."

I left the office, heading back downstairs toward the parking garage, stopping at the newsstand for a cup of tea and a bag of almonds before heading out into the cold. As I waited for my drink, I checked the Link-Media website for follow-up on my article. As always, the mix of comments ranged from complimentary to wackadoodle hate speech. I was constantly stunned at the vitriol of online commentators. Particularly offensive were the derogatory comments about Skylar herself. "Looks like a slut to me. Musta had it comin." "Guess her old man wanted a younger model." How did people get this callous and hateful? The woman had been murdered, and these idiots couldn't show an ounce of empathy. Borkowski and I needed to have another conversation about moderating these posts. The line between free speech and hate was uncomfortably thin.

I tabbed over to Twitter, bracing myself for the ugliness in my own account. I'd posted an obligatory link earlier but hated the platform, finding it petty and mean. Unfortunately, it was now an essential element of my industry and often the source of critical breaking news. A post on my feed stopped me cold. "That's what happens to women with big mouths."

W*here are you?*
I shot a quick text to Michael. Images of the two dead women flashed unbidden into my consciousness as I typed. It was the same killer; I had no doubts. But if Gavin Wright had ordered a murder-for-hire, were we to assume that Oliver Hayes had done the same and used the same killer?

I needed to see those emails. Pacing the lobby outside the newsstand, I waited for a response. Who else could I tap? What other favors could I call in to find out how close CPD was to identifying the man they believed to be the hired killer?

Near the Art Institute. Why? Michael responded.

Can we meet? I asked, growing agitated when an answer didn't appear instantly.

Almost wrapped up. I have a few minutes if you're close.

Great. Meet me at The Gage whenever you can.

I left my car in the ramp and walked the eight blocks to Michigan and Monroe, my thoughts so wrapped up in the case that I barely felt the cold.

Luckily, it was a Monday, and the normally busy restaurant

wasn't fully booked. It was a little more upscale than I was in the mood for, but I knew I could sit here for an extended period without the waitstaff giving me dirty looks because they weren't turning the table. I ordered a Pellegrino and asked the waitress to come back when my guest had arrived.

As I sipped my drink, my mind tried to process the connections between Elyse Wright's murder and Skylar Hayes's murder. The cause of death was identical, and as I saw from the autopsy photos, so were the cut marks to their mouths. Both women were involved in nasty, contentious divorces, and they shared an attorney. Both women were the higher-income spouse. Both were known to be strong, opinionated women and were roughly the same age. It was impossible not to connect their murders. But who would have done it, and why?

If I stuck with the CPD's theory that Gavin Wright had hired a hit man to kill his wife, then Oliver Hayes had hired the same hit man and had a similar motive. Get her out of the way before divorce ended his career and finances.

I had no idea how one went about finding someone willing to commit murder for money, but it couldn't be easy. These men were well-off professionals. What exposure did they have to the dregs of society? Maybe I was being hasty. Oliver had a cocaine habit. It wasn't inconceivable that his dealer could have made an introduction. But that still left me with a missing connection between Gavin Wright and Oliver Hayes. For the theory to be accurate, somehow these men needed to know each other or needed to have a mutual acquaintance for referral.

From what I could tell, Hayes was just a run-of-the-mill crappy husband with a drug problem and a penchant for sleazy sex. It was the stuff that kept private eyes and divorce attorneys in business. The part I didn't know was how badly he wanted to keep his dirty laundry private and whether his wife was the vindictive type. Had she been hell-bent on revenge, or would an advantageous financial settlement have convinced her to keep the ugliness out of discoverable public documents? I'd have to call Victor.

"What a nice surprise, seeing you in the middle of the day. It's not the Friday night dinner you blew off, but I'll take it."

I'd been so lost in thought, I hadn't even noticed Michael arrive.

I smiled, thoughts of murder set aside for the moment, but feeling just a little sheepish about his reference to Friday. Michael bent down for a kiss, and I could smell the faint aroma of sandalwood.

Once he settled into his seat, the waitress came over for a drink order and left us with menus. I zeroed in on the first thing that looked appealing, waiting for Michael to do the same before hitting him up with talk of death.

"I was expecting to have to eat a bland turkey sandwich with Janek. This is certainly an upgrade," Michael said after we ordered. "Are you doing okay? It's been a dramatic few days." He laid a hand on my forearm, concern etched in his eyes.

"I think so," I said. "I'm confused, sad, anxious to know what's happened to these women." I didn't add anything about fighting for my company or how unnerved I was by my own flirtations with Ryan or terrified that my indecision in my relationship with Michael would send him packing. All were subjects that needed far more self-reflection than I was prepared for at the moment.

"Have you gotten any closer to identifying Elyse Wright's killer?" I couldn't contain myself. I also didn't want to make this a where-do-*we*-stand chat. The questions I had about the murders were streaming too fast.

"Come on, Andrea. You know I can't give you inside information on our investigation. It isn't fair for you to ask."

"Is it fair to pretend to the public that these two murders are not connected? Let the people help you find this guy. Someone saw something or heard something. I don't understand how it helps anyone for you to continue to play out this ridiculous carjacking explanation."

I sipped my drink and adjusted a nonexistent twist in my sleeve, taking a moment.

"Yes, there are similarities in the manner of death, I admit that. But that doesn't mean we have firm evidence, or that if we did, we're ready to make it public. We'll issue a statement when we're prepared to do so. I don't need to explain myself to you."

There was an edge in his voice I hadn't heard before. He was annoyed with me for pushing him. And likely annoyed with me for a few other things as well.

"No, you don't," I said, feeling that we were discussing work as well as our relationship. Michael was still hurt and angry over my reaction to his suggestion of a change in our living situations. But he was the one who walked out on the conversation. I hadn't been given the opportunity to explain last week, nor had I been asked. Had I wanted to be? Once again, I recognized the contradictions in my feelings for Michael. If I didn't know how I felt, how could he possibly be expected to interpret my behavior? Maybe this was the first real test of our relationship. If we couldn't communicate over something as important as a decision to live together, then there was likely pain ahead. But this wasn't the time for a deep heart-to-heart. I came here to discuss the murders.

"Michael, I've seen the autopsy photos." He stopped mid-bite into his poutine and looked at me, eyes fiery. "I understand that there is some kind of protocol we're trying to sort through, balancing our relationship with work demands, but please don't take me for one of the reporters who's going to read the statement verbatim from the press liaison and call it a day. You know me better than that. There are connections between these women that go even deeper than the knife that sliced them open. What I don't know is what the connections are between the husbands. I hoped that you would speak to me about it. What was in the emails that convinced you Wright hired someone to kill his wife? What leads do you have on the killer? Have you found anything that indicates Oliver Hayes wanted to take out his wife, too?"

"I can't do this. I can't release information just because you ask. I have people I answer to and internal strategies we're working with. Discussing it could compromise the investigation. When we have an official statement, you'll get that along with everyone else."

"Okay, but at some point you'll need to explain why CPD would apparently prefer to frighten the women of Chicago, letting them think a random serial killer is on the loose, rather than connect the murders. I have my job to do as well, and I don't need your permission to go public."

He looked at me, his eyes sad. I wasn't giving him the response he wanted. "I can't discuss it with you," he said quietly.

"Fine. Lunch is on me. I'm sure you need to get back to work." We looked at each other for what seemed like an eternity, neither of us having the willingness or the time to say all that we had to say.

He took a drink of water, put on his jacket, and left. My eyes filled with tears as I watched him walk away. Had I done the right thing? Or had I just made the biggest mistake of my life?

25

W hat had I done?

I put my head in my hands, wrestling with the urge to call Michael, to ask him to come back to the restaurant and talk this through, but my mind wasn't clear enough to understand what I wanted. I needed the distance, and so did Michael. It felt as though we were at a point of either ending whatever this was between us or, if we could talk this through, moving to a new stage. At the moment I couldn't tell which, and we were both too close to it to see clearly.

I ordered another Pellegrino and nibbled on my crab-and-avocado toast while I struggled to shift my thoughts back to the murders. I stared at the Pellegrino label, a thought forming. Could the connection be Elyse Wright's advertising agency? I grabbed my phone and put in a call to Tanya's cell.

"It's Andrea Kellner again. This is going to seem out of left field, but do you know if Skylar's employer used any advertising agencies?"

"Sure," she said, sounding a little more together than she had earlier. "The agency did some direct-to-consumer work, Facebook ads, things like that to build up demand. But most of the company advertising was print ads in trade magazines. They were targeting retail buyers, usually just before market week."

"What's that?"

"That's when all the trade shows run. Merchants fly in to New York or LA to discover new product lines or to make their buys. So the ads are focused on enticing buyers who've never placed orders or showing off new items to people already familiar with the company. There are also a lot of postcard mailers, with booth numbers, reminders to set appointments. It's kind of a last-minute memory jog or a way to highlight new designs."

"Did Skylar go to these shows?"

"All the time. Sometimes her clients preferred to work the line at the shows so they could balance their purchases out with other orders they'd written, and some would only see the line if she came to them. All depended on a store's budget and time. She didn't care as long as they left paper. Sorry, that's 'orders' in layman's terms."

"Do you know what agency the company used?"

"No, you'd have to ask the corporate office about that, but Skylar did have a connection there. A couple months ago, she told me that she'd spoken to one of the employees who worked on the digital media end, but that was about a personal issue."

"Do you know what the issue was?" My question seemed prying, but under the circumstances, any little detail could be relevant.

"She was getting a lot of ugly crap on her Twitter account. She'd block them, but others kept popping up. It scared her. She was trying to find out if she should call the cops. I guess the comments got pretty bad, woman-hate stuff."

Another connective thread. Both women had been the target of nasty Twitter tirades. Did that mean something? Woman hate. Sexism had again reared its ugly head.

"Thanks, Tanya. I appreciate your help." I flagged my waitress for the check.

What about my own situation? Was sexism at the core of Ramelli's plan? And what *did* I want? Sooner or later I was going to have to answer Ryan's question, if only just for myself. Right now, my priority was to maintain my options. I wanted to be the one to decide my own future. And if I left, I wanted it to be on my terms, not theirs. After last Friday, I knew I didn't trust these guys. There was an ulterior motive, or three, and it was time to get my head out of the sand and deal with it.

I picked up my phone and made an appointment with my attorney for first thing in the morning. A review of my contract would help me understand my vulnerability.

A text popped up. Brynn.

Can you meet me downstairs in the coffee shop in five minutes?

I'll need ten, but I'm on my way. My gut clenched. What now? I laid some cash on the table and headed out to flag a cab.

She was at a back booth when I arrived, her normal monster cup of java in front of her and a slice of chocolate layer cake big enough for four. But that was the only thing that looked normal. Her eyes were rimmed red, and she seemed to have shrunken into the booth.

"I haven't seen you all day. Sorry about that. What's up? You look like you've lost your best friend." I slid into the booth, removed my coat, and tossed it on the bench beside me. Whatever Brynn was upset about needed undivided attention.

She wrapped her hands around her mug and stared over my shoulder before answering. "I just spent a couple hours with that consultant, Ryan Molina. I didn't want him and Borkowski seeing me run right to you afterward. Things are tense enough, I don't need to get in the middle of this turf war."

"How bad was it?" I asked, steeling myself for the worst.

She bit her lower lip and looked at me. "They canned me."

"What? They can't." I was so stunned and angry, I couldn't form a complete sentence. I stared at Brynn, questions bombarding my brain, unable to understand what Borkowski had just done or why. How could he have fired her without consulting me?

"I spent about an hour and half just with Molina," Brynn continued. "He asked all kinds of questions about what I was working on right now, how I structured my day. Real stupid stuff. He had no interest in my background or what I wanted out of the job. Actually, most of his questions tied back to you."

"About me? What kind of questions?"

"What projects you had on your plate? What work was I doing for you? And a whole bunch of questions about whether Borkowski had approved that work." She looked at me as if there was something else she wanted to say but didn't know if she should.

"There's more?"

"He asked a question I found particularly odd." She paused for a drink of coffee. "He wanted to know about Detective Hewitt. Whether you were friends."

Although I hadn't said anything to Brynn, or anyone else at work for that matter, about my romantic life, I could tell by her expression that she knew. I hadn't been silent because I was hiding anything; it simply hadn't seemed important to share.

"And what did you say?"

"I told him the truth. That I knew you were acquainted, but if he has more questions about your friends, he should ask you himself."

I laughed. "I'm sure that was well received."

"What else was I going to say? Men can be such cowards. Anyway, when the meeting was over, Borkowski called me into his office and told me I had two weeks. Said he was doing some reorganization of the staff and I wasn't needed anymore. I said fine, asked him if I'd still get my vacation pay. And that's how we ended it."

"I don't know what to say, Brynn. I'm so angry I can't see straight. He completely blindsided me."

I'd given Borkowski responsibility for staffing when he took over as general manager, but if there was a need to reduce head count, that was not a decision to be made without me, let alone making Brynn the first target. It did confirm that Borkowski was fully in bed with Ramelli, or he was being used. Either way, this was a power move intended to undermine me.

"I know you had nothing to do with this, and you'd never have handled it so poorly. It's just that with my mom and all, money is really tight. I guess my decision about looking for another job is being made for me."

I pulled out my wallet. "Don't argue," I said, handing her a check. "It will give you a little cushion. If I can't work out something with Borkowski, I'll put in some calls for you, and you'll have the most glowing reference your new employer will have ever heard."

Tears ran down Brynn's face and mine as I stood and gave her a hug.

"You might want to stay down here for a while," I said, grabbing my coat. "The windows are going to be rattling when I get ahold of that backstabbing son of a bitch."

26

I stormed back into the office filled with rage. Who the hell did Borkowski think he was, firing Brynn without even consulting me? This was my damn company! I looked around the room, hoping to catch both him and Ryan still in the office. The staff shot me confused looks as I stomped through the space. I didn't imagine I was hiding my anger terribly well.

"Where's Borkowski?" I barked at Raquel, the poor admin stationed outside his office and therefore stuck with my abuse.

"He and Mr. Molina left a few minutes ago," she said, her brows drawn.

"Are they coming back?"

"I don't think so," she mumbled. "Mr. Borkowski said something about a meeting. Should I put you on his calendar for tomorrow morning?" She barely looked up, probably afraid to hear my answer.

"Block out his schedule first thing in the morning. Unless I get to him first, in which case he'll be on crutches."

Her mouth dropped open, but she caught herself. "Yes, ma'am. Is there anything else?"

"I'll take care of everything else myself. Thank you."

As I turned, the employees within earshot quickly busied themselves in their work, pretending they'd heard nothing. I was too mad to care.

I was on the phone again with my attorney's assistant even before I'd reached my office, asking that he call me at home this evening instead. I may have been naïve about the games Ramelli was willing to play, but I was a fast learner. The future of my company was at stake.

Too pissed off to be in the office, I grabbed my coat and texted Cai. I needed an intervention, could she spare ten minutes for coffee?

My phone rang seconds after I stepped out of the Link-Media building.

"What's wrong?"

"Borkowski just stabbed me in the back. Looks like he's on the Ramelli team. The SOB just fired Brynn without consulting me. Do you have some time?" I marched east on Erie toward Wells, keeping my eyes open for a cab, oblivious to the puddles on the sidewalk.

"Sorry. I'm prepping for a trial tomorrow, so I'm chained to my desk for the duration. Tomorrow night? Maybe a glass of wine?"

"No problem. I'm just feeling stupid and naïve that Ramelli is getting the upper hand and using my own employees against me. Let's talk tomorrow. In the meantime, I'll go fashion up a voodoo doll or something. Good luck with your case."

Now what? If I couldn't yell at Borkowski or download to Cai, what was I going to do with all the nervous energy and anger running through my veins? Walk until I came up with another option or until my feet froze, I guessed. I crossed Wells, moving vaguely in the direction of Eataly. By the time I got there, I'd either be halfway frostbitten or ready for a very large

Cabernet. Either way, I could pick up takeout and remove the dinner debate from my decision list.

Whatever Ramelli's end game was, clearly I had underestimated the urgency of the situation. Why hadn't I met with my attorney immediately? I'd also underestimated Borkowski. I could only imagine he'd been promised something big to play the role of hatchet man. His involvement burned me most of all. I'd promoted the man, and now he was teaming up with Ramelli to get me out of the business.

But what about Ryan? I knew he'd been competitive with Erik. Was this just one last win when Erik wasn't around anymore to do something about it? Was that why he'd come on so strong Friday night—I'd become a prize?

As I stomped through the slush, a text came through from one of my inside sources, a clerk at the courthouse. "You might want to get down here. Last-minute schedule change. They are sneaking in Wright's arraignment."

I jumped the snowbank and flagged the first cab I saw. Time to send her another case of champagne.

The crowd had already built up outside the courthouse by the time I arrived, just minutes after the call. My source had been good, but her timing lagged. This arraignment was already underway. Damn!

Whatever the legal team thought they were accomplishing by trying to keep attention focused elsewhere was obviously in vain. The word was clearly out. A throng of reporters and various legal groupies huddled around the entrance. From the looks of it, well over a hundred people were crowded around, trying to get a line of sight to the door.

Police officers were stationed around Daley Plaza, keeping observers at bay while the press panned the crowd. Security personnel stood stationed at the entrances inside the glass-walled lobby, denying anyone without official business access. It was late in the day for trial activity, so that meant no one was getting in.

I scanned the area, looking for better positioning and familiar faces. It wasn't unusual for people who had connections to a case to show up for key moments, giving me the ability to snag an impromptu interview.

As I maneuvered into position next to a pillar under the overhang, hoping to get a good camera shot of Wright as he was escorted out of the building and back to jail, voices rose behind me. About thirty people were marching north on Dearborn toward the building. I could see them across the street as they began to cross over into Daley Plaza. I could make out the angry tone of their chant but not the words.

As they filed into the plaza, the first thing I noticed were the homemade signs lifted in their hands and waving above their heads. Then I heard them. "Men will not be denied." "Know your place." "It's God's will." "Women will be subservient." "Free Gavin."

I tensed with disgust. It was only then that I looked more closely at the group. Men, most of whom I guessed to be in their thirties. And all Caucasian. Anger invaded their rhetoric as they chanted and waved their hate-filled signs.

I tapped the video app on my phone and pointed the camera, feeling the hatred and anger emanating from the men. My chest tightened as they stormed toward the entrance, pushing their way through the press as more cameras turned. They walked en masse until the police presence slowed them down, then stood in formation, making their voices heard, spouting ugliness and supporting a man accused of killing his wife.

As the crowd shifted ever closer to the doors, I was pinned between the pillar and the hate-filled men as they grew agitated. For the moment, the men were too distracted by their mission to pay any attention to me, but I was vulnerable, and a rush of fear ran up my spine.

A commotion at the front of the courthouse caused me to swing my camera. Two officers led the way, followed by Gavin Wright, hands cuffed behind his back, eyes to the ground, alongside his defense attorney. Additional officers were at his flank. The men next to me cheered when they saw him, then chanted even louder as Wright was led toward a police van waiting at the curb. As I pivoted my camera toward the vehicle, one of the protesters caught my eye. A familiar face.

In the middle of the group, five feet in front of me, Marcus Bennett stood shoulder to shoulder with the other men spewing hateful things about women and male superiority. With their target now in sight, the men cheered, chanting, "She deserved what she got" as I filmed the entire exchange.

Adrenaline surged in my chest as the men rallied. Ignoring my discomfort, I slid between the bodies, holding my camera high to keep Wright in the frame. As he was led to the vehicle, the mob became frustrated with their restraints, pushing forward and pulling at the cops. An elbow landed in my back. Bodies were shoved around me, arms reached out. I swung my head, looking for an exit path, uncertain which direction was safe as all of us, protestors and journalists, were caught in the fracas.

Additional officers rushed in, holding the line as the men struggled to get at Wright. As the cops pushed back, the chanting grew louder and bodies in front of me stumbled. A man was shoved back into my chest, my body breaking his fall. I wobbled but regained my footing, and we stood face-to-face. Marcus Bennett.

"You bitch," he growled, before turning and disappearing back into the crowd.

27

P lans of takeout from Eataly long forgotten, I was nestled safely back in my apartment after my encounter at Daley Plaza with a glass of Cabernet and Walter on my lap, contemplating what the hell I was going to do now.

The first issue was a relatively easy one. Victor needed to know about the ugly viewpoint Marcus Bennett espoused. This was beyond a brief moment of subtle chauvinism. It was public hate, verging on violence. The palpable anger and hostility I felt from the group of men protesting the fact that one of their own had been sent to jail was terrifying. Had these men claimed Wright, a man of mixed race, as one of their own after assuming that he had taken charge of the woman in his life? Normally, I would've expected this type of hate group to be as racist as they were misogynistic. Perhaps in their minds, his bold move of getting his wayward wife out of the way trumped the tint of his skin.

I'd seen no indication that Wright himself had ever displayed such archaic views of women's roles. Perhaps it had nothing to do with Wright specifically and everything to do with a man putting *his* woman in her place. I was disgusted, and angered, and fearful of what I had witnessed today. It was a terrifying reminder that despite all the advances women had made, hate and misogyny were as alive and well as racism. It simply hid under the surface until someone felt emboldened enough to express it publicly. Or it took strength in numbers to say things publicly that would never be said otherwise.

Regardless, Victor could not continue to have this man in his employ. He could not let these archaic and horrific views be released anywhere near his clients, nor could he allow these viewpoints to influence the work his office performed. I hated to insert myself in the running of his business, but there was absolutely no choice. Victor needed to know and would do the right thing. I picked up the phone, getting him on the second ring.

"Victor, I'm sorry to call you this time of night, you're probably getting ready for dinner, but I needed to share something, and it couldn't wait until the morning."

"Not a problem, Andrea. What is it? I've just gotten home. You're not interrupting anything."

"I was at the courthouse late this afternoon. Were you aware that Gavin Wright was arraigned today?"

"Yes, I was informed."

"Do you know where Marcus Bennett was this afternoon?"

"I know that he left early, something about an appointment." I could hear the puzzlement in his voice. "But quite frankly, I don't keep track of those things. My office manager handles scheduling requests. Is there something wrong?"

"Yes, unfortunately. He left early to come to the courthouse."

"Why would he take off work to see Gavin Wright arraigned? I don't understand."

"He was there as a private citizen, expressing his viewpoints. He and about twenty other men. White men," I added. "They were at Gavin's arraignment protesting his arrest. The group of them were aggressive, ugly, and chanted things like 'She deserved what she got.'"

"What?"

"I was there. I was in the middle of it all, and this appears to be a group who believe men are superior to women. Masters of their house, if you will." I paused for a moment, letting what I was saying sink in. "It was really ugly, Victor."

"And my Marcus, my paralegal, was part of this group? He was part of this hate speech?"

"I'm afraid so. And I have him on film. I'm going to email you the clip. There is no question Bennett was not only a part of this group but a loud, vocal, willing participant. I knew you'd want to know."

"No, that is absolutely not something I ever wanted to know about one of my own employees." His voice was filled with disgust. "I couldn't possibly tolerate that kind of behavior. That kind of thought. Good Lord. I knew he had very conservative viewpoints, but this is beyond comprehension. I don't suppose you were the only one who filmed this?"

"No, I'm afraid not. Obviously, we don't know yet whether his face will be visible in whatever news clips are used, but I wanted to give you advance notice."

"Well, there goes my quiet evening." He sighed. "Send me the file. Then I'm going to fire that little bastard faster than he can have his wife bring him his slippers and his pipe. I'm appalled, but thank you for telling me, Andrea. I couldn't possibly have such hateful views publicly attached to my business. I'd never get another female client again. And I have no interest in changing my business name to Chauvinists 'R' Us."

"Sorry, Victor. I'll speak to you soon."

And speaking of ugly men, I was tempted to call Borkowski and hand him his pink slip too, but being impulsive wouldn't get me anywhere. Firing him wouldn't get Ramelli off my back. If I was going to beat these guys, I would need to beat them at their own game.

I lifted Walter off of my lap, replenished my wine, then went to my office to take a call from my attorney, bringing him up to speed on the latest developments.

My anxiety partially allayed, I stared at the notes I'd tacked to my bulletin board on the Wright case, then added a few Post-its, new developments since I'd last been in the office. Sorting the notes into columns, I lay out what I knew about the female victims and their husbands.

What was the connection? The common denominator between the women seemed to be divorce, badly behaved husbands, and personalities that could best be described as feisty. But so far I'd found no indication that the women knew each other or had anything else in common. No mutual friends, no charity work, no professional involvement. Regarding the husbands, their connection still wasn't clear.

I opened a browser window and went back into search mode on Oliver Hayes. An hour later, I'd fleshed out a few more tidbits about his professional background, but the tie-in between the men eluded me.

My phone buzzed. The doorman letting me know I had a visitor. Michael. I pulled the clip out of my hair and fluffed it loose, then went to the door. Was this going to be a "Let's make up" or a "We're done" conversation?

He stood in the entryway, his brown curls wet with fresh snow. My heart raced. Confused, anxious, I didn't know where to begin to describe the emotions jumbling my mind.

"I hope it's okay that I stopped by without calling. I was afraid you'd say no."

"Of course it's okay. Come in."

I closed the door behind him and took his wet coat to the closet. Michael was on the couch when I returned. I sat next to him, tucking my legs underneath me. Walter parked himself on the floor by my feet, readying himself for attack mode.

"Are you still mad at me?"

"Did I say I was mad?" He tilted his head, and I could again smell the sandalwood soap I knew he used, bringing thoughts of tenderness and love and passion.

"No, but there were a few other indications." I laughed.

"I think you're right that this overlap of work and romance is getting a little confusing. I don't have experience with this. My ex-wife certainly never asked details about my cases, other than when was I going to give up all the dangerous stuff and get a desk job. You're challenging me, and I'm not used to it."

His voice was measured, as if he weren't experienced at sorting through his emotions. I watched him futz with the clasp of his watch as I battled my own emotions.

"And you don't really like it," I added.

"It frustrates me, would be more accurate. I love your independence, but..."

"Just not when it challenges your own work."

"Maybe that's it, if I'm being honest with myself. Maybe I just need time to adjust. Maybe you and I need to have different conversations about what we can talk about, what we can't. I think I've been naïve about the complications. It's something we probably both need to think about."

He finally pulled his gaze up from his wrist and shifted his body, angling toward me. Getting the words out seemed to take the tension out of his shoulders.

"You know I would never push you to be someone you're not," I said, choosing each word as if it were the only one I'd get. "I respect you and admire your career choice. But I need you to do the same for me, even when it's uncomfortable. Particularly when it's uncomfortable. So, yes, I think we both have a lot to think about. It's complicated, and we need to respect that."

"Fair enough." He nodded. "Don't expect perfection, but I'll try." He squeezed my hand and didn't let go. "What were you doing tonight before I invited myself in?"

"Working, what else?" We both laughed. "I know you don't really want to talk about this, but I have a hypothetical question."

"Hypothetical?" This time he shook his head, sighed, and rolled his eyes. "In the spirit of goodwill and communication, go ahead."

"I'll preface it with a statement, which you won't react to. Okay?"

He nodded, looking at me skeptically.

"I believe Elyse Wright and Skylar Hayes were probably killed by the same man. But one of the things that confuses me is how their husbands would have gone about finding the same guy to do the deed. So far, I can't find any other connection between the men. You don't have to comment on that theory; I'm just laying it out as groundwork. But, assuming I'm correct, how would a professional man like Gavin Wright go about finding someone he could pay to kill his wife? How is it done, theoretically? It's not like there's a killer-for-hire category on Craigslist. How would Gavin Wright begin to know where to look? As a cop, educate me on what you've seen, how these things work."

"That's like asking a nature-versus-nurture question."

"I'm asking because I can't imagine it. What do you do, sit at a biker bar in a rough part of town, hoping you get lucky and the right guy just happens to come along? That's absurd."

"It shouldn't be surprising to you, but a lot of people have shady individuals in their past. Someone who knows someone, who knows someone, who knows someone. It's this behind-the-scenes informal referral network, for lack of a better way to put it."

"So, Oliver Hayes had a coke habit. He might have inquired

of his dealer, who inquired of someone else, and before you know it, the wife is dead. Hypothetically, of course."

"Yeah, more or less. You just keep uncovering the rocks until eventually you find a snake underneath."

"So do you know who Hayes's dealer was?" I couldn't resist and had to slip in the question.

"That's a 'no comment,' Ms. Kellner. You're not keeping to hypotheticals."

My eyes went back to Michael's wrist. The bracelet. Elyse Wright's bracelet was missing. "Michael, was Skylar missing anything? A personal item—jewelry, perhaps? Something that she normally wore every day."

"Where are you going with this? I see your mind running off into uncomfortable territory again."

"Humor me for a minute."

"Apparently, she wore a necklace that her mother had given her. A thin gold chain with a single drop pearl. It wasn't found on her person or anywhere near her body. Her husband asked about it, said she never took it off."

"Remember how Elyse Wright had a missing bracelet? I'd be willing to bet that that necklace is in the same place as Elyse Wright's bracelet."

28

I t wasn't yet 8:30, but already I felt as though I'd put in a half-day of work. I'd sent a copy of the video I'd captured following Gavin Wright's arraignment to Borkowski for editing, along with my write-up, then I'd followed that with round two of the conversation with my attorney. We'd spent nearly thirty minutes clarifying a strategy. Although it depended on how aggressive Ramelli and company decided to play, my contract and ownership position gave me a fighting chance.

I couldn't control whether Ryan was going to make a run at the business, with Ramelli's participation, of course, but I didn't have to accept their terms. And with legal help, I could put enough obstacles in their way to prevent the takeover from being a sure thing. It didn't answer the question of what I *did* want, but it helped me obtain time and space for choices.

For the moment, dealing with Borkowski's actions would have to satisfy me. I grabbed my tea and headed straight to the back corner. Borkowski would be expecting me. But he may not be expecting the fury he had unleashed.

Raquel shrunk visibly when she saw me approach her desk.

"He's waiting for you," she managed to mumble. I had a

feeling that the minute the door was closed she'd have a sudden urge for a long coffee break.

He was sitting at his desk, shirtsleeves rolled, tie loose, papers strewn over the surface, and a red pen in hand. It was one of Borkowski's holdovers from his newspaper days. Editing via paper printout and red ink.

"Sit," he said, not looking up. "I'll be just a second."

I slid into the chair and leaned back, crossing my arms. I'd walked in the door feeling under control, but now that I was here, my anger was spilling over again.

"So, is this about Brynn? You're not going to get all huffy, are you?" He looked at me over the top of his readers, the pen still wedged between his fingers. "We gotta cut back on overhead. I know you two have a relationship, but there are adjustments we need to make. You'll just have to do your own research from here on out. We have to tighten things up. Cut back expenses across the board. Cut the nonessentials. You've seen the numbers."

I let him rant, knowing that it was the most effective way to handle the man.

"And nowhere in that thought process did you even think to consult me?" I said, not caring if I sounded shrill. "Brynn has been with me from the beginning. How dare you make a unilateral decision like that without involving me? I had a right to be involved in that decision since I'm the one that works with her on a daily basis."

"You put me in here to be the manager. I'm managing. Staffing and budgets are what I do. Being second-guessed for every decision is not the way this works."

Borkowski flushed at the collar, and I imagined my own cheeks were showing their own heat.

"I'm not second-guessing your every decision," I shot back. "I'm demanding respect. Brynn works for me a good fifty percent of the time, yet you didn't have the courtesy to even have a conversation with me? How am I to take that? And speaking of job responsibilities, I'm the one who gave you this job. I know it hasn't always been easy to differentiate where your job ends and mine begins, but like it or not, I still own this business. You will get on the phone, apologize profusely to her, get her to agree to stay on, and give her a ten percent raise. If not, then you and I should have conversations about your own position with this company."

"Well, the board may have a different position on who's in charge." He tossed his pen in the drawer, then slammed it closed.

"Get her back on the payroll." I left his office. The fight was on.

I flopped into my desk chair with a huff, feeling battered and attacked. My attorney would be ready, should there be legal action to defend, but for the moment the only thing that made sense was for me to do my job and be ready.

Opening my email, I saw a note from our video editor asking me to review the clip of Wright I'd sent in before she loaded it to the website. I clicked, then hit play. The piece had been cut to just shy of sixty seconds. I ran through it once for impact, judging the viewer experience. The chaos and fear rolled back through me as I watched. The chanting, the shouts, the walk as Gavin Wright moved from the courthouse to the waiting vehicle. I'd gotten a clear shot of not only his face but the surrounding atmosphere. Great. So wrapped up in the energy of the moment, I hadn't noted whether Marcus Bennett was identifiable. I hit play again, pausing every few seconds to scan the faces in the crowd.

Sure enough, there he was about twenty seconds into the tape. I hit pause. It wasn't a full-face, dead-on shot, but close enough that anyone who knew him could tag him. To his left, facing my camera, was another face that caught my attention.

Also familiar. I searched my memory. It was the forensic accountant, Leon Rutkowski. Bennett had introduced him right before
Elyse was murdered. No wonder the two of them got along.
Victor wasn't going to be happy. At least this guy was a hired
consultant, not an employee, so his connection to Kirkland and
McCullough wasn't public. Bennett had likely already been
fired, but I was going to have to give Victor the bad news.
Bennett and Rutkowski were both having their fifteen minutes
of fame.

29

Yes, Victor, your woman-hating employee was going to make the midday news.

I'd phoned, giving him the bad news about Marcus Bennett. Apparently, he'd felt guilty about axing the guy over the phone, so he had waited to do it in person first thing this morning. Not surprisingly, Bennett hadn't taken his termination well, storming out of the office after using up all the curse words he knew.

At least it was over with, provided Bennett didn't conclude he had some wrongful termination suit. It was never the smartest strategy to try to sue an attorney, but some people needed to learn the hard way. I didn't imagine Victor was concerned; it seemed hard to argue in support of such hateful viewpoints, particularly when a number of celebrities had recently lost endorsements or jobs over lesser offenses.

I sat at my desk after the call, thinking about what had transpired the day before in Daley Plaza and imagining that some of Gavin Wright's arrogance had been knocked off his shoulders. Was he aware that he had become a hero to a group of women-hating white guys? And if the charging of Gavin Wright was going to bring out the crazy haters, the identity of Skylar Hayes's killer would likely have the same effect—that is, if CPD ever came out and charged anyone.

But who were these guys, the protesters? They seemed organized. Had managed to assemble quickly. Even with an inside source, I'd had less than fifteen minutes' notice. I assumed some type of Twitter brigade was their call to action. And if they could get a couple dozen guys to show up within minutes, how many more were there?

I got up and flagged Brynn into my office. She'd taken the balance of the day off yesterday but was back in this morning, believing to be on her two-week countdown.

"Did you get any sleep last night?"

Judging by the extra-large mug in her hands, my guess was not much. She set the cup on the edge of my desk, took a seat, then rubbed the bridge of her nose.

"Barely two hours. We had a late-night visit to the emergency room. My mom was having heart palpitations. Luckily, it was just a false alarm, but that didn't make much time for frivolous things like rest. That's why coffee was invented." She patted the handle of her mug. "Cup number three. I figure if I keep up this pace, I can make it to the weekend before I crash."

"That's awful. Is your mom okay?"

"Yeah, she's fine now. The stress makes her a bit of a worrier. Doesn't help her medical condition, but she panics. Speaking of panicking, did you leave Borkowski bruised and huddled in a corner?"

"Well, I don't know if anything bruises him, but I didn't hold back. It isn't fair, you just got caught in the crossfire of some bigger power plays. I'm doing everything I can to right the ship."

Brynn didn't deserve this, didn't deserve to be used as a pawn in Ramelli and Ryan's scheme. I didn't fault Borkowski's logic; we did have issues to address in the business, but firing Brynn wasn't the solution. It was a wedge.

"Well, I'm on the payroll for two more weeks. I'm not going to do anything stupid, like walk out." She shrugged.

"Great, because I have a project for you."

"Thank goodness. I expected to be staring at an empty inbox for two weeks. What do you have?"

"It's about that demonstration yesterday at Wright's arraignment. You're the Twitter guru, see if you can find the call-to-action thread. I can't tell if this is some small impromptu group that latched on to Gavin or if there's something bigger, more organized behind it."

"And why would a group of crazy-ass misogynistic white men be on Twitter? Duh! That's exactly where these whackos find their peeps." She rolled her eyes, grabbed her mug, and stood.

"And take a look at Skylar Hayes's feed, if it's still up. Apparently, she was also a victim of the trolls."

"You got it. Great video, by the way. Yell if you need anything else."

That settled, I pulled my mind back to Elyse Wright. Since CPD was still playing coy with Skylar Hayes's murder, focusing on Elyse seemed the smarter strategy. The aspect I had yet to figure out was why she'd been spying on her husband. The common reason, an affair, seemed to have no merit; surely if she'd had any suspicions, there was no reason to have hidden it from her divorce attorney. The only other thing that came to mind was perhaps she had some inkling of the embezzlement or there was someone else who had come to her with allegations of her husband's sexual assault. Spying seemed like an intelligence-gathering move.

Was it possible that Elyse knew about the embezzlement but pretended not to? After all, her reputation was equally important to her. Perhaps she had gambled that awareness would equate with guilt in the eyes of the court? I ran the legal strategy through my mind and found it viable. As it was, no evidence had been presented connecting Elyse to her husband's crimes, yet she'd been forced to spend a fair amount of time in the months preceding her death defending herself and her reputation. If she'd discovered something, something that she was uncertain about, and had hired surveillance, the time between her discovery and sharing that with authorities would be questioned. It was a dilemma, largely a damned-if-you-do-damned-if-you-don't situation. Knowing what I did about Elyse, I could easily imagine her trying to gather evidence before going public with the allegations. Perhaps Sikora's death occurred before she had adequate evidence?

I spent a couple hours sifting through Lexis-Nexis, looking at entries about Skylar Hayes's husband before strained eyesight and hunger got the better of me. The weather was milder today and I craved movement, so I grabbed my coat and my bag and headed downstairs, intending to make a run over to Eataly. Ever since my aborted trip yesterday, I'd been in the mood for linguine with clams.

Slipping on my gloves, I headed east, thrilled to see sunshine. I was only five feet outside the front door of the building when I saw him. Bennett leaned against a beat-up Dodge Caravan parked in a spot at the curb. He moved the minute he saw me, coming at me fast. I froze, pausing for a second too long debating his intent. Then he was on me, standing inches away, invading my space. His face a blotched circle of anger. Instinctually, I stepped back, and he matched my stride until I was against the brick of the building.

"Back off," I shouted.

"Who the hell do you think you are? What right do you have to get in my business and get me fired?" he screamed at me, so close that I could smell the coffee on his breath and feel his spittle on my face.

"You got yourself fired by making a public demonstration of hate," I said, working to control my voice, fearing that my anger would escalate his. I looked around me for an escape plan, but the sidewalk was empty. As I edged closer to the door, he followed, and I saw nothing but venom in his eyes.

"Women like you are the scourge of the earth. You don't know your place. That ex-husband of yours should have shown you the truth. Should have trained you better."

I said nothing but kept my gaze firm, noting every word, watching for any telltale sign of what he might do next. His views of women in the world made me nauseous, but debating the subject wasn't an option. I needed to get away from him.

Slowly I reached into my coat pocket, remembering I'd left my house keys there. I intertwined my fingers between the blades and drew out my hand, ready to use them as a weapon if I needed.

He continued to yell his ugly rhetoric about a woman's place and how I didn't know mine, but I refused to engage, suspecting that any sign of weakness would only increase my vulnerability. He seemed to be baiting me, expecting me to lash out at him, growing more enraged when I didn't cower or scream. I knew Bennett was on the edge of losing control. I scanned the sidewalk, again calculating whether I could knock him unsteady and make a run for the door.

I shifted my feet to brace myself before I shoved into his body, then saw his hands come up to strike me. I swung for his face with everything I had. Unable to avoid contact, I reached him just as he reached me. His blow sent me back into the brick, my head snapping against the hard surface. As I crouched to avoid another hit, I saw blood in the trail marks my keys had left along his jaw.

"Hey!" I heard a male voice yell as I swung back at Bennett. Before I could turn, a large man shoved his way between Bennett and me, grabbing my attacker by the arm.

"I called 911," someone else yelled.

Bennett gave the man an elbow in the ribs and pushed away, running toward his van.

I leaned against the wall, heart pounding, sweat dripping down my neck, watching him go.

"You're going to pay for that, bitch," he screamed before getting in his car and speeding off.

30

D amn! My head felt as if I had a hot poker embedded in my skull.

I sat on the sidewalk, leaning against the building, trying to control my racing heart. The man who had stepped between Bennett and me stood at the curb, flagging down the police vehicle that had just turned the corner onto Erie. A woman kneeled next to me, confused about what to do. Hovering, she asked if I wanted to lie down or if she could get something for me. She had pulled a package of tissues from her purse, and I was using them to press against the back of my skull. It hurt like hell to touch, so I had a feeling there was more blood in my hair than on the tissue.

A cold compress in a darkened room was probably on the agenda for the evening. This headache had a long way to go before reaching its peak. The one positive about my adrenaline rush was that I wasn't feeling the February temperature.

A police officer joined the woman next to me.

"The ambulance will be here in a minute," he said. "Lean forward, if you can, so I can take a look at the damage."

I did as I was told, but even the smallest movement made my head feel like molten Jell-O.

"Doesn't look too bad. Probably won't even need stitches." He handed me a sturdier compress. "Do you want to tell me what happened?"

"This guy was trying to beat the shit out of her!"

The man who'd inserted himself into the altercation piped up, telling the officer what he'd seen, and his female companion jumped in, adding her perspective. They were both in their twenties and, based on their attire, probably worked in the neighborhood. They spoke so rapidly that the officer needed to ask them to take turns so he could follow the chain of events.

I was still feeling winded, so I let them talk. Hearing them describe what they saw sounded substantially more ominous than the perspective I had while experiencing it.

I'd been focused on how to tamp down Bennett's anger, but hearing these two describe the altercation made a chill run down my spine. I was lucky they had come along and luckier still to be sitting here with what felt like nothing more than a monster headache and a bandaged head.

Lights flashing, siren at full volume, an ambulance pulled up, drawing attention to our little party. The officer stood and continued speaking to the couple that had intervened while an EMT came over and began to remove debris from my wound. I sat quietly, leaning my head on my knees while he gently dabbed at the blood and cleaned the laceration.

I didn't know Bennett well, but the impression I'd had of him as mild mannered had just flown out the window. Not only did the man have a serious temper, but he was obviously capable of violence.

And he blamed me for his firing.

The EMT placed a cold pack on the back of my head, securing it in place with an Ace bandage he wrapped around my forehead. He then asked me to lean back and pulled out a small flashlight to check my pupils for signs of a concussion. When he finished, Michael was crouched alongside him.

I looked up into his worried brown eyes. "I can think of better ways to get attention," he said.

I gave him a weak smile. "Let me guess, you have the entire police force tuned in to call you if I'm ever in trouble."

"You caught me. Guilty as charged. I pay them in beer. We even have a code name for you." He smiled, but I had a feeling it was an effort. "Do you want to tell me what happened?"

The EMT stepped away, satisfied that I didn't have a concussion, trading places with the first officer.

"Give me a minute." I called over the couple that had intervened and thanked them profusely, asking for contact information. The least I could do was to treat them to a nice dinner or something. When they'd gone, I filled Michael in on the background story.

"He was waiting for me outside the building when I walked out. His name is Marcus Bennett."

"Wait, you know the guy? The guy who attacked you?" Michael asked, his forehead furrowed.

"I know *of* him would be a better way to put it. He is a paralegal for Victor Kirkland."

"Victor Kirkland, the divorce attorney? The Victor Kirkland who represented both of the murder victims?" Michael asked, his voice now grave.

I could see the anger bubble up inside of him. Anger at Bennett? Or anger at me for what he imagined had instigated the attack?

The responding officer stood nearby, listening to the details but not completely understanding the connections.

"Yes, that Victor Kirkland," I said, adjusting my legs as my foot started to cramp. "Bennett was fired this morning, and he blames me."

"I'm confused already," the responding officer added, throwing up his hands.

"Forgive the obvious question, but why? Why exactly does he believe you interfered in his employment situation?" Michael asked.

"Let me start from the beginning. Bennett was one of the guys protesting outside of Gavin Wright's arraignment yesterday. He, and two dozen of his women-hating friends, screamed and yelled and called Wright a hero for taking out his wife. Well, I was there, and I filmed it. When I realized one of Victor's employees was screaming hate speech publicly, and I had it on tape, I had no choice but to share it with Victor. Thankfully, Victor responded as any rational employer would, and he fired the SOB. Therefore, Bennett blames me. And he came here specifically to let me know."

"What did he say?"

"He ranted like a lunatic. Said delightful things like I hadn't been properly 'trained by my husband.' Sweet, isn't it? He's an off-the-wall, eighteenth-century misogynist." I was shifting from shock to anger, which I took as a good sign. "And, get this, he threatened that I would pay for what I've done."

Michael's jaw clenched, and I saw the look on his face shift from cop to boyfriend.

Like it or not, it wasn't possible to isolate those roles anymore.

"Michael, it's time for us to have a straight conversation about the connection between these two murders."

31

"Are you tired of playing knight in shining armor?"

Having been given the all-clear by the EMTs, Michael escorted me back to my apartment.

"Apparently, someone needs to," he teased. "Now, off to bed with you. Rest, I mean it, or I'll haul you off to a lovely private cell at the Cook County jail. Trust me, you won't like the food, so I suggest you behave."

He led me down the hall to my bedroom, propping the pillows on my bed while I stripped down to my undies. I crawled in to the smooth, cool sheets while Michael ran off for supplies. He returned with water, Advil, an ice pack, and a towel that he laid on my pillows for protection. Walter followed him in, watching suspiciously from the end of the bed.

"Drink." He handed me two pills and the water bottle.

"Yes, Dad." I smiled, then gave him a kiss.

"Your cell is here on the nightstand. Call me if you need anything, okay?"

I nodded.

"I'll check in later, maybe bring you some soup if you're up to eating."

I reached for his hand. "Thank you."

He winked and smiled.

I settled back on the pillows, positioned the ice pack, and adjusted the comforter around me. With Michael gone, Walter curled up next to my leg, purring contentedly.

Despite the headache, I was wired. How had Marcus Bennett come to these viewpoints on women? What childhood trauma or backward parenting was responsible for these hateful beliefs? And how did his wife tolerate it? The extreme misogyny was beyond comprehension, at least to me, but that was an issue for mental health professionals. I closed my eyes and shut out the thoughts, letting sleep work its healing magic.

When I woke, the sky had gone dark. I switched on the lamp and removed the long-since thawed ice pack. Feeling grimy and sweaty, I stripped and stepped into the shower, letting the warm water rinse away the dried blood and the stink of old adrenaline.

Feeling more refreshed, I dressed in yoga gear, hit my hair with just enough warm air to keep it from dripping, then rebandaged my wound.

Walter followed me into the kitchen while I turned on the teapot and opened my phone to see what messages I had missed.

A call from Borkowski, who'd been contacted by the police. And a text from Michael asking if he needed to pick up anything before he came over. I sent him back a note saying I was fine, popped a few more Advil, then took my tea to the living room. Sinking deep into the down cushions with a throw over my legs and the thriller I'd just started, I flipped the switch on the gas fireplace.

I'd barely cracked the spine when my cell phone rang. The doorman calling to say I had a visitor. Ryan Molina.

What was he doing here? I told the doorman to send him up,

but I had every intention of turning him back around quickly. I couldn't handle whatever he was selling, not tonight.

Hearing the ding of the elevator, I opened the door. Ryan stood in the doorway, droplets of snow melting on his cashmere coat.

"Are you all right? I just heard what happened." His face was creased with worry as he looked at me, taking hold of my arm as he spoke.

My mind flitted between the real concern I saw in his face and the knowledge that he was a backstabbing pig intent on stealing my company out from under me.

"No serious damage. I just need rest," I said, but made no effort to invite him in. I didn't trust him and certainly didn't trust his motives. "I'm sure I'll be fine in the morning."

"What can I do?"

His gaze was penetrating, to the point that I felt exposed. I gripped the door, wanting to slam it closed and escape from his intensity.

"You look so, so vulnerable. Surely there's something I can do." He lifted a hand and caressed my cheek.

"I'm..." I paused midsentence at the sound of the elevator doors opening again.

Michael stepped out, stopping in his tracks as he saw us. He looked from me to Ryan and then back to me again, anger in his eyes.

Ryan removed his hand, sensing the new tension, but didn't flinch. Looking squarely at Michael, he extended a hand. "I'm Ryan Molina, an old friend of Andrea's. It sounds like she's had quite a scare today."

I introduced Michael but didn't explain our relationship. The three of us stood in the vestibule, silent, as if this were a battle of wills to see who would walk away first.

"Get some rest, Andrea," Ryan said, running his fingers

through his hair. "I'll check in with you in the morning." He nodded to Michael and stepped into the elevator.

I opened the door, but instead of giving me a kiss, Michael went straight to the kitchen, leaving me to follow. He set down the brown bag he'd brought in and began removing takeout containers.

"Can I take your coat?"

"Obviously you're feeling better," he said, his voice biting. He slipped off his coat and handed it to me before turning back to the food.

I wasn't in the mood for jealousy or petty arguments based on an assumption, not fact. After hanging his coat, I returned to the sofa and my tea, leaving Michael to pout on his own.

Moments later, Michael joined me on the sofa. "Who was that?" he asked, wasting no time with frivolous questions.

"Ryan is a consultant who's been hired to do some work at Link-Media. He's also an old friend of Erik's."

"It looked more like he was an old friend of yours."

"Please don't go there, not tonight." I didn't have the energy for an argument and would likely say something I'd regret. "Can we restart? I'm not trying to be evasive, but now is not the time. Please, just sit with me. We can enjoy the fire, you can have some scotch, I'll have my tea, we'll eat something, and we'll both be better in the morning. I'll tell you all about Ryan another time."

"I was just surprised," Michael said, his voice softer. "I'm sorry, but the way he was touching you made me defensive and protective, but I can let it go. I'll get that drink."

As he moved toward the kitchen, I laid my head back, thankful that I had averted a tense moment but also still feeling the heat of Ryan's touch on my cheek. What was I doing?

Michael returned with his glass. He bent down and gave me a kiss before sitting next to me on the couch. "Better?"

"Much. Did you find Bennett?" I asked.

"Not yet, but it won't take long." He twirled the ice in glass. "We did speak to his wife. She didn't know where he was, nor that he had been fired."

"That means Bennett's going to be mad at you, too. He seems like the kind of guy who'd prefer to control the narrative on how he lost his job. What did you think of the wife?"

"Unusual. I felt like I was talking to June Cleaver, complete with an apron and pearls, or maybe a Stepford wife. She smiled at me the whole time, like there was a button on the back of her head she had to manually turn off."

"I don't know what their story is, but I'm surprised she spoke to you at all. I think whatever lifestyle they're into, they've got some funky rules about women being alone with a man."

"I wasn't alone with her. Her father stood behind her the whole time, and there were two young kids hiding behind her skirt."

The image of Bennett as he raged at me came into my mind again. Twice now I had seen and felt his palpable anger.

"Are you certain Wright hired someone to kill his wife?" I couldn't hold back. A thought was gnawing at me. "Bennett has shown hate toward women and that he's capable of violence. He's also a common link between both victims. What if his hatred went too far? What if he is the one who killed both women?"

"That's crazy." Michael stared at me. "You have to stop this. Let Janek and me do our jobs. I can't debate the details of a police investigation with you."

"Is it really that farfetched? Those guys yesterday were militant. They believe men are superior beings, and they have dim views of successful women. Do we really know how far a guy like that would go?"

32

Elyse Wright's terrified eyes flashed in my mind, and I awoke with a start.

After a fitful night, I had finally fallen into a deep sleep around 4:00 a.m. Between the uncomfortable icepack and the headache that wanted to make my skull explode, rest had eluded me. My bedside clock said 9:00 a.m.

Shaking off the image, I moved toward the bathroom. Walter followed, watching me as I removed the head wrapping that had shifted loose in my sleep. He sat on the counter, meowing at me.

"You're right. I look like hell."

Michael had been kind and thoughtful and caring last night, but the minute I challenged him on the cases, he'd shut down, refusing to entertain my theory. We'd eaten our meal in near silence, and he'd left shortly after rather than spending the night. I didn't know how to feel about it, other than feeling very alone and confused this morning. I knew he was walking a thin line that went one way, Janek's, but to refuse to entertain any alternative thought meant CPD could be looking in the wrong direction.

I settled into my morning routine, although my movements

were slow and stiff. Every shift of my head brought a new stab of pain. As I dressed, I thought about Marcus Bennett. Victor had hired him, so it was safe to assume his references and work ethic were stable. But it wouldn't be difficult to hide extreme viewpoints in the workplace, particularly given the demanding schedules of the legal industry.

I'd heard firsthand some of his derogatory viewpoints on women and had now seen a violent undercurrent. Was that violent streak a result of losing his job? A onetime event? Or was it a thread throughout his life? I didn't know enough to have an opinion.

My cell rang as I was settling into my office.

"Andrea, are you okay?" Victor said the minute I picked up. "I just found out what Marcus did to you. The police were here first thing this morning asking questions. I can't believe he would do this."

"I'll be fine. Just a bump on the head, no concussion. But Bennett is facing assault charges." I added Bennett's name to my pin board as we spoke. "It's hard to predict who's going to react badly to being fired. I'm certain you didn't anticipate this."

"What a stupid thing to do. I always saw him as having dated views of the world, but I never imagined he would ever hurt anyone."

The memory of how Bennett had spoken to his wife, the tone he'd used, the hatred in his voice, all flashed back into my mind. I sat back on the edge of my desk and looked at the board. Was I off-base to consider Bennett as a suspect?

"Victor, have you ever known Bennett to raise his voice or to lose his temper?"

"The police asked me the same thing. I know him to be a pretty quiet, mild-mannered guy. I think he's got wonky views of marital roles, but the arrangement he has with his wife is certainly none of my business."

"What do you mean by that? What are his positions on marriage?"

"He has that decades-old viewpoint that a man is the king of his castle and that a woman's role is home and children. I was aware of it only because some of the female staff overheard him make comments to his wife on the phone. They were concerned that he might say something derogatory in front of a client. Anyway, I spoke to him and made it clear that that language was not to enter the workplace. I knew it wouldn't change his point of view, and his relationship with his wife is certainly not my problem, but sharing it in the office wasn't something I could tolerate. I thought we understood each other. That is, until you told me what you had overheard."

"Does he have a religious affiliation that you're aware of?" I asked, remembering the exchange I'd witnessed outside Victor's office. "I saw his wife the other day, and her dress and demeanor made me wonder if they might be following some modesty protocol for religious reasons."

"Frankly, their religion hasn't come up. He simply described her as a quote-unquote traditional wife. Whatever the hell that means."

Where had I heard that expression before?

"Thanks, Victor. I'm sure CPD will be in touch if they have any additional questions."

The phrase stuck with me. Traditional wife. I'd heard it used somewhere before. I opened a browser window and typed the phrase into the search field. A slew of results filled my screen. Yes, there it was, a *New York Times* article.

I scanned through the text, refreshing my memory. Apparently, the phrase was code, actually an alt-right movement in its own right, complete with a Twitter hashtag, #tradwife. The belief centered around the idea that by embodying traditional feminine and wifely qualities, such as meekness and chastity and submission to their husbands, women would live the perfect life. That the difficulties of modern society would be avoided.

My stomach knotted at the thought. And what did men get out of it?

The more I read, the uglier it got. The theme underlying the movement seemed to be largely one of white male supremacy. Followers also believed that corruption of the white race was responsible for all of society's ills and the only way around it was racial and gender role purity. Feeling nauseous, I moved to Twitter, scrolling through endless posts pleading for women to submit to their husbands and extolling the virtues of motherhood and homeschooling, but only because then children could not be corrupted through exposure to alternative thinking.

Men need to feel admired by their women. Women were created to do what men can't. Smart women who want to increase their options adapt. The Twitter posts were an endless barrage of brainwashing.

How could this exist? It was a cult of hate and all-in racism wrapped up in false packaging. Images of smiling white women and children, in their Betty Crocker kitchens and *Leave It to Beaver* homes, waiting for Daddy to come home and take care of them, filled the internet. It was as if they wanted to live their lives with the emotional blindness of cartoon figures. A house, a husband who took care of everything, and a baby were all that was required for happiness. How could this exist in this day and age? How could women tolerate it? And what kind of man advocated this lifestyle?

I got up from the desk, my skin crawling. I had never come across such toxic misogyny or such poorly disguised racism. What I found most revolting was the willing participation of the women who seemed content and even grateful to have no expectation of equality.

Is this what defined the Bennetts' relationship? And if it did, so what? His marriage was not the issue. But was hate of women a factor? Neither Elyse nor Skylar had had much personal contact with Bennett, although he worked on their cases in a supporting role. Both were strong, opinionated women with higher incomes than their spouses, but that applied to many women. Why single out these two? Had they insulted him in some way?

The extreme viewpoint was certainly disturbing but, in and of itself, not much of a motive. There was something personal in these killings, the close proximity, murdered in their homes, the slashing of their mouths. He wanted both a literal and figurative silencing. Yes, it was personal.

33

The house was a yellow-ocher seventies split-level showing its age. Rangy junipers framed the door, and rotted asphalt shingles threatened water damage. I guess the #tradmarriage only applied to women, because Marcus Bennett was woefully inadequate at home maintenance. I sat in my car outside their home, watching for signs of life.

I wasn't exactly sure what I was doing here, or what I intended to do if I saw Bennett, but curiosity had gotten the better of me. I grabbed my phone.

"Hi, it's me," I said when Michael answered.

"What a surprise. I expected you to sleep until noon. I would have called, but I didn't want to wake you. Did you make it through the night?"

"More or less, it wasn't the most restful night, but I'm doing fine. Taking it easy." I knew he was assuming I was still at home in my jammies, and I had no intention of correcting him. Why invite argument about my fitness for duty? Or my involvement in the case?

"Do you need anything? I'm pretty deep in a case today, but I can bring dinner over again tonight, if you want." I heard caution in his voice, as if he thought I might reject him. Or maybe he was wondering about Ryan. Although he had calmed down quickly after the moment of jealousy, I suspected that he had gone all cop last night and spent the evening digging into the guy's background. Maybe we could compare files?

"Why don't we touch base later, see how your case is going, see how I feel? Is that okay?" I wasn't avoiding, just buying time until I figured out why I was here.

"Yeah, sure," he said, but I could hear the disappointment.

"Have you been able to find Bennett?" I asked, looking at the house again for signs of life.

"Not yet. And his family isn't cooperating. I think he's hiding out, and the wife knows it."

"Think about it. You've embarrassed him. You were the one to tell her and her dad-in-law, that Marcus lost his job before he could come up with his own version, one that exonerates him. He's off trying to get his story straight."

"Or maybe they know where he is and are helping him avoid us. That's the more logical scenario. The perp makes up a doozy of a story, and the family falls for it hook, line, and sinker and starts protecting him. Guy says the cops are the ones lying. The dummies never understand that it just makes everything worse. Hard to claim you're innocent when you hide."

I caught a flash as sunlight glinted off the front door. Someone was leaving the Bennett house.

"Let me know if you find him," I said to Michael. "I'll give you a call later."

The front door of the Bennett home had opened. Mrs. Bennett appeared to be leaving, and she was alone. She pulled her knit hat down lower on her ears and adjusted the matching scarf around her neck, then began walking toward the street. I watched the door and the curtains in the windows to see if she was traveling alone or if anyone was watching her movements from inside. No sign of anyone. When she got to the sidewalk, she made a right turn. Now what?

I hesitated only a moment, then followed her. She didn't seem hurried as she walked, nor was there any signal that she thought she might have company.

The neighborhood had a distinctly suburban feel, moderate homes on small parcels. There was evidence of children everywhere, snow-covered swing sets or snowmen in the front yards. Edison Park was a neighborhood near O'Hare along the I-90 corridor and just inside the Chicago city limits. It provided safety, decent schools, and an easy commute into downtown. It also meant pedestrians were few and far between on the sidewalk in February, and I was feeling as if I had a big red sign that said "stalker" on my head.

I kept my pace slow and plodding, matching Mrs. Bennett's stride, staying about half a block behind her. She wore a long navy puffer coat and tall fleece-lined boots, so she was far more prepared for the weather than I was, but I didn't have the impression she was out for a hike. With little ones at home, and with what I had learned of the traditional-wife concept, this was likely a short trip.

I trailed her for another three blocks, wondering why I hadn't just stayed in the car and driven like the rest of suburbia. I had at least brought gloves, but this kind of surveillance required thermal long johns and hand warmers. At the next corner, she turned again. By the time I reached the intersection, I could no longer see her. Glancing from side to side, I looked for fresh footprints or signs of a door closing. Nothing. However, the street was lined with cars, and two women were heading into a square brick building mid-block. I assessed my options.

Was this a community center? A colorful handwritten sign planted in the snow bank said Women's Group Open House. I looked more closely at the building. A discreet plaque on the

door said New World Congregation with a small cross underneath. Apparently, this was a church but indistinct. Purpose-
fully? Or simply an adapted use of the building? Regardless, this
had to be Mrs. Bennett's destination.

Seeing no downside, I followed a woman with a plate of
cookies through the door into a large reception area. The room
was set up with about two dozen folding chairs arranged in rows
in an alcove. A card table covered with a gingham tablecloth was
loaded with trays of pastries and sweets while a second held
liquid refreshments. I stopped for a moment, scanning the room
for Mrs. Bennett.

"Welcome." A woman approached me with an enthusiastic
smile. "You can hang your coat right here." She pointed. "Then
get yourself a name tag and help yourself to refreshments. We'll
be starting the meeting in about fifteen minutes." I smiled shyly
and thanked her, trying to blend in. Thankfully, she moved on to
assist others. What the hell, I was here.

I put my coat on a hook, scribbled my first name on a sticker
with a Sharpie, placed it on my chest, then filled a Styrofoam
cup with weak, tepid tea. The homemade cookie plates over-
flowed with choices. I guess these women had to do something
with their suppressed frustrations.

I winced as I took a sip of the lukewarm liquid, reminding
myself to stop the tea snobbery. This didn't seem like a crowd
that would appreciate the distinction between an Earl Grey with
a strong bergamot finish and a first-flush Darjeeling. Besides, I
wasn't here for the refreshments.

Standing against the wall, I pretended to sip and watched
the women as they mingled. Most seemed to know each other,
gathering in small groups. The assembled women were largely
in their twenties and thirties, which made sense—prime child-
bearing decades. Only one woman wasn't as pale as the snow

outside, and she, too, seemed to have wandered in not fully aware of what she was walking into.

And skin color wasn't the only common denominator. Whatever fashion gods had dictated that shirt dresses, mid-calf skirts, and sweater sets were dead hadn't spent any time in this crowd. Where did they buy this stuff? Dressed in skinny jeans, black motorcycle boots, and a chunky fisherman's sweater, my garb alone told the group I wasn't one of them. At least I wasn't showing skin; it was as close to their version of modest as I got.

"Hi, I'm Martha." A woman approached me, a printed flyer in her hand. "Thank you for coming. Are you new in the neighborhood?"

"Yes, just a couple weeks," I lied, smiling politely. As expected, I'd been pegged as a newbie.

"That's great. We're always excited to meet new women of quality." She handed me the printout. "We meet here every second Wednesday at eleven thirty."

I glanced at the flyer. Handmade by one of the women, no doubt, extolling the virtues of family and tradition. Martha prattled on about timing the meetings so as not to conflict with getting kids to school or supper on the table, while I pretended to agree, catching sight of Mrs. Bennett as she spoke.

"How many children do you have?" Martha asked.

"Can you excuse me for a moment? I need to find the ladies' room." The trick to this type of recon work was to fake engagement while avoiding answering any personal questions. And Martha had just gotten personal.

"Of course, get that in before the meeting starts. Just down that back hall." She smiled and flicked her hand toward the far wall.

I nodded and tucked her flyer into my bag, then moved to find a more neutral territory. My plan, such that it was, was to get as close to Mrs. Bennett as I could, chat her up, and see what I could learn about her husband.

I had my opportunity a few minutes later when Mrs. Bennett's companion stepped away.

"Hi, I'm Andrea," I said, extending a hand. She took it, looking at me long enough to catch that I wasn't one of the converted.

"Jill. Are you new?" She looked at me expectantly, fingering the pearls resting against her jewel neck sweater.

Gone was the downturned head I'd seen outside of Victor's office. Here she seemed relaxed, comfortable in her skin.

I nodded. The less detail given the better. "Have you been part of these meetings for a long time?" I asked.

The question seemed to warm her up. I was gathering that the purpose of the meeting was an intro to the lifestyle and that established members were here to recruit, whitewashing reality, of course. Maybe conversion was the better word. Suddenly the Scientology TV network came to mind, although this was a substantially lower-budget operation.

"I've been coming since before my babies were born. Marcus, that's my husband, likes that I socialize with like-minded women. As long as it doesn't interfere with my other duties, of course."

"Of course. How many children do you have?"

"Three, all under five. Hopefully God will bless me with at least a few more."

I cringed inwardly, guessing her to be only in her late twenties. She'd likely never known a life alone as a single woman or supported herself, and if she was going the baby-machine route, that was unlikely to change. I was conscious of my own bias, my own fears of dependence, as I thought about what her life must be like. I was making judgments about these women and the life that they had chosen, but the traditional-wife lifestyle wasn't the reason I was here.

"Does your husband share your desire to have more children?"

She gave me a confused look. "Of course. If it's God's will, who are we to challenge?"

"I only asked because it must be hard, financially. Chicago is not an inexpensive place to live on one income."

"My husband has an excellent job. We manage nicely." Her face pinked up as she spoke, and her eyes suddenly would not meet mine. The woman was a terrible liar. "Well, if you'll excuse me, I should get to my seat," she said. "Nice meeting you."

Conversation over. I watched her join two women she clearly knew who were already seated. As the group was called to assemble, I took a chair in the back where I could observe Jill Bennett.

The speaker began by welcoming new and prospective members, then droned on about family values, the importance of motherly love, and the endless threats modern society placed on women's roles as caregivers. I had to clench the sides of my chair to keep from screaming about how insulting I found these antiquated concepts. Was my face betraying me? I looked around, concluding I was safe. All attention was on the speaker.

I shot my eyes back over to Jill. She appeared unruffled. Her reaction told me they hadn't yet settled on a story about her husband's dismissal so had chosen denial. I wondered what they would say to the neighbors after he was charged with assault?

Thankfully, I managed to keep my cool through the balance of the recruiting speech. The Hispanic woman I'd noticed earlier caught my eye and smiled. She hadn't taken the bait either. The official presentation ending, I gathered my bag, watching Jill Bennett out of the corner of my eye. She was heading for the door, fast. I followed.

She was already out the door as I slipped on my coat. As I exited the building, I found myself cornered by Martha, the woman who had greeted me initially. Taking her recruiting role to heart, she peppered me with questions about my impressions of the meeting. I answered noncommittally, excusing myself to intercept Jill before she left.

"Jill?"

She turned at the sound of her name.

"I wanted to catch you before you left. I was wondering if I could talk to you some more about the group?"

"Well, I really should get home. The little ones need their mommy. I'm sure Martha can answer any questions."

She was edging toward the street as she spoke.

"Jill."

Marcus Bennett waited at the end of the walk, and she scurried to meet him.

Now what? He hadn't noticed me yet, but would momentarily. And after yesterday's incident, I had no idea how he'd react. Would he feel emboldened and attack me again in front of this group? Should I text Michael that I had found the guy? No, then I'd have to explain what the hell I was doing here.

They stood together on the walk, Marcus saying something to her I couldn't hear. Realizing my options were to hide or confront him, I stepped forward, getting within ten paces of the couple before Bennett turned and looked at me. I wasn't sure what I was going to say to him, but something would come to me.

Bennett looked from me to his wife, then back at me again. He beelined toward me, his face red and eyes hot.

"Now you're hassling my wife? Haven't you done enough? You're coming after my family now? How dare you! This is not your business."

"It becomes my business when you slam me into a brick wall."

I glanced at Jill, certain that her husband hadn't told her about the assault. She stood mute, her hand gripping the fabric of her coat, looking like a child being chastised.

Silence was the price she paid for a roof over her head and all the babies she could handle.

We were no longer alone on the sidewalk as the women from the meeting exited, not knowing they were walking into an argument or any of the history behind it. They stopped and looked at each other, confused about what was going on and what, if anything, they were supposed to do about it. Not a single one of them said a word, deciding it was none of their business.

"Leave us alone," Bennett shouted. "Go back to your immoral lifestyle. Don't come here to corrupt us. This is what happens when women don't know their place, haven't learned to submit!"

My outrage exploded.

"Submit? To whom? Is that why Elyse Wright is dead? Because she didn't submit? She didn't submit to you?"

Bennett's fury boiled over, and he rushed at me. I slid to my right to avoid him, tripping in the process and landing on the sidewalk. But before Bennett could regroup, a squad car roared up to the curb. Two officers rushed over. Grabbing Bennett's arms and cuffing them behind his back while he hurled insults at me.

"Mr. Bennett, you are under arrest for assault. Adding a second charge isn't going to help you," one of the officers said.

With Bennett secured, the other officer stepped toward me, helping me to my feet. "Ms. Kellner, I recognized you from the police report. I don't know what you're doing here, but you might consider staying the hell away from this guy. I don't think he's a fan."

As the officer began to take my statement, Bennett was led to the squad car. A second later, the sound of a body being slammed into metal interrupted us, and the officer ran to assist his partner. Bennett bucked and kicked, trying to release himself from the cop's grip, and both officers wrestled him facedown on the ground.

His wife stood stone faced, staring at the spectacle of her husband cuffed and spread-eagle.

Bennett was lifted none too gently to his feet, and his eyes bore into me as he hissed, "You whore. You deserve to die."

34

"Have you completely stopped answering your phone?" Borkowski stood in front of me, arms crossed over his chest. "I have to learn from the police that you were assaulted outside of the office last night, then I don't hear from you all night, and now you stroll in here at one o'clock? Had it occurred to you to let somebody know what was going on?"

So much had gone on that I didn't know where to begin to explain. But he was right. My head was too full of thoughts to even make sense of what had happened over the last twenty-four hours. After taking my statement, the officers had taken Bennett in for processing, and I was now back at work with lots of suspicions and a story that felt as if it had just taken a dramatic new turn.

Not only had Bennett shoved me into a wall, but he had threatened my life. As an attorney, I knew that words mattered, and although there was a legal difference between "You should die" and "I'm going to kill you," it was a threat nonetheless. And the question now was whether Marcus Bennett was capable of murder. Were his misogynistic views motive enough? No, of course not, but he did know both women and had clearly expressed his hate-filled viewpoint. The next question was had there been something specific about these two women, their cases, or their interaction with Bennett that might have angered him to such a level?

"I apologize," I said, sitting on the edge of my desk. "I should have called in. I had such a terrible headache last night, and I just wanted to sleep. That's no excuse. I should've sent you a text letting you know I was okay. Thank you for checking on me."

He relaxed a little. "And so this morning you just slept the day away? Forgetting that people might be worried? You have a head injury. For all we knew, you were on the floor of your apartment, passed out."

"I don't have an excuse. At least not a valid one. I was feeling well enough that I went to follow up on a lead. And the morning took a turn."

"A turn? Let me guess, you pissed off someone else?"

"No, just the same guy I pissed off yesterday." I shrugged and crossed my arms.

I saw Michael barreling through the Link-Media office toward me. He wasn't happy.

"Well?" Borkowski said as Michael reached my office.

He hovered in the doorway. I stood, turned to Borkowski. "It's complicated. I'll fill you in a little later." Borkowski swung his head toward Michael's scowl, raised an eyebrow, and looked back at me. "Complicated, is it? I'll bet." He turned and left.

Michael closed the door behind him, and we stood face-to-face.

"What the hell, Andrea? Were you lying to me about being at home? Is this all some big game to you? What are you doing going after the guy? He just tossed you into a wall like you were a snowball. God knows what he would have done if someone hadn't come along to stop him. And still you lie to me and secretly go after him today?"

"I admit I withheld information," I said, trying unsuccessfully to rationalize my actions. "You made an assumption that I was at home, and I didn't correct you."

"Let me get this straight. After Marcus Bennett attacked you, nearly gives you a concussion, you decide to drive out to his house and confront him. Is that about right?"

"I didn't drive out to see Bennett. I went to see his wife." I stepped back to the desk and sat on the edge, my headache resurfacing.

"His wife?" Michael paused, looking at me with confusion. "Why?"

"Curiosity. They have this weird man-in-charge, traditional-wife thing going. That in itself is creepy and possibly relevant. I wanted to ask her where Marcus was when the killings occurred."

"You were checking his alibi? So now you think this guy stabbed these women to death just because he's a misogynist?"

"Michael, have you not considered it? Anger issues, violent tendencies, he worked with both of the victims. And this isn't run-of-the-mill misogyny. This guy believes women need to submit to their husbands. That they need to be trained. Helluva personality profile, don't you think?"

"So, the guy's a whack job. I'll give you that. But he's also just been fired, and he blames you. That doesn't make him a killer." He paced the small room as he chastised me. "More importantly, it doesn't give you license to go after the guy just because you hate how they live."

"You're making it sound like this is some personal grievance. I think their viewpoint is repugnant, but that's not what this is about. Think about it, Michael. These two women were both more successful than their husbands. They both initiated divorce proceedings. They both effectively took down their husbands by exposing their misdeeds. Do you think a man like Marcus Bennett, who believes women need to be trained and subservient, wouldn't view these two women as needing to be taught a lesson?"

"Look, there are people in the world with crazy-ass views. Marcus Bennett and his wife and their traditional-wife concepts are some of them. It's ugly, it's hateful, and he may have even despised these women, but we work on proof. Hateful thought doesn't always translate to hateful deed."

"So you don't think he's capable?" I said, crossing my arms over my chest, getting irritated.

"That's not what I said. He probably is whacked out enough to hurt someone. And right now, the someone he's got his eyes on is you."

We were both quiet for a moment, letting our thoughts gel, trying to separate our feelings for each other from the logic of our jobs.

"So what will you do from here? With Bennett?"

"We'll start with the crime we have—assault. After that, I can't answer."

Michael stepped forward and stood in front of me. "Please, Andrea, let us do our jobs. There are procedures I need to follow," he said, his voice softening. "And I can't take another night of worrying that you're safe."

I closed my eyes and let out a breath, fighting tears that welled in my eyes, not knowing what to say. A knock on the glass of my door jolted me back.

"I heard about last night." Ryan had opened the door without waiting for an invitation or without stopping to consider his bad timing. Or because he just didn't care about either.

"I'm just fine, thank you," I said, keeping my eyes on Michael.

He shot Ryan a glance that could have cut glass. If Ryan noticed, he was pretending not to.

"Are you sure you should be in the office?" Ryan asked, stepping into the room as if he had a right to be there.

Michael glared at me. "Obviously you have things to do," he said, walking out the door in a huff and leaving me unable to counter. Why was the man always walking out?

"Sorry, did I interrupt something?" Ryan asked when Michael had gone.

Who was he kidding with the false concern? He'd known he was interrupting before he walked in the door. It had been purposeful.

I ignored the question, not trusting myself to contain my anger. I was mad at Ryan, mad at Michael, and mad at myself for being in the situation at all. "Were you just checking in, or is there something you needed from me?"

"Of course I was concerned. Some crazy guy attempted to hurt you."

"Really, I'm fine. But behind on some work, so if you'll excuse me." I turned away and walked behind my desk, lifting the lid on the laptop.

"Sure, of course. But please take it easy. We wouldn't want you to hurt that pretty little head of yours any further."

I couldn't even manage a fake smile. The patronizing tone nauseated me. I had had enough of men who pretended to be protective all while stabbing me in the back.

"Can you close the door on your way out?" I asked, not lifting my head up from my computer.

Attractive or not, sexy or not, Ryan Molina was just more of the same. I turned my attention to my screen and opened up the video file from Gavin Wright's arraignment. I wanted another look at the man's behavior. I took a sip of tea, waited for Ryan to be gone, then clicked play.

In my dealings with Bennett, I had seen a mild-mannered, somewhat mousey kind of man. Yet there was something more, something hidden. I let the tape run, pausing periodically, looking for Bennett in the crowd of men, listening for his voice. Scanning faces, reactions, analyzing the word choice in their hate speech. First, I played the edited clip, which had appeared on the Link-Media website, then I opened my original file and did the same. Had Bennett appeared anywhere other than the brief moment when the crowd got heated?

I found Bennett in one other frame, standing shoulder to shoulder with the other men. Anger was etched on their faces as they chanted in unison. Freezing the image, I studied the faces of the men, pondering the cause and depth of their hate. How did they function in their jobs, in their lives? Did they blame women for positions usurped, for rewards not given? Was their resentment so strong that it would lead to violence? These were the thoughts that ran through my mind as I studied these white male faces.

I rewound about thirty seconds of tape, then hit play. The man to Bennett's left was Leon Rutkowski. In all the craziness of the last twenty-four hours, I had forgotten that Rutkowski had been in the crowd. I continued looking at the frames, only seeing him again in the same shot where I had captured Bennett's face directly. His expression held an anger, a hatred that seemed even more palpable than Bennett's. I knew nothing of the man. Clearly they had a connection through Victor's firm.

Beyond hate for women, were there other connections?

35

Was Rutkowski involved?

I knew little of the man, other than his work as a forensic accountant. But it was a start. I hated to keep bugging Victor, but he had firsthand knowledge. I'd left the office shortly after reviewing the video, swallowed a couple more Advil, and was now about to interrupt his day yet again. Maybe I did need to put him on retainer.

"Sorry, Nancy, I need to see him again." She gave me a small smile, nodded, then picked up the phone. I walked to the conference room. No need to wait for an escort—I was part of the Kirkland and McCullough family after all of this.

"How's your head?" Victor said, hurrying into the room. His tie was loosened, his sleeves were rolled. Clearly I'd caught him in the middle of something mentally taxing.

"Nothing that won't heal," I said. "Oh, CPD picked up Bennett this morning. He won't be held for long, but maybe a night in jail will give him something to think about." I didn't bother sharing the details of the arrest; it would only make Victor feel more guilty than he already did.

"The whole thing makes me sad, but thank goodness. I've

been so worried. I wish I had fired him months ago. I'm just too softhearted on these kinds of things. Or maybe just too damn busy."

"Don't beat yourself up. Marcus Bennett's issues have nothing to do with you. I promise, my injuries are minor. And you've done the right thing by terminating him."

"Please, sit. You didn't run over here just to tell me that." Victor pulled out a chair.

I pulled off my coat and joined him, Marcus Bennett's threatening words fresh in my mind.

"I'm sorry I keep running to you, but this new information on Bennett has given me more questions than answers. I'm hoping you can help me make sense of it," I said.

"I'll do what I can, but I'm pretty damn confused myself."

"As we're starting to see, his views on women are pretty extreme. He's been harboring a lot of hate, and I'm wondering if there were signs that we've missed. Can you remember any incidents where Elyse Wright or Skylar Hayes might have challenged him or gotten into some kind of disagreement with him? Was there any tension in the relationships that he had with these two women?"

Victor scrunched his eyes for a moment.

"There certainly was never any type of argument. I would have known about that immediately and never would have tolerated an employee raising their voice to a client. But I guess in hindsight, I would say that both women had concerns about promptness. Attention to detail. They both seemed to feel that, at moments, Marcus was slow-walking aspects of their cases."

"In what way?"

"Apparently, information wasn't always passed on promptly, documents sometimes seemed out of order or difficult to locate. I didn't think much of it at the time. This is a busy law firm, and while we do our best, there are always moments where we don't perform at one hundred and ten percent. I recall speaking to Marcus on a couple of occasions about it and assuring our clients that we were making every effort. But quite frankly, it never crossed my mind that there might be anything intentional about the acts. But I suppose it's possible that Marcus was letting his personal viewpoints influence the work he did. I hate to say it, but in light of what we know now, it is a possibility."

"Rather passive-aggressive," I said, thinking out loud. "What about your staff? Did you notice any differences in how Bennett responded to you or other men at the firm versus the women that he worked with?"

"Again, I can't say I noticed anything, but as I think back, my perspective may have changed a bit. As you know, the firm is largely staffed with women, and I'm certainly aware that he was on his best behavior around me. But it's my firm, and that's the behavior I would expect. The male clients seemed to love him. Were very complimentary of his efficiency. It was never obvious that he might be slanting his work product in favor of male clients, or maybe that was just my own male perspective on the world."

I could sense he was struggling. Struggling with guilt, struggling to reflect on his own observations and perhaps his own preconditioning as a white man in the world now faced with hate and female oppression in a way he couldn't ignore.

"How were his interactions with your forensic accountant?"

"They have a good relationship. Leon Rutkowski is a free-lance provider that I pull in only when the situation is warranted and usually for very specific tasks."

"Do you remember how you came to use his services?"

"Let me think. If I remember correctly, he was someone Marcus referred. I believe they knew each other from college and then had some type of work association after."

That made sense. They'd probably been building this bond of misogyny since college.

"When did you start working with him?"

"Not terribly long ago, a couple of years at most. I believe I started working with him somewhere around the time your case was kicking off, but there was nothing in your situation that warranted his services. If I recall correctly, I tested him with a small case and got references from the accounting firm he had been employed with before going out on his own. I use him several times a year. Why do you ask?"

"Did Rutkowski work on both Elyse Wright's case and Skylar Hayes's?"

"Yes, he did. Given the financial complexity of both cases, I hired him to do a deep dive." He paused, crossed his arms over his chest. "You're making me nervous. I'm not sure I like where you seem to be going with this."

"Frankly, I'm not sure where I'm going with this. I didn't mention this the other day, but after looking at the videotape again, it's clear that Rutkowski shares some of Bennett's viewpoints. He was at the protest screaming ugly hate speech about women too. I don't know if that means anything, but it seems worth looking into."

"I can't say I feel I know the guy or his personal points of view. I hired him for a task, and he performed. I have no complaints about the quality of the work that he provided for me."

"Has your staff given you any inkling of sexist behavior or language coming out of Rutkowski?"

"No, but as we're learning, I may be the last to know this stuff." He sighed. "Hold on for a minute. Let me get Nancy in here. Other than Marcus, she's the one who had the most contact with him."

As Victor stepped out, I wondered about the friendship

between Bennett and Leon Rutkowski, imagining both of them steeped in a false life where fifties role models reigned and men were men. I pictured Leon with a matching wife in her shirt dress, pearls, and apron, living blocks from the Bennetts, sharing barbecues with their brood of children. A self-created world where bad things would never happen because men were in charge and women waited on their every need.

Victor came back into the room. Nancy followed, looking a bit uncomfortable, but she joined us at the table.

"Nancy, Andrea has some questions about our forensic accountant, Mr. Rutkowski. I brought you in since you've had more contact with him than anyone other than Marcus. Would that be okay?"

"Yes, of course. I'm happy to help." She looked at Victor, then at me, trying to figure out where this was going.

"I'm wondering if you ever witnessed any behavior or language from Mr. Rutkowski that seemed misogynistic or hateful toward women?"

She hesitated, looked at Victor expectantly. He nodded.

"Only every time I came into contact with him," she said.

"Can you be more specific?" I asked.

Victor was silent but lifted his brows. I imagined it was disconcerting for him to be made aware of things that his staff felt uncomfortable sharing with him.

"I know Mr. Kirkland likes him," she began. "Thinks he does a good job and all, but as far as I'm concerned, it's all an act. With me, he's rude and dismissive. There are people who act that way when they come in—after all, I'm just the secretary, and divorce is a tough thing—but Mr. Rutkowski has been outright mean. He speaks to all the women like we're just around to do his bidding. Sorry, Mr. Kirkland, if I'm the first to tell you this."

"It's okay, Nancy, just tell us the truth."

"Can you give me some examples of how Rutkowski behaved toward women?" I asked.

"A couple months ago, he asked out Catherine, one of our young attorneys. When she said no, he called her a frigid lesbian bitch. And I'm quoting; I was there. He asked her out while standing in the middle of the reception area. Didn't matter to him that anyone was there hearing the whole thing. Catherine was uncomfortable, but she was polite, hardly rude, simply said no thank you. Said that she didn't mix work with her personal life. There was no cause for him to get so angry. The way he responded, you'd think she'd been insulting or mean. But the guy couldn't handle the rejection and snapped at her. He's been extra rude to her ever since, even going out of his way to be around her so he can say something hurtful. At least the last part is what she's told me."

"He's not married?" I asked. "For some reason I assumed he was." Interesting. I had him pegged firmly in the traditional-wife crowd with his newspaper and scotch waiting for him the moment he returned from work, towheaded children clamoring for attention at his knees.

"No, more like the kind of guy who can't get a date and then blames women because he's rude and socially awkward."

"Thank you, Nancy, I appreciate your honesty. That's all I needed."

She left, but Victor and I stayed for a moment. I imagined he was processing the disconnect between the relationship he thought he had with his staff and the new reality he was learning. And I was thinking about Rutkowski's hatred of women in a whole new way.

"The boss is always the last one to know," he said, running his hand over the top of his head. "I don't know what else to say. There are always things your staff keep to themselves, but I had no idea this was going on. I'm appalled that the women in this firm have been subjected to this. Why didn't they say anything?" Victor asked, shaking his head and not really expecting an answer from me.

I could hear the sadness and confusion in his voice. It was a difficult concept for men to wrap their heads around, the fact that women were used to abuse in one form or another and, more often than not, simply dealt with it on their own. Victor was no different than most; he hadn't experienced it, so he wasn't tuned in to look for it, then was shocked when it slapped him in the face. Perhaps this was the sensitivity training he needed to find ways to open the dialogue for women to express themselves in his office.

"It sounds like you've been given a gift. I'm sure there are a number of women on your staff who would like to hear those same words."

"And they will." He sighed. "Well, Rutkowski's off the list. Luckily, he just finished his work on the Hayes case, and I won't be forced to look that jackass in the eye any longer, either."

As I wrapped up the conversation with Victor, another question formed in my mind. Being mid-divorce, Elyse and Skylar had both been single, sort of. Maybe Rutkowski thought he had a shot? Was it possible that he had made advances on both women and been rejected?

36

Ordinary hate wasn't enough. What was the personal component?

I was beating my head against the wall, trying to figure out if there was anything more that connected these men than their mutual hate for women. Whoever killed Elyse Wright and Skylar Hayes was making a statement about their willingness to talk. And what had they both been vocal about? Their husbands' wrongdoing. I had firsthand experience with Bennett's willingness to inflict physical violence, but what about Rutkowski? Did he have similar tendencies? Or did he limit his hate to name-calling and false slut-shaming?

I'd picked up a bowl of chicken-and-rice soup at the deli downstairs on my way back into the office and was waiting for Brynn while I sipped.

"I thought you hated their soup," Brynn said, peering into my cardboard container, laptop in hand.

"It's just like my mother used to make. Canned." I rolled my eyes. "I didn't have time to be a foodie today. The kitchen closes at two thirty, and they wouldn't make me a salad."

She chuckled and parked herself in the chair, elbows on her

knees. "Mr. Marcus Bennett doesn't like you much, does he?"

"I don't like him, either, so we're even. So, Twitter. Talk to me."

"They should rename it Trolls 'R' Us. Sorry, I know you have to use it, but I hate the platform. Anyway, I started some background work. Give me a second while I pull my notes."

"I may use it, but don't ask me to understand how to do anything other than post something simple."

I took another sip of soup, cringing from the sodium content and rice now turned to mush, my thoughts on possible motives for the murders. If Bennett or Rutkowski were the killer, perhaps understanding why would help me prove the case.

Was it the outrage of two men being taken down by the women who were supposed to bow to their husbands' authority? Lesser indignities had driven men to kill, but I couldn't let go of the idea that these murders were personal. The intimacy of the murders and the postmortem slashes to the mouths said that the killer had a relationship, even loosely, with the victims. They weren't simply symbols of society's ills.

"Okay, when I looked into Skylar's account, she wasn't a big user. And never used it for business. There wasn't anywhere close to the amount of content that Elyse Wright posted. I took some screenshots. Give me a second to run through them. Are you looking for anything in particular or just the general sexist bullshit that creeps seem to dish out?" she asked as she scrolled.

"I'm wondering if there were any threats or tweets that seemed particularly ugly. One of her coworkers mentioned she'd been concerned." A new thought popped into my mind. "Is there a way to see if the same Twitter handle can be found in comments on both women's accounts? Maybe the same guy got nasty with both of them? I know that's a little more work than a quick glance, but if he did, it might give me something to work with. I'm hitting a brick wall, so take a look into it for me."

"I'd be more than happy to out one of these creeps. I can't stand the way they hide in the background. Cowards, all of them. Not one of them would say any of this shit to someone's face."

"You're right about that."

Unfortunately, I had no choice but to participate in the drivel. Occasionally it yielded a source or a lead or, at the very least, was often the fastest way to get news out.

"When I was going through Elyse Wright's feed, I made a list of the handles of the guys who were the most obnoxious to her," Brynn said. "The worst was this guy, @mstrxxx. He's the one who tweeted the pic with the X across Elyse's face. His avatar is some stupid cartoon fist. I'll have to poke around to see if I can track him to Skylar, too."

As we spoke, a youngish man in a helmet and serious biking gear appeared in my office doorway. Had to be a messenger, as no one else would be stupid enough to try riding a bike through the streets of Chicago in February.

"Can I help you?"

"You Andrea Kellner?" he asked, reading from a clipboard. "I have a package for you."

After I confirmed my identity, he lifted the flap on the messenger bag slung across his chest. The bag dinged as its many metal buttons were disturbed with the effort. He lifted an envelope out of the pocket, glanced at the front, and then laid it on the top of my desk.

"I need you to sign this," he said, then placed his clipboard in front of me. I scribbled my name, and he was off.

"Sorry about that," I said to Brynn. "When do you think you could get back to me?" I asked, lifting up the manila envelope the messenger had left. My name was scrawled across the front, but there were no other markings. I tore open the flap as Brynn discussed her timing. I looked into the envelope and pulled out the contents.

"What the hell? Oh, my God." I dropped the documents in horror and jumped to my feet.

"What's wrong?" She looked at me, then at the top of my desk.

"Someone sent me photos. Photos of Elyse Wright and Skylar Hayes, dead. These are from the crime scenes," I said, my voice getting shrill and my body beginning to shake. "There's a third photo—of me."

We stood together, staring in disbelief at an image of me pulled from the company website, a red X drawn over my mouth.

I grabbed the images splayed across my desk and flipped them over, looking for a note or markings of any kind to see who might have sent them. Even opening the envelope again to see if I had missed something. Nothing.

"Who was he?" Brynn took my arm. "The messenger? Did you see where he was from? Andrea, you need to call the police, right now."

"These images had to have been taken by the killer," I said, frozen in place, my eyes locked on the two faces of death. "I guess the message is that I'm next."

I looked at Brynn and then again at the photos on my desk, then ran toward the elevator. The messenger was nowhere in sight, and the elevator sat untouched. The stairs. I ran down onto the street, frantically looking for the biker, but there was no sign of him. I trudged back into the building and asked employees closest to the door if he had said anything when he arrived. Asking if anyone noted the company he worked for, learning only that he had asked for me by name.

No one had noticed what company he worked for. And neither had I.

37

Michael stood next to my desk, watching a technician dust the photographs and envelope for prints while I watched them through the glass. An officer had grilled me on what the guy had said, what he looked like, the usual describe-the-guy-so-we-can-find-him questions. I wasn't much help.

The officer was now going through the same routine with others in the office while I stood on the sidelines, helpless, trying to assess how scared I was. Damn scared.

"There you go again. You always have to be the center of attention." Borkowski stood next to me. Despite his playful tone, I could see the concern on his face. "At least we can get a story out of it. Since everyone around here is distracted by our men in blue, we're going to need it."

"Thanks. We can always count on you for your well-developed empathy," I shot back, more sarcastically than I intended. This was the banter—minus my attitude, anyway—that had been part of our relationship prior to Ryan Molina and Wade Ramelli turning my future upside down. It seemed false now. Knowing them, they'd try to use this to pile on another reason I needed to go. Can't have a threat to the staff around the office every day.

Borkowski may have a prickly exterior, but I knew that underneath it he had a big heart. Was he softening on whatever secret deal he'd struck with the two of them, or was this just a little guilt shining through? More likely, I was just overthinking.

"Why is this taking so long?" I paced and huffed like a four-year-old forced to stand in line at the DMV.

Finally, the technician seemed to be wrapping up. I watched him bag the photos and start packing up his kit. Michael came out to give me the update.

"No prints. Other than yours, that is."

"These photos, they were taken by the killer, weren't they?" I pressed him.

"Possibly."

"Come on, Michael, give me a break. Could you give any more of a non-answer than that? The only other option is someone got ahold of the photos your guys took. Do you think a cop sent these to me? Is that a likely scenario? When was the last time you had leaks of this kind in your forensics department?"

I was badgering him, my voice agitated and loud, maybe even bordering on hysterical, and I knew it, but I was sick to death of the evasiveness he kept dishing out. Whatever he was doing to set boundaries between his job and our relationship was failing miserably, in my opinion.

Borkowski kept his face neutral as he listened to me rant but made no effort to leave. He was probably waiting to see if I'd need to be escorted out of the building.

"I'm just asking that you stop jumping to conclusions without evidence and let CPD do the police work. If this isn't a sign that you've been overstepping, I don't know what is. You've made yourself a target. And now I have to worry about someone coming after you when you don't even have the good sense to be cautious."

"Apparently I'll need to wait until someone tries to kill me before you're ready to have a conversation about reality!"

I stormed into my office, slamming the door behind me, not caring that I was making a scene. My life had just been threatened; I was entitled. Michael and Borkowski and the rest of the staff would just have to deal with it.

I buried my head in an internet search on Rutkowski while I tried to get a grip and clear my head enough to think this through. Bennett was in jail, at least for a few more hours, but he could have arranged the messenger earlier. Rutkowski had no such obstacles. For all I knew, maybe he'd been standing across the street, watching the whole damn thing and laughing. Would upping the pressure on the men push one of them out into the open? Or just get me killed?

Rutkowski was the one who intrigued me. I picked up the phone and called Kirkland and McCullough, asking for a meeting with Catherine, the young attorney Rutkowski had been hassling. I was told she was down at the courthouse. I grabbed my coat and bag and headed out to find a cab.

————

DIVORCE CASES WERE HEARD by the circuit court of Cook County housed in the Daley Center. Catherine was trying a case before Judge Powers in room 202. It was impossible to gauge the timing. I could be waiting five minutes or five hours. I pulled up her photo from the Kirkland website.

Divorce cases were generally a long series of delicate negotiations back and forth between the parties, up to and sometimes after the time set for trial. It was a process, like many in the legal world, designed to get the two parties to come to an agreement on their own, while the legal team played negotiator.

I took a seat outside of the courtroom and watched, not certain which mediation rooms had been assigned. After about forty-five minutes of sitting on the hard bench, I was starting to lose feeling in my tush, so I stood and paced the hallway for a bit. Hushed conversation floated over from the side hallway, a sign that someone might be wrapping up for the day. Moments later Catherine appeared, laden with a thick, battered briefcase that probably weighed over thirty pounds. A distraught woman walked by her side, sniffing and dabbing at her eyes.

I remembered the feeling.

I watched for a moment, not wanting to intrude on an emotional exchange. Few wanted this moment of pain witnessed publicly, even in this building. The client nodded sadly several times while Catherine tried to reassure her before they both went their respective ways.

"Catherine?"

She looked at me, trying to place my face. She was a small woman and looked like she belonged in a Crest commercial. Blond and blue-eyed, just like the #tradwife ideal, but her eyes held a fierceness that overshadowed her frame. "Yes. Do I know you?"

"No, but I'm a friend and former client of your firm. My name is Andrea Kellner." I handed her a card. "I was speaking to Victor and Nancy earlier today, and they told me about an interaction that you had with Leon Rutkowski. I hope you don't mind, but they told me you had some uncomfortable experiences with him, and I wanted to talk to you about it."

"I'm not in the habit of discussing these things with strangers. I'm sure you understand." She began to walk away.

"Forgive me, I didn't explain myself properly. This is in regards to the death of Elyse Wright and Skylar Hayes," I said.

She stopped and waited for me to continue. "I don't know if you were involved with their cases, but I'm sure you're aware of their murders. Marcus Bennett attacked me and has threatened my life. I understand that both Bennett and Rutkowski were involved with the work in these two cases, and both shared a rather disturbing trait. Their hatred of women. I'd appreciate it if you would talk to me about your experience. It might help solve the murders."

Catherine reacted visibly, drawing in a breath and bringing a hand to her mouth. I took that as permission to continue.

"I understand from Nancy that she witnessed Rutkowski displaying aggressive tendencies toward you," I said. "And I'm trying to find out—"

"You think he was involved in their deaths?" she jumped in.

"I don't know that, but he is one of the connections between the women. I thought it was worth speaking to you. I want to understand more about how he operates, what he does with that hatred. So, long story, but that's why I'm here. I'm just trying to uncover what I can and see where it leads."

"Okay, let's sit. I could never live with myself if someone else died."

Or was she at risk herself? I didn't want to scare her, but she would likely draw her own conclusions. We took a seat on a bench outside the courtroom.

"I'm going to assume Nancy filled you in on what she witnessed when he asked me out," she said, removing the wire-rimmed glasses she wore.

"Yes, I've got the basics. What happened after you rejected him?"

"It started out pretty childish. He'd mutter things under his breath, derogatory things, called me names. Usually something related to my 'snobby' attitude. He was never loud enough for anyone else to hear. He's one of those guys who seems to feel women owe him something." She shrugged.

"Anyway, I pulled him aside one day after this had been going on for nearly a month. I told him to knock it off. That he was being unprofessional. That he needed to stop or I would have to have a conversation with Mr. Kirkland. He was making my work environment a problem, and I was tired of avoiding the guy. There's enough to do around here without his childish male ego in the way."

"And how did he respond?"

"The way guys like this always do. He called me a frigid bitch and stormed out. But he stopped saying things when others were around."

"But he didn't stop altogether?"

"Even though he stopped the name-calling, there's been this underlying hostility. I feel it anytime he looks at me. I've done everything I can to avoid him."

"So, he had a tantrum and now he's pouting, but he's basically left you alone."

"Not exactly. I can't prove this, but right around then, I started getting some really ugly stuff on my Twitter feed. I don't know that it's him, and if it weren't for the murders, I wouldn't mention it at all, but I do think Rutkowski was probably the one posting."

"By ugly stuff, what do you mean?"

"Whoever posted, it was whacked-out women-hate rhetoric. He blamed women for his inability to get a date. Describes himself as an incel, involuntarily celibate. I guess it's a thing. Creepy guys who hate women because they can't get laid. He even used language that said women should be assigned. Like a charity handout to the needy, if you can believe that. In their warped minds, it's some weird entitlement program. It's totally sick stuff. I blocked the guy after the first few ugly tweets, but more have popped up. Look, I don't know for certain that it was Rutkowski who started it. It could just be that the Twittersphere has attracted other idiots, or maybe it's the same guy who's changed his handle and keeps coming at me. I don't know. I just keep blocking the assholes."

"Do you remember the initial Twitter handle?"

"I'll never forget it. It's @mstrxxx."

38

One of these two men was the killer. I was certain of it.

I sat on my sofa, a second glass of Cabernet in hand, trying to sort through the information. My notes were spread out on the coffee table in front of me, and I picked up piece after piece, struggling to find something I had missed, an approach that I hadn't yet thought of.

Walter, of course, sprawled in the middle of it all, desperate to be included, the way only a cat could. I lifted one of his paws and slid out a legal pad.

After speaking with Catherine, Brynn and I had done a dive into the concept of incels, finding an online group of men who'd branded themselves with the handle. Involuntarily celibate men who were not having sex because women constantly rebuffed their advances. Warped though the thinking was, they blamed women rather than looking at their own attitudes and approaches. We'd found documented cases of these self-described incels taking out their anger and exerting revenge violently on women. Was Leon Rutkowski such a man?

Bennett was married, but his hatred wasn't rooted in sexual rejection; it was rooted in a worldview that defined women essentially as property. I knew that he resented women who earned more, achieved more, and were more socially superior to men. Had he extracted some misguided revenge because these two women had dared to expose the flaws in their husbands? Because they had extracted their own version of justice by assisting in their prosecution versus hiding behind and blindly supporting them the way Jill Bennett had done?

As I thought about it, either scenario was possible. As was the possibility that the two men together were responsible. But I needed evidence. And I didn't have it.

I took another sip of my wine and drummed my pencil on my notepad, hoping for inspiration, while Walter stared at me, eyes half-closed, purring.

My cell phone rang. The front desk.

"Ms. Kellner, we have a flower delivery. Would you like me to send them up?"

"Yes, go ahead." It was rather late for a delivery, but given our recent tension, I assumed Michael was sending a bouquet. Thrilled with the thought, I got up, grabbed tip money, and went to the door.

As the elevator opened, a woman in a dark coat and knit hat exited, a glass vase of red roses in hand.

She mumbled hello and handed me the flowers.

"Just a second, let me put this down." I took the package from her hands and stepped inside to place it on the console table near the door, then pulled the tip money out of my pocket. When I turned, she had followed me in and was closing the door.

I paused for a moment, confused by her behavior, then reached out to give her the tip. Perhaps she'd been worried about Walter escaping? She ignored the money in my hand and instead looked around the apartment as she stepped inside further.

"I'm sorry, is there something else?" I asked, her brazenness raising the hair on the back of my neck.

She pulled off her cap, shoved it in her coat pocket, then unzipped her bulky coat.

"This is an awfully large apartment for one woman. Are you barren?"

I stared back into Jill Bennett's eyes.

What was going on? I said nothing, wanting a moment to figure out why she was here, but my mind was locked in a loop. Was this about her husband's termination? She calmly stepped further into the living room, removed her coat, and laid it on the back of a chair as if invited. Gone was the sweet floral dress I'd last seen her in, replaced by a bulky sweater, jeans, and snow boots.

"I asked you a question. Are you barren?" Her tone had grown harsh, as had the look in her eyes.

"That's hardly any of your business. What do you want? If you're here to ask me to help your husband get his job back, I'm not going to do that. His behavior was appalling and public."

She walked around the room slowly, looking at every item, stopping to run her hand over the upholstery as if evaluating my choices.

"I wanted to see how you lived. To see the emptiness of a life alone and unloved. It's as hollow as I expected it to be. You have all of this and no one to share it with. No one to cook for, to care for." She turned hate-filled eyes back to me. "Yet you think nothing of those that do. You live your life selfish, destroying the fabric of our society, destroying the true nature of women. I came to see your empty, selfish life."

"I'd like you to leave," I said, sensing rage under the surface of her controlled tone. She said the words without inflection, as if reading from a script, but her eyes were filled with loathing. "How I live my life is none of your concern. And yours is none of mine, so please leave, or I'll be forced to call the police."

My threat seemed to have no impact, and her preaching continued unabated.

"Perhaps you hate men? Are you one of those lesbians? Are you perverted and unholy? God's way is clear. Women exist to serve our husbands. Our job, our fulfillment, is bearing children, yet you have neither."

"I said, I'd like you to leave." I stepped forward and picked my phone up from the coffee table.

She matched my pace, knocking the phone from my hand. Walter ran, frightened by the noise.

"Jill, calm down." I opened my mouth to say more, but the jingle of a bracelet around her wrist caught my attention. I looked down. Then up at her neck.

No.

My breath caught in my throat.

"Good, I see you noticed my jewelry," Jill said. "They really weren't worthy of such nice things. They were harlots. They didn't know their place in the world. Just like you don't know yours."

She reached into the back of her jeans, and when her arm came out, I saw the knife.

She thrust forward at my stomach in a rage, but I was faster, knocking away her blow. She spun, unsteady in her footing, but didn't lose her grip on the knife. I lunged again for my phone, now lying on the floor, but she kicked it out of the way, thrusting again, this time making contact with my side. As I yelped in pain and doubled over, she came at me. I threw my right shoulder into hers with everything I had, knocked her sideways, then kicked at her as she wobbled. The knife clattered to the floor.

I dove, the pain in my side forgotten with the adrenaline, reaching for the handle, feeling my hands flail against the edge but not quite touching it. Jill came at me, grabbing for the knife, pushing my hands out of range.

I kicked my legs wildly at her, doing anything I could to make contact, anything to get free and recover the knife as she towered over me, delivering blows to my legs and trapping me on the floor. As I stretched my fingers forward, I kicked at her knees feeling her buckle. As she struggled to maintain her footing, she let loose, jamming her boot into my wound.

As I screamed in pain from the impact, my fingertips felt the hilt of the knife.

She came at me again, outraged, flailing, kicking, screaming, pummeling me any way she could as I tried to get a grip on the knife. Filled with adrenaline, I inched myself forward as her blows continued. Getting my hands on the hilt, I turned onto my back, gripping the knife with both hands, knowing my life depended on it.

She lunged again, and with every ounce of strength I could muster, I kicked again at her legs. Felt her stumble and fall on top of me, an elbow jamming into my throat. I pushed her off, instinctively pulling away and coughing as I tried to regain my breath, but the only sound I heard from her was the gurgle of blood as it pooled in her mouth.

She lay on her side. Her eyes wide, pleading, terrified. And the knife was buried firmly in her chest.

As I struggled to sit up, I watched the last bit of light fade from her eyes.

39

My body shook uncontrollably as exhaustion and adrenaline flooded my veins, and I could do nothing to control it.

I lay in a hospital bed at Northwestern, twenty-five stitches in my left side, pillows cradling my head, and ice packs across my incision. My wound was just a low throb at the moment, but that would change soon enough as the pain meds wore off.

Michael appeared in the doorway. I gave him a half-smile, which was the best I could manage, given the drugs. He pulled a chair over to the side of the bed and clasped my hand.

"What do you need? A drink? Another pillow?"

"Can you find me another blanket?"

He stepped out for a moment, then returned with a nurse who had bedding in her arms. Michael gently wrapped the blanket around my shoulders, tucking it under my chin, cocooning me in the scratchy acrylic as if I were an infant needing to feel safe. He wasn't far off.

I wrestled a hand out of the covers, took his, and brought it to my mouth for a kiss.

"I'm glad you're here."

"I wouldn't be anywhere else."

We sat this way, inches apart, our eyes saying everything that needed to be said, until Janek arrived, bringing reality with him. Michael sat up but didn't let go of my hand.

"She's dead, isn't she?" I asked, looking at Janek's steely eyes, knowing it was true but needing him to say it.

"The knife pierced her liver," he said, nodding. "She didn't have a chance."

"Irony, isn't it?" I said, not expecting an answer. "The same fatal blow she delivered to Elyse and Skylar."

The look in Elyse's eyes as she lay dying came back into my mind. Had she and Jill shared the same last thoughts?

"What happens now?" I asked.

"We'll confirm everything you described, of course, and Marcus Bennett is going to face some difficult questions, but unless there are surprises, this case is over," Janek said, allowing a hint of satisfaction to cross his face. One more bad guy off the streets.

"Murder charges against Gavin Wright have been dropped," Michael added. "We've traced the emails discussing the contract hit to some gangbanger in Gary, Indiana. He followed Elyse a few times, just to get a handle on her schedule and figure out his bid. She seemed on to him, so he got scared and walked. We're continuing to watch the guy, but it seems both of these schmucks were new to the game and got cold feet."

"And Elyse assumed, correctly, that Gavin was behind it and started her own surveillance," I said, the missing piece falling into place. "Well, Gavin's still facing a class-one felony for embezzlement, which could mean as much as thirty years behind bars, even if he didn't follow through on her murder. And what about Bennett and Rutkowski? What happens to them?" I asked, uncertain of how to feel. They hadn't been directly responsible for Jill's actions. Legally they would suffer no consequences, but what was the role of environment?

"Bennett still has to face the outstanding assault charges against you," Janek said. "But unless we discover that he had advance knowledge or something else we didn't expect, that will be the end of it. You can't prosecute someone for creating an environment of hate."

"No, of course not," I said. "It's hard to grasp that there are men with such hate for women roaming freely in the world." I paused for a moment, sorting through my emotions, wondering how many men in these online groups would eagerly turn violent for their cause.

"I'd like to drop the charges against Bennett," I said. "His children need their father now."

"Are you sure?" Michael asked, squeezing my hand, his face again twisted with concern. "He threatened you, he assaulted you. Why would you let him off?"

"Because his wife's actions are the consequence of his hate," I said, looking into Michael's eyes. "Being a single parent is the penalty he must suffer, and he has a tough lesson in gender roles ahead of him as he has to be both mom and dad to his kids. It's wishful thinking, but perhaps in time he'll come to appreciate a new vision of family and throw out some of those arcane views. Perhaps the cycle of misogyny will end when dad has to also be mom."

————

A WEEK after Jill Bennett died, I walked back into my office at Link-Media. My wound was still sore when the muscles were stressed, but it had been my psyche that needed the additional healing. During my recovery, I had realized how tired I'd become of living unsettled. My home was a jumble of boxes and empty spaces I hadn't yet furnished. First it had been the divorce, then the remodeling; I was living as if every tomorrow would bring another uncertainty, another reason not to make plans.

My office was no different—worse, perhaps, because I'd felt like an imposter in it. Initially I told myself it was because I was new in the career, then because I hadn't earned my ownership of the company. The net result was that I'd treated the space as if it were nothing more than a functional room, disconnected from my mood and who I was as a human being, certain to disappear or change like so much else over the past few years. I'd put off bringing in items to warm it up, to make it more personal, afraid that it was simply a matter of time before I would be gone.

Vowing to find my footing, I'd reveled in the ease of internet shopping over the past week and had begun working on my want list. I'd filled a bag of new acquisitions to bring with me to the office.

I set down my travel mug of tea, hung my coat, and then opened the suitcase. As I arranged small pieces of framed art on my bookshelf, Borkowski walked in.

"Nice touch," he said. "It's good to have you back." He looked at me as if he wanted to say more or simply expected me to infer by his pregnant pause that our past tension was water under the bridge.

"Is it?" I picked up my tea and sat on the edge of my desk, waiting for a reaction. This one he'd actually have to say out loud.

"I suppose I deserve that," he said, then closed the door. "I wanted to talk to you last week but..." He trailed off. "You had enough to worry about. Anyway, it's taken me a while to understand, but it seems Ramelli and Molina have got something cooked up. Some secret business entity. This consulting thing, it's not about efficiency or restructuring. They're trying to take over. They've got a plan to force you out and have been lying the whole time. Manipulating the both of us." He shook his head and let out a breath. "I feel like an idiot for trusting Ramelli, but he was always loyal to Erik. It just didn't cross my mind that he would try to stab you in the back."

I let him have his say, seeing the pride stripped away from a man who never expected he could be played. I took a sip of tea and waited for him to finish, waiting for the discomfort of the moment to stretch on for a bit longer than necessary.

"I know all about it. I've known almost from the beginning. I just didn't know whose side you were on."

Borkowski stared at me, letting the revelation sink in, and then shoved his hands deep into his pockets. "You'd think I would know to be a little more suspicious." He shrugged and bit down on his lip. "Hmm. I guess you're the better journalist. What did you think, that they had paid me off to participate?"

I paused, considering my words. "I entertained the possibility that promises had been made, let's put it that way."

"I understand." He nodded. "I don't know if this was the politically correct move, but I called Molina this morning and told him his services were no longer required. We'd pay off the balance as it was laid out in his contract, but we would take it from here on our own. I don't doubt he was on the phone to Ramelli half a second later, so be prepared for that angry phone call."

"I don't think there will be one. My attorney delivered a letter last night pointing out that Mr. Ramelli violated his contract when he entered into a side business relationship with Molina. He's been removed from the board."

Borkowski looked at me, confusion on his face, then let out the biggest laugh I'd ever heard from him.

"Well, aren't you full of surprises? I think you just made my year. You're not a woman to piss off." He looked at me with a smile and new respect in his eyes.

There was a knock on the door. Brynn. I motioned her in and gave her a big hug. Then I turned toward Borkowski.

"I called her before I called Molina," he said. "And yes, I gave her a raise too. We'll figure out how to trim back nonessentials elsewhere. Together."

I stepped over and gave him a hug, something I'd never done before. At first he was stiff and uncomfortable, not knowing how to respond. Then he let out another chuckle and put his arm around Brynn, drawing her into the group embrace.

"Don't get any ideas," I said to Borkowski, grinning. "Technically, I'm still your boss; traditional gender roles be damned!"

DID YOU ENJOY THE BOOK?

Thank you so much for reading LIES OF MEN. I'm truly honored that you've spent your time with me.

Reviews are the most powerful tool in an authors' arsenal for getting attention to our books to other readers. If you've enjoyed the story, I would be very grateful if you could spend a moment leaving an honest review.

You can leave your review by visiting Amazon or Goodreads.

NEXT IN THE SERIES

GET INFORMATION ON THE NEXT ANDREA KELLNER
STORY

<u>Also by Dana Killion</u>
    Fatal Choices - a free prequel short story
    Lies in High Places - Andrea Kellner Book 1
    The Last Lie - Andrea Kellner Book 2
    Lies of Men - Andrea Kellner Book 3 - March 2019

I love to hear from my readers. Did you have a favorite scene?
Have an idea for who I should kill off next? Jot me a note. I occasionally send newsletters with details on the next release,
special offers, and other bits of news about the series.

Sign up for my Mailing List at www.danakillion.com

ACKNOWLEDGMENTS

Writing a novel involves months, sometimes years, of plotting, planning, and fretting over every word, and this book was no different. It also involves the support and dedication of good friends and loyal fans.

My heartfelt thanks to the readers who have have stuck with me through this wonderful journey. Your encouragement and kind words are priceless.

To my wonderful new editor Kate Schomaker, thank you for your enthusiasm, for tightening my prose, and for your patience with my refusal to learn the proper placement of commas.

To my boys, Alex and Zach, I hope you live dreams of your own. And finally, to my husband Theo, thank you for continually reminding me of your love and that making the tough choice was worth it. xoxo

ABOUT THE AUTHOR

Dana Killion grew up in a small town in northern Wisconsin, reading Nancy Drew and dreaming of living surrounded by tall buildings. A career in the apparel industry satisfied her city living urge and Nancy Drew evolved into Cornwell, Fairstein, and Evanovich.

One day, frustrated that her favorite authors weren't writing fast enough, an insane thought crossed her mind. "Maybe I could write a novel?"

Silly, naïve, downright ludicrous. But she did it. She plotted and planned and got 80,000 words on the page. That manuscript lives permanently in the back of a closet. But the writing bug had bitten.

Lies of Men is her third novel. Dana lives in Chicago and Florida with her husband and her kitty, Isabel, happily avoiding temperatures below fifty.

DanaKillion.com

Made in the USA
Coppell, TX
02 October 2020